Anderson in Bloom

Also by Jennifer Dugan

The Ride of Her Life
Love at First Set

Anderson in Bloom

A Novel

JENNIFER DUGAN

AVON

An Imprint of HarperCollins*Publishers*

Without limiting the exclusive rights of any author, contributor or the publisher of this publication, any unauthorized use of this publication to train generative artificial intelligence (AI) technologies is expressly prohibited. HarperCollins also exercise their rights under Article 4(3) of the Digital Single Market Directive 2019/790 and expressly reserve this publication from the text and data mining exception.

This is a work of fiction. Names, characters, places, and incidents are products of the author's imagination or are used fictitiously and are not to be construed as real. Any resemblance to actual events, locales, organizations, or persons, living or dead, is entirely coincidental.

ANDERSON IN BLOOM. Copyright © 2026 by Jennifer Lynn Dugan. All rights reserved. No part of this book may be used or reproduced in any manner whatsoever without written permission except in the case of brief quotations embodied in critical articles and reviews. For information, address HarperCollins Publishers, 195 Broadway, New York, NY 10007. In Europe, HarperCollins Publishers, Macken House, 39/40 Mayor Street Upper, Dublin 1, DO1 C9W8, Ireland.

HarperCollins books may be purchased for educational, business, or sales promotional use. For information, please email the Special Markets Department at SPsales@harpercollins.com.

Avon, Avon & logo, and Avon Books & logo are registered trademarks of HarperCollins Publishers in the United States of America and other countries.

hc.com

FIRST EDITION

Interior text design by Diahann Sturge-Campbell

Floral illustration © Jung Suk Hyun/Stock.Adobe.com

Library of Congress Cataloging-in-Publication Data has been applied for.

ISBN 978-0-06-342031-1

Printed and bound in the UK using 100% Renewable Electricity at CPI Group (UK) Ltd

26 CPI 2

To anyone who's ever had to figure it out the hard way

Chapter One

In Which the Fear of Being Known Results in Free Flowers

The woman in the plaid coat eyes the carnations wearily, checking and rechecking the price, picking up first one color and then another. I glance up at her from behind the front counter of this too-warm flower shop that I call home—literally, I rent out the tiny studio upstairs—and try to gauge if I'm needed. The way she frowns and immediately looks away when our eyes meet tells me I'm probably not. Fine, but don't come crying to me when you make your "celebratory bouquet" with a bunch of flowers that mean "I hate you."

I scoff to myself and go back to dragging my rose stripper down the stems of the latest delivery. The sharp blade rips the thorns and leaves off with a satisfying slicing sound that almost lets me forget the truth of it all—which is that my job here is to smooth out all their wildness, file down their rough edges, and make them more palatable. The plant version of what I've been trying to do to myself my whole damn life, with mixed results.

God forbid anybody ever appreciates anything in its natural state—thorns and all—and saves me some scratches. Nope. People want all of the beauty, but none of the pain. It's the same everywhere, even out here in this little town by the sea, where it's about flowers and sand, instead of back there, where it's about bodies and fame.

But we're not talking about *back there*. Especially not today of all days, on the five-year anniversary of my escape to the East Coast. Today is for celebrating. Cel-e-brating. But first, I need to make a sale.

I scrunch my eyes shut in a hard reset and grab another stem, trying to will the woman to buy something through powers of hypnosis and compulsion that I definitely don't have, but pretended to once, in a pilot that never aired. *You know you want one, do it, pull the trigger, buy the flower, buy something, buy anything, buy it, come on buy it*, repeats in my head so hard I'm getting a headache. It's probably about as effective now as it was then, which is to say not at all.

I don't even care if she just gets that lone shitty carnation in her hand. I just need something, anything, to show for the fact that I dragged myself down the stairs and have been perched at this counter since ten o'clock in the morning—ripping leaves off stems because I've already fulfilled all the specialty orders and no new ones have come in yet.

It's been a slow day, and by slow, I mean empty, and by day, I mean week, and by week, I mean month, if I'm being honest. The worry lines and dark circles surrounding my boss—and best friend—Regan's eyes have been noticeably more present lately, and I hate it.

Apparently In Bloom Flowers and Gifts has been a staple in the Town of Clayborn for decades—I remember seeing it when I came here on vacation in a past life—but Regan only took it over about six years ago, after her grandma retired and fucked off to Florida, swearing off the cold Maine winters forever. I came on the scene only a year later, fresh from LA and ready to do something, anything, new—and while it was already slow then, it wasn't *this* bad.

I'm pretty sure that the rent I pay Regan, and my specialty bouquets that we ship out to event planners, are the only things keeping the lights on around here. And if that means I occasionally overpay my rent during the leaner months, even if Regan protests, so be it.

I don't mind, though. Friends help each other out, and god knows Regan shows up for me just as often. Besides, the cash sitting in my old accounts feels like dirty money these days—the least I can do is let it help someone. Better that than putting it up my nose or investing it in the latest crypto Ponzi scheme like some of the other failed former child actors my age do. Who knows where I would have ended up if Regan hadn't taken me under her wing, back when I first showed up in all my "I'm not running away, just starting over" glory.

I was fresh off the biggest heartbreak of my life—crashing in a rental cabin full of sand, barely eating or sleeping, and definitely drinking too much. I probably made every bad choice a person could make back then. After a lifetime of only doing what I should, of always being the responsible one in my relationships, I guess that felt like *freedom* to me. Unfortunately, it also felt like crap.

Walking into In Bloom and asking for an application was just about the only thing I did right when I first moved here. I got lucky. Most people probably would have turned me away in the state I was in, but not Regan. She took one look at the exhausted, depressed disaster in front of her and decided I wasn't just worthy of being an employee but also of being her friend. If my old agent could get 15 percent for finding me the jobs that made up my past life, I figure it's the least Regan deserves for actually *saving* it.

My old agent. The same one who sent my career down the toilet when he—

"Dammit!" Blood spills down my hand, a new gash glaring up at me from the side of my finger, and suddenly that slicing sound doesn't sound so relaxing anymore. That's what I get for letting my mind wander into such dangerous territory. I grab a paper towel off the rack, wrap it as tight as I can, and then grab a few more when it immediately soaks through. Perfect. Just what I need. More blood spilled in the name of beauty.

"Are you okay?"

I snap my eyes up from my hand in time to see Ms. Plaid Coat sliding the carnation back into its bucket. Not good. I still want this sale. "I'm great!" I say, too cheerfully.

Be cool, I tell myself. *Come on, I'm an actor, or used to be. And, as they say, the show must go on.*

Sure, the acting might look a little different these days—more customer service smile than red carpet looks—but still, selling yourself is selling yourself. I can be lovable. I can be delightful. I'm still Anderson goddamn Ducharme after all.

With a deep breath, I turn the dial inside my head from "recluse" to "amiable charmer," grab a few more paper towels and attempt to approach Ms. Plaid Jacket. This is for In Bloom. I can be pleasant and sociable for In Bloom.

"Aren't carnations beautiful?" I try as an opening volley.

"They're cheap is what I like about them," the woman answers gruffly, her eyes drifting to my paper-towel-wrapped hand.

Okay, I think, *okay*, and I switch gears. "Yes, very practical too! Did you know that every color has its own meaning?" I study the rack of flowers for a moment before pulling out a few in coordinating celebratory colors. Understanding the language of flowers has been an obsession of mine since I was a little kid daydreaming in my mother's massive gardens. "What's the occasion? I could help you craft a bouquet that expresses whatever you're trying to say without breaking the bank to do it." I jiggle the stems I'm holding in my paper towel hand in her direction. "We're all about affordability here."

Oh my god, what does that even mean?! Stop waving your bloody hand around.

"I'll take four of the yellow ones and call it a day," she says. "You know you can just superglue whatever's bleeding under there if you don't want to pay for stitches, right?"

And wait, did this just work? Are we bonding over being too cheap for medical bills?

"Good idea," I say, meaning it too. I'd rather bathe in superglue than risk going to urgent care, where I have to fill out forms with my actual legal name and worry about them being leaked. There's just one problem . . . "What is this for, though? Because yellow means—"

The woman turns to look at me, probably opening her mouth

to tell me she doesn't care, when a look of recognition dawns across her features. And *oh, oh no.* I slide my attempt at an arrangement back in with the others and hastily grab four of the bright yellow blooms.

"Never mind! I'm sure yellow's perfect!"

"Wait, do I know you?" the woman asks, leaning a bit closer. I realize too late that she's not as old as I thought. Probably not quite young enough to be a part of my former fan base, but not far enough off for me to feel safe. Especially if she has any younger siblings. Shit.

"I have a . . . common face," I say, wincing at how awkward it sounds. I mean, what's the alternative: admitting that yes, once upon a time I *was* the costar of a wildly popular teen sitcom on the megawatt children's network that everybody knows and loves? That yes, I *am* the very same girl who disappeared without a trace five years ago, tired of only being offered bit parts in high school dramas despite already being twenty-three? And that yes, all of those things, combined with my desperate desire for a clean break with my ex, led to me washing up in this very same dingy town where Ms. Plaid Jacket is currently buying apology carnations from without even bothering to know the meaning of them?

No. I'll take awkward any day.

Plaid Jacket narrows her eyes. "Aren't you that girl from that show? What was it called again? God, it's on the tip of my tongue . . ."

My body flushes hot, and I'm instantly brought back to a session with my old therapist in LA. "Where do you feel the anxiety in your body, Andy?" she would always say, because back then I *was* Andy, not little Annie who spends all day de-thorning roses in this tourist trap of a coastal Maine town.

I feel it fucking everywhere, Janet, is how I always answered that question—and how I would answer it now, if I could afford to. And if therapist Janet wasn't on the exact opposite coast . . . along with the rest of my old life.

"Nope," I say, rushing the sad little carnations over to the counter.

"No, you definitely are! Oh my god, can I get a selfie? My little sister will flip!" she says, following me, already pulling out her phone. "She was obsessed with you. Especially when she found out you and Nikki weren't just—"

"It's not me," I say, cutting her off, and then lean conspiratorially over the counter. "But can you keep a secret?"

"Probably."

"Andy is my cousin." The lie falls off my tongue so easily it feels like the truth, but isn't that all acting is anyway? Just a giant lie in a gorgeous production package?

"No way, seriously?"

"Yep, obviously the genes are strong on that side of the family," I say, waving my hand casually toward my face and then holding my breath for her reaction.

"So you grew up with Andy, then? *The* Andy, from *The Nikki and Andy Show*?"

"Mmmhmmm," I say, glad that my ruse seems to be working. It's not often that I get recognized anymore, and I'd like to keep it that way.

"Do you still talk to her, or did she cut you off like she cut off—"

"All the time," I say, and force on a smile.

Plaid Jacket's face lights up and I mentally kick myself. "Then you know where she is?"

"No!" I say, a little too fast. "We don't . . . we don't really talk about that. She's just out there, somewhere, finding herself." *I mean, it's not technically a lie.*

Disappointment etches itself across Plaid Jacket's features. "Sounds like she still sucks just as much as she used to then."

"What?" I jerk back. "No, She's great. Perfect, actually. I love her." And then, because I can't stop myself: "You don't even know her."

"Sorry," the woman says, holding up her hands. She's clearly taken aback by my little outburst. "I just meant, you know, there were all those stories about her online before she took off and here we are, years later, and she's still 'finding herself'? Not even telling her own family where she is?" She gestures toward me. "You are way cooler about that than I would be if it was my cousin."

"Can I wrap these for you?" I ask, desperate to change the subject before my rapidly clenching fists snap her carnation stems. "I'll even throw in some baby's breath for free to punch it up a little."

That's not all I want to punch up right now.

"Oh, thanks, yeah, that'd be great," the woman says, momentarily distracted by the allure of a good deal. Most people around here are. It's not a very wealthy town, after all, especially not during the off-season.

I force the pathetic arrangement of sad carnations and wispy baby's breath to look prettier than it has any right to be—while still being careful not to bleed all over it—and then usher the woman out the door with her five-dollars-plus-tax purchase as fast as I can.

I'm still patting myself on the back for the bullet (barely) dodged when Regan steps out of the back room, where she's been breaking down boxes from today's delivery. Gouda, my fluffy gray gremlin of a cat that I rescued from a dumpster nearly seven years ago, follows right behind her, meowing for food even though it's not even close to feeding time.

"Did I just hear you give away flowers for free?" Regan asks, arching her eyebrows when she sees me using floral tape to wrap fresh paper towels around my hand. "Don't tell me you cut yourself again."

A tinge of guilt has me biting my lip. "Just a scratch this time," I lie. "And I only gave her a few sprigs of baby's breath, which I'll cover. Let me just run up and grab my wallet."

"Relax," Regan says. "It's like twenty-five cents. I know you're good for it. How'd that happen, though? You're usually worse than me about the bottom line."

I snort at that, even though I know it's true. I guess there's just something about having everything stolen from me, aside from the legally mandated Coogan Account and its paltry balance—15 percent of everything I earned as a minor safe and sound under federal law—that has me checking and rechecking the books here. Fool me once, shame on you. Fool me twice . . .

"Was she cute?" Regan teases, sliding the rest of the roses over to finish them up herself. It's almost closing time, and as much as I'm happy to stay here twenty-four-seven, because god knows I have nothing else to do, I know Regan is anxious to get home. Besides, it would be almost impossible for me to finish stripping the stems now that my hand is wrapped up like a Bounty boxing glove.

"God, I wish. No, she thought I looked *familiar*," I admit eventually. "I needed to distract her and send her on her way."

"Ahh," Regan says with a sigh. "Did you go with the distant cousin lie or the 'everyone has a doppelgänger and it's *so* annoying that mine was on TV' one?"

"Cousin."

"Good, that one's way more believable." She pauses, studying my face. "It's been a little while since that's happened. You okay?"

"Yeah," I say, not meeting her eyes, because we both understand the answer to that question has been *not really* for most of my life.

Regan knows the truth of who I am and who I used to be, because of course she does. I still remember working up the courage to come clean, and how worried I was that it would change something between us . . . but when the time came, it was kind of underwhelming.

Turns out she had figured it out almost immediately, back when I was still renting cabin six from Mrs. Sanderson and spending way too long shaking sand out of my clothes. Regan didn't care one bit, although she did admit to streaming every episode once I officially moved into her rental upstairs. She said it was part of her "background check," and I was desperate enough for a friend that I laughed it off, even though it was deeply mortifying.

Once I realized my secret really was safe with her, I signed a one-year lease and decided I was staying. The place isn't much, especially compared to what I was used to on the left coast—barely a one bedroom thanks to a hastily added wall—but I love that it's *just* mine. Well, mine and Gouda's—who, as if on cue, lets out another yowl before curling up on the heating vent.

Sometimes I wonder if Gouda misses LA, the sounds and smells and sunshine she used to soak up through the window of the fourth-floor condo we shared with my rotten ex, the feel of real marble and hardwood under her paws, rather than linoleum or laminate, but if she does, she hasn't complained in any real discernible way.

Besides, she hated my last girlfriend even more than I did by the end. While I'm sure Gouda could have done without the impromptu cross-country road trip, and she definitely could have done without me driving straight to the beach the second we pulled into town, I'd like to think she's happier here.

I know I am, even if my ex-celebrity status has kind of become a running joke around my friends. Like when I sign the same printed-out time sheet that In Bloom has been using weekly since it opened in 1980, Regan always says she's going to take *THE* Anderson Ducharme's autograph and put it on eBay, or when Johnny, Regan's other best friend and the town mechanic, dressed up as my old character for our three-person Halloween party last year. It's ridiculous, sure, but I don't really mind anymore...

Because it means that someone found out—two someones, actually—and the world didn't end. They're still my friends, they don't care about any of the Hollywood bullshit, and I don't I have to keep my past a secret. I breathed a little bit easier after that.

I probably would breathe a lot better now if I wasn't still worried about everyone else on this planet finding out, but oh well. It's just hard knowing that anyone in the entire universe can google the worst moments of my life at a second's notice once they realize who I really am.

It's why I don't get too close with anyone else around here. I can't trust it, not really. Which means that Regan does the bulk of the deliveries and *all* of the farmers markets, while I handle the inventory and custom orders. It works out well. She's an extrovert who gets antsy in the silence of the store . . . and silence is what I came here for. Isn't it?

I know what it sounds like—it sounds like I'm hiding, and like Regan and Johnny have been aiding and abetting me these last few years. But I'm not. I swear, I'm not.

This place gave me a *chance to start fresh*. A chance to figure out who I was on my own terms, despite everything from my old life telling me that who I was *was not enough*. That I could only ever be a speck of dust overshadowed by someone else's light, never standing on my own. Never being seen for who I truly am.

I had to leave. I had to choose myself for once. So I packed up what little I owned and left, ditching the warm West Coast for the ice-cold East in the middle of March. I was reborn in those frigid waters—with my cat yowling from her carrier in the front seat of my car, surrounded by expensive luggage and garbage bags full of my belongings; an odd mix, just like me.

I had walked onto the beach that night in sneakers and leggings and an old concert hoodie I still have in the back of my closet. I kept going until the water skimmed my hips and then my belly and then my chin. And when I finally turned and bolted back up the sand, wet and shivering and feeling totally wrung out—I knew I was already becoming something new. Something just for me.

Andy was gone. Andy had to die.

Long live Annie, future florist, instead.

Chapter Two

TMZ Will Break Your Heart

I shouldn't be doing this.

I should *not* be doing this.

And I'm not just talking about the fact that I've just superglued two of my fingers together in an effort to close my cut from earlier that definitely could have used a stitch or two. No, I'm talking about the other, worse thing: cyberstalking my old life.

I can't help it. Being almost recognized by that woman at the flower shop has sent my head spiraling six thousand miles, and more than a couple years back, to the land of beauty and fame—or tabloids and garbage, to be more accurate. I get that all this is going to do is toss my mental health in the toilet and then double flush, but I can't stop.

(Even though I should *absolutely* stop and in fact paid a lot of money for Janet to teach me how to stop. *TMZ will break your heart* was a frequent mantra of ours once upon a time.)

But damn it, Janet, if even superglue won't keep me away, I don't know what will.

It starts as a small niggle in the back of my brain when I first walk into my silent apartment, having left Gouda downstairs to finish out her nap on the vent. Just a gentle pressure to look, see, consume that grows into a gnawing headache I can't escape from, no matter how hard I distract myself with the task of tending wounds. It's possible, I realize, that what happened to me, what Nikki *did* to me, what they *all* did to me, will always be the biggest wound, and that perhaps there is not enough superglue in the world to fix it.

So I scroll. I scroll as I fix my bleeding fingers or make them worse, because the truth is, the need to know has filled my entire body up to the brim. I'm a live grenade so terrified someone's gonna pull my pin that I just go ahead and do it myself.

It always starts with a simple google, having long since deleted the alerts on my name. I sigh and try to pry my fingers apart while the results load, most of them old and outdated—I pretend that's a relief and not a disappointment. Why would anyone be posting an article about me now anyway? What would they even say? "Failed Actor Turned Recluse Still Reclusing"?

My parents long ago reassured everyone from NBC to TMZ that, despite my sudden disappearance and the deletion of all my social media accounts, I was still alive and well and just "taking a break." Pretty soon most people stopped caring. You stop commodifying yourself, they all just move on to the next person who will.

Like I said, I should be relieved.

I *should*. But I'm not.

I click over to Google Images, just to see if there's anything I should be "worried about." That's what I said last time Regan caught me checking—that I just needed to make sure everything was on the up-and-up.

A few years ago, I went grocery shopping with my dad during a holiday visit. One of the creeps I went to high school with snapped a picture with their phone and sold it—suddenly an image of me weighing brussels sprouts with no makeup on and glaring three-inch roots was *everywhere*.

Each headline was worse than the last. First there was "She Lives!" Then "From Major to Meijer" and, most embarrassingly, in a nod to a running joke about my former character's hatred of all things green, "Sprouting from the Dead: Kiddie Star Finally Eats Her Veggies."

Then it just got mean. The few people who still talk about me on social media started suggesting that I leaked the photo myself to stay relevant—as if I purposely wanted to be associated with the most hated vegetable on earth for all eternity. (Okay, so maybe that joke about not liking vegetables was based on a true story.) It was so insulting. If I was going to leak anything, it would be a picture of me looking hot next to one of my kick-ass floral arrangements, thank you very much.

Giving up on both Google and ever getting my fingers unstuck from each other, I head over to Instagram. I have one heavily locked down account that I only use to stalk my old "friends" as they live their most fabulous—read: manufactured—lives for the cameras. I only very occasionally comment on their posts, and it's never mean. (Okay, fine, sometimes I post a hundred eyeball emojis when they post something obviously fake, but I'm only human.)

It's just that I literally can't believe no one has figured out

Kendra's "private plane" is a rental set. The girl flew Southwest when I knew her, for god's sake—a fact that I vowed to take to my grave after she threatened to shove her red-bottomed heel into my eye if I ever told. (Honestly, if anyone was going to commit murder via extravagant apparel, it would be her.)

Then there's Demarco, who pretends to be a perfectly vanilla hetero boy next door, the ideal ageless, sexless leading man for Hallmark mothers to pine over . . . the same Demarco who is actually a darling bisexual like me and Nikki, and who's so deep in the kink scene that he's a member of not one but two of the most elite dungeons in LA.

I still remember when we bumped into him at one of them. Nikki had taken me there to "research" the latest spicy fanfic-turned-industry-smash that was in the studio's pipeline . . . she never booked the job, but at least we got a lot of great new ideas from it. We also got an eyeful of Demarco we were *not* expecting.

I click to his profile first. Of all the friends I had back then—or thought I had—he's the only one I've actually missed. I take a deep breath and a swig of cheap beer, almost snorting it out my nose when I see Demarco's latest post. He's gushing about getting the starring role in a Christmas movie on the new ultra-conservative holiday channel. You know, the one that thought Hallmark was *too progressive*. Yikes. Second thought, maybe I don't miss him all that much.

I shake my head and steel my nerves when I see *who* Insta is suggesting I follow next. A name that still makes my stomach swoop even after all these years and a face that makes my blood turn to cold fury. Because suddenly there she is, in all her blue-check-verified, hot-shit, 18.3M-followers-and-counting celebrity glory: Nikki Colletti.

Nikki wasn't just the costar of *The Nikki and Andy Show*, but also of my entire former freaking life—the very ex I had to fling myself across the entire country to finally be rid of. I guess you could say it was a pretty bad breakup—well, for me, at least. Nikki didn't waste much time scooping up an Oscar and, if TMZ is to be believed, an entire cast of lovers to go along with it.

I don't dare click on her stories, scared that she'll somehow figure out that my "Mallory Malbone" account is really me, even if I did use a picture of one of my best clients as the profile pic—a sweet little horse rancher a state over with a propensity for event planning and flowers. That rancher probably single-handedly saved In Bloom this year, finding us after one of my floral arrangements went viral on TikTok.

Sorry, Molly, but I had to.

(Do I feel guilty for using her picture to spy on my old friends? Yes. Am I going to stop? Probably not. Did I at least change her name? Sort of? Besides, everybody has a doppelgänger, right? Hers just happens to be . . . well, my fake Instagram profile. Besides, from what I know of her, she'd get it. Probably even support it.)

I click over and scroll down Nikki's grid, looking at all the artful selfies and random blurry shots that are just enough of an enigma to leave her fans commenting guesses as to where she is and what she's doing—gaming the algorithms, always.

Jealousy stirs deep in my belly as I keep scrolling—who's taking the faraway shots? I know she doesn't know how to use a timer—but then swiftly swirls into something else, something we're not going to talk about, or even think about, as my scrolling finger stutter-stops on a close-up of her skin.

You can't see her face, but I don't need to. There was a time when my fingertips had felt every inch of her; when I knew her bones as well as I knew my own, could map her pores and freckles from memory—and while our fingerprints have long since washed off each other's bodies, they haven't washed out of my mind.

I'd know that collarbone anywhere.

I stare at the way the beads of water and sand trail down her skin in the picture, dipping lower and lower until they disappear beneath the fabric of her tiny bikini—the same bikini I've tied and untied for her a thousand times, with the taste of sea salt on our tongues and our laughter giving way to sandy kisses.

I shift in my seat and swallow hard, trying to forget that I once knew every bit of her, inside and out, and now I don't know her at all. I may have been the one who ultimately cut the line and ran, but that doesn't mean I wanted to. That doesn't mean her hooks aren't still in me.

I take another swig from the bottle, and then another, picking at stray bits of glue on my fingers even though it hurts, trying to distract myself from all the questions I shouldn't be thinking. Does she ever miss my laugh the way I do hers? Or the taste of my skin on her tongue?

God, this is embarrassing.

I hate her, I remind myself, *a lot. A lot a lot.* Everything I'm feeling right now? Everything I'm thinking? It's just chemicals, brain chemistry, crossed lines from past lives, because now, in this one, *I. Hate. Her.* She's the devil, the evil empire, Kylo Ren pre-redemption arc but *worse*. She's the Wicked Witch of the West, and I'd do well to remember it.

I huff out a breath, polish off the beer in record time, and click over to TikTok, switching from the In Bloom store account I manage to my "super-secret, very bad, do not use" account that I only let myself pull up on the worst of brain days. The evil algorithm instantly rewards me with clip after clip of my old show. I pick one, slumping in my seat as I watch the younger version of myself burst into the living room stage set with a boisterous, "Honey, I'm home!"

I can't help but cringe.

My character was always the loud, ridiculous one—the comic foil designed to reassure parents that they didn't have to worry, that things would never get *too* serious around here. Meanwhile Nikki's character was the sweet, quiet, thoughtful one—the one you rooted for.

I had tried out for that role too, but they said my "face wasn't quite right for the part." I had heard that before—had spent hours in the mirror wishing my eyes were less owlish, my features more delicate. When I saw Nikki on set the first day, I got it, though. She was *perfect*. A classic beauty even at seventeen—able to seamlessly morph between looking like the girl next door and a silver screen starlet with a flick of her makeup brush.

As if on cue, Nikki appears in the clip with a wide grin on her face. This is from early in the first season, when the show was still trying to decide if we were going for slapstick or snarky and when Nikki and I were just getting comfortable enough with each other to flirt.

I catch myself smiling at the younger version of us, even if I *am* on-screen carrying a comically large movie theater soda and popcorn destined for disaster. Naturally, they had me trip over an ill-placed backpack that Nikki's character had been warning me not to step on. In the time-honored tradition of cheesy kids' comedy, everything goes flying everywhere . . . but especially all over *her*.

I vividly remember filming this one.

Nikki's supposed to be furious after getting covered in my soda and snacks, her straitlaced stick-up-the-ass character still not sold on being friends with such a clown . . . but she couldn't be. Not back then, when it was all brand-new butterflies between us. Little me winks at the camera—my character's signature move—and Nikki exaggerates her pout in attempt to not break character once again.

This was the seventh take, the first six ruined when my giggling triggered hers. The director was getting angry, as were the producers, right along with Nikki's agent, Eliza, who was always ready to ruin our fun. She was twice the stage mom Nikki's real mom was, and getting paid for the privilege.

Screw Eliza and screw the director and producers too.

Maybe they should try being seventeen on an ice-cold set, dousing their crush in soda over and over again until her shirt clings to her like a second skin and her bra loses the battle to contain freezing nipples. I dare them not to blush. Not to giggle nervously as they notice. Not to worry about the heat pooling deep in their bellies and whether everyone on set can tell. Whether the whole world could tell.

The canned laugh track rips me out of my thoughts, and god,

how I hate that sound now. Back then, I used to pretend that it was real. I obsessively watched each episode when it aired, trying to find ways to do better and convincing myself that the laugh track meant that I had pleased the studio execs and other gods of Hollywood—*that I was doing a good job*. Surely they wouldn't add laughter if the episode sucked, right?

I was so hungry for approval and praise back then, like a dog begging for pats whenever anybody looked my way. I just wanted to be accepted, you know? To be loved. But love is fickle, anyone in Hollywood will tell you. And the quickest way to make Hollywood fall out of love with you is to outlive your usefulness.

So I tried, desperately at times, to stay useful, even if that meant doing double or triple the amount of work on our show than Nikki did. God, she was barely even on set the last couple of seasons, her star rising so fast it outpaced mine and then all of ours, long before any of us wanted it to. Blink and we're costars, blink again and she'd become the sun itself.

She never even said thank you for all the times I covered for her—I don't think it ever even occurred to her that she should. Yet to most of the world, *I'm* the awful one—because I'm the one who left.

I swipe up again, just about ready to switch back to the florist account, when I see Nikki—not past Nikki, but current. It looks to be a teaser for an upcoming E! exclusive interview that's going to go up tomorrow. They've sat her in an all-white room, and whatever intern is in charge of random TikTok graphics has even stuck an annoying "breaking news" gif on top of it. It flashes gaudily in the corner of the screen, ruining whatever effect they were going for with the colorless background. I'm about to scroll by—my eyes already rolling at what I assume is the latest casting news for some indie movie that's much cooler than anything I ever did—when I hear it.

"I don't know if I would call it a tell-all," she says with a laugh, "but it's definitely a tell-*most*. It might even clear up a few *mysteries* for my fans." And then she does it, the wink. The wink that I came up with for my character all on my own, but never got credit for—the fourth-wall-breaking wink that made our show iconic and left the writers scrambling to look like they did it on purpose. The wink that then went on to become my signature move, not just on our sitcom but at every red carpet and comic con signing table I graced before I disappeared for good. *My wink*. Not hers. Hasn't she taken enough?

And, what, is that supposed to imply she's talking about us? Me? Not just *her* time on the show, but *mine* as well? I swear to god, she better be sitting on some other whole-ass mystery, because if she even thinks she's going to use me leaving her, leaving Hollywood, as memoir clickbait . . . then she's not just a bad person, she's *evil*.

I check the timestamp on the TikTok—seven minutes ago. This really is breaking news. I click over to google her again, this time adding words like "book" and "memoir." The results start piling up, mostly social media stitches of people reacting to her quickly-becoming-viral TikTok in real time. But they're not talking about her, they're talking about . . . me. Reveling in the idea that they'll finally get their answers, their pound of flesh for me daring to take back my life. My quiet anonymity is threatened in the blink of an eye, and even Gouda scratching at the door to be let in—evidently done with napping in the shop—can't pull me away.

Because she's really doing it. She's writing a memoir, telling *her* version of *our* story—and it is our story, judging by all the winks and comments she's sending to everyone freaking out beneath the post. It has to be a public spectacle with her, always. How very typical. *How very Nikki.*

The urge to unblock her number long enough to scream at her for doing this *again*, for talking over me *again*, wells up inside me. I even get so far as to pick up my phone . . . but good sense wins out at the last minute, and I call Regan instead.

"She's writing a book!" I practically screech the second the call connects, trying to hide the hurt and fear behind my anger.

"Who is? What are you talking about?"

"Nikki! She's writing a book about growing up in Hollywood and her time on the show. She even did the wink. My fucking wink."

"Are you okay?"

"She's going to ruin everything!" I try to run my hand through my hair, remembering too late the predicament with my hand when the crunchy glue snags my strands. "Also, I may have superglued my hand together."

"You . . . never mind. I'll be right there," Regan says. In the background, Johnny asks, "What's going on?" because of course he's at her house. They're in love, Your Honor, I'll swear to it even if they pretend they're not—but none of that matters right now.

"Thanks," I say. It comes out more plaintive than I mean it to, and I can't decide what I hate more: that Nikki's writing a book or that my past still has this much power over me.

* * *

I DON'T HAVE to wait long for them to arrive, seeing as how Regan lives barely a block and a half away. The fact that Johnny's right behind her bearing pizza and more beer is a welcome surprise, as is the acetone Regan brought for my fingers. I must have interrupted a date night . . . not that they would ever call it that.

"Who needs to get slapped?" Johnny asks. "The publisher for agreeing to this, the TikTok gods who put it on your For You page, or can I *finally* go straight to the source?"

I shrug and accept his one-armed hug while Regan gets busy putting away the beer. To say that Johnny hates Nikki would be an understatement. He's taken on the role of a protective big-brother type after we somehow managed to turn a drunken one-night stand into an actual yearslong friendship.

I think it was that protectiveness, mixed with his special blend of bluntness and honesty, that had me ready to jump into his bed that night. I wasn't used to that sort of thing after being surrounded by fast-talking, double-tongued Hollywood types who would sell you out on a dime, and I was intrigued. I suppose the fact that we also closed down the bar didn't hurt. I wouldn't say we regretted it the next morning, but we both knew sleeping together was a mistake.

Regan told me not to worry about it when, not long after hiring me, I confessed that I had slept with someone she obviously considered a close friend. She said Johnny was basically part of the town's welcome basket: here's a map of the farmers market, here's one of Janey's pies, and don't forget your complimentary dicking down, courtesy of the owner of Main Street Mechanics.

Plus that was long, long before I realized that Johnny was head over heels for Regan, and that she was pretending not to return the feeling. They weren't as obvious back then as they are now.

"No one's slapping anyone," Regan says, handing me a plate and carrying the box into the living room while Johnny is preoccupied with soaking a paper towel in acetone.

"Yet," he says, which makes me laugh even though I feel like my stomach is about to come up my throat.

"Yet," she amends when she finally gets a chance to look at me. I don't miss her wince. I rub my hand over my eyes, embarrassed, as she yanks me into a tight hug. It's true. I may have cried a little, or a lot, in the ten minutes or so it took them to come over. I'm sure I look like garbage and I'm probably giving them flashbacks to when we first met.

Regan leads me over the big armchair in the living room and sits me down so Johnny can get to work gently dissolving the superglue. He's exceedingly careful to avoid the actual injury, and if someone doesn't say something soon, that alone is going to start up the waterworks again.

"You guys want to see?" I ask, holding up the iPad with my free hand and pushing play before either of them answers. They watch obediently, Johnny's jaw clenched and Regan letting out a sigh as the clip finishes. I drop into my chair, my head hanging back in defeat as Johnny wipes my hands down and goes to the kitchen to put everything away.

"Well, damn," he says, returning quickly with another beer.

"Well, damn," I agree, clinking my bottle against his in the most depressing cheers I've ever been a part of. At least my fingers are unstuck now.

"Maybe this won't change anything," Regan says, trying to be logical, trying to keep me from losing it.

"If that wink means what I think it means, I don't see how it couldn't."

"No one knows you're here."

I shake my head. "You really believe that?"

Johnny takes a sip of his beer. "What do you mean?"

"You really think you two are the only ones who live here who've ever recognized me? Because I think people eventually did but have just kept it quiet because nobody really cared about me anymore. That woman at the flower shop is going to realize I'm not a distant cousin once my face is back on TMZ all the time. Nikki's about to send a lot of eyes in my direction, and I'm sure one of the gossip sites will pay good money for someone to sell me out."

"So what?" Regan says. "Let them look. Who cares? You're doing good. You're making a solid life for yourself with your floral designs. Forget all the noise, Annie. It doesn't matter."

She's right, I know she's right . . . or rather I know that she should be. But I'm not ready for this. I'm not ready for any of it. It feels too much like the first time, like when everyone found out their favorite child actors were actually queer—long before Nikki and I were ready to come out. Only this time it's not just my sexuality being exposed, but my entire freaking life.

And yeah, maybe I told myself—and keep telling myself—that this was a fresh start, a new life; that I'm not hiding here but rebuilding . . . but the truth of the matter is that I *am* hiding. I have been for a long time, and just like years and years ago, when reporters came around set desperate to expose my private life, I'm not ready. I'm not ready to reconcile that Andy was a part of Annie and vice versa—and I shouldn't have to just because Nikki decides it's time.

"You know we have your back, right?" Johnny says, stuffing a second slice of pizza into his mouth and chewing thoughtfully. "Whatever you want to do, however you want to handle this."

"Yeah," Regan agrees. "Always."

"Especially if it involves ending you-know-who," he adds with a cheeky little smile. Regan smacks his arm, and he grabs her in a gentle headlock as I look away. Normally, I bask in their warmth, enjoying watching them skate around the idea of being in love, inching toward it instead of barreling. It almost makes me believe in it all over again. But not today.

Today their warmth only highlights how cold I feel. Forget love. Forget all of this.

I finish my second beer, my head comfortably buzzing, as I grab a slice of pizza for myself. I don't drink all that often. Nikki scared me away from all of that, the way it took over her life—because the better parties *always* brought with them the better booze, the better pills, the better fun. But I have to admit that tonight, I don't really care about unhealthy coping mechanisms. I just want to forget for a little while that Nikki put my whole life in a blender with her bullshit memoir. Forget the wink and the smiles and the laugh tracks. Forget her warm skin and her cold heart and what she did to me.

Regan puts on my favorite trashy reality show and drags me over to the couch so she can rest her head on my shoulder as Johnny clears our plates. He covers us with my fuzziest blanket when he comes back, not even complaining that I stole his place on the couch, just settling into my old spot on the chair and passing me another beer and another and another, until I can finally breathe for a second. Until I can believe that in some universe, this might all end up okay.

Of course, that only lasts until the room starts to spin and I commandeer the TV again, drunkenly casting TikToks and reels to the fifty-five-inch screen. I make them sit through countless clips of my old show and interviews, as well as ones I've found of people ripping into Nikki for her various scandals over the years.

I punctuate each one by saying things like "See, she's evil, right?" and "Don't you think I should've gotten an Oscar instead of her?" until Regan declares it's bedtime and Johnny, the traitor that he is, agrees.

I begin my forced march to brush my teeth and apply my night serums, skincare being the one habit I've never given up from my Hollywood days. I'm interrupted only briefly by a quick visit to the porcelain gods, my stomach rebelling from too many bad beers and greasy slices of pizza while Johnny paces outside of the bathroom and Regan holds my hair. Normally, this would bother me, but I'm past the point of caring about anything right now.

"You know what?" I announce, dropping on top of my comforter after brushing my teeth for the second time. "I'm gonna call Nikki and tell her exactly what I think about her doing this. Put her right in her place for once."

"No, you're not," Johnny says gently, helping Regan tuck me into bed properly. She's careful to pull my phone from my hand, placing it on the charger across the room—the one I put there in an effort to spend *less* nights googling.

"You're going to get some rest, and when you wake up, I'm going to have a fresh bottle of water and some ibuprofen waiting for you and your hangover." Regan smiles. "Now sleep."

"Yeah," I mumble. "S'probably not her number anymore anyway." I pull my blankets up to my chin and let my eyes slip shut. "Love you guys," I say, like we always do before leaving.

"Love you too," Regan says, shutting the door to my bedroom once she's satisfied I'm not getting up.

I hear the hall closet door open and shut as I start to drift off and I smile to myself, knowing that sound means one, if not both of them, will be in my living room when I wake up, snuggled under one of the countless blankets I keep in there. Maybe I can even convince them we have time for a quick breakfast at our favorite diner before we all leave to open up our respective shops.

It's almost enough. Almost.

But right before I fully tip over into dreamland, it hits me—Nikki probably *has* changed her number. God knows she changed it all the time when were together, especially whenever her more . . . passionate . . . fans got ahold of it. So, what's the harm in texting her to tell her off? It's not like she'd see it anyway, and whoever owns the number now will probably just delete it assuming it's a wrong number.

I could get a little closure for my own benefit, no harm, no foul. Sure, maybe it's the epitome of drunk logic, but doesn't it, on some level, make absolute perfect sense? I roll over to my side, taking a minute to think this through. One single sober brain cell tries to argue that it's a bad idea, but the rest of me, especially my heart, decides that it does, in fact, make perfect sense to tell a random wrong number to get wrecked in the name of closure.

Pleased with my "perfect" plan, I creep out of bed, careful not to make a sound. I don't want Regan or Johnny to come check on me and blow the whole thing. I get just close enough to reach it, and then snatch my phone off the charger, rushing back under my covers dramatically, like a kid sneaking screen time after curfew.

I scroll to the name I haven't dared touch in years and blow out the longest, deepest breath. My finger hesitates just for a second as I hit unblock, but it's far, far too late to back out now.

> **Me:** I doubt this is still your number but fuck you and your book

The perfect opening volley, and pretty much all I have to say. Three dots instantly appear, and I grin, expecting them to say something like "Who is this?" or "Wrong number" or "Fuck you too, whoever you are."

But then the words from the reply flash across my screen. A frown yanks my lips down as I struggle to process what I'm reading.

> **Nikki:** Holy shit Andy???? Where are you??? Where have you been?!!!

No. No, no, no, this is not the closure I promised myself. This is the opposite of closure. This isn't drunk logic, this is a *drunk fucking fuckup for the ages*. I flop back on my pillow. *What the hell do I do now?* I shouldn't write back. I can't write back.

I have to, though, right? I mean, I can't let her know she upset me, even though she did. I mean, yes, I wanted her to know, sure, but not *really*. Now I just look pathetic. I can fix this. I have to fix this. Okay, I just need to make it sound like I'm doing great without her. Because I am. Aren't I? I am! Right? I'm living the goddamn dream. I am doing the thing. Like Regan said, I have a great life! And I'm going to tell her just that.

> **Me:** Living the dream obvs

I don't wait for the dots to appear. I don't even wait for it to say delivered. Instead, I turn my phone off and pull the blankets tight under my chin, feeling prouder of myself than I have any right to.

I finally got the last word with her after all.

Chapter Three
Just When You Think It Can't Get Worse

Waking up the next day is not peaceful nor is it gentle. It's bolting upright in bed with a pounding headache and enough misplaced adrenaline in my body to flip my stomach upside down. *What did I do last night?*

I groan as the memories come back into focus, the thousand TikToks I forced on my friends, the superglued fingers . . . the text. The text!

"Oh no. No, no, no, no, no, no!" I say, scrambling through my comforter to find my phone. Please, gods, goddesses, universe, whatever's out there, let my memory of texting Nikki have just been a horrible, horrible nightmare. My hands shake as they wrap around the cold glass of my cracked iPhone and flip it over—the screen is flooded with a string of notifications. I flop back on my pillow and squeeze my eyes shut when I realize they're mostly from Nikki.

"Shit, shit, shit, shit!" I yelp, tangling in my sheets as I rush to get out of bed and fall hard on my ass in the process. Gouda looks on from the doorway, unimpressed. I've barely gotten myself to sitting when the phone rings in my hand. I drop it in terror, watching it vibrate beside my naked thigh—I must have shimmied out of my sweats at some point last night in my drunken haze. I take a deep breath and flip over the phone, praying it's not Nikki. I breathe a sigh of relief to see it's Regan calling instead.

I fall back against the hardwood floor, knocking my already sore head against the ground in the process, and accept the call. "Hey, Regan," I say, my voice gravelly from disuse, my throat more than a little sore after last night's unfortunate episode while brushing my teeth. I've always had a sensitive gag reflex.

"Are you okay up there?"

"Why wouldn't I be?" I ask, my voice squeaking up an octave, because I am *not* about to tell Regan what I did. No. I need to block Nikki and pretend like none of this ever happened. Ever.

"Because I just heard banging? What was that? It sounded like you dropped a ton of bricks on the floor."

"Oh, that was me!" I chirp, relieved to have an easy explanation at the ready.

"Did you faint? Or pass out or something? I knew I should have stayed, but Johnny had to get to the garage, and it was getting late—are you okay?"

"I'm fine. I tripped getting out of bed. Wait, what time is it?" I ask, noticing for the first time the way the sun is blazing through my bedroom windows. That only happens in the afternoon. Did my alarm not go off?

"It's about one fifteen," she says.

"Oh my god, Regan, I am so, *so*, sorry I'm"—I do the math

quickly in my head—"three hours late?! You should have woken me up!"

Regan chuckles into the phone. "You looked like you needed the rest when I checked in on you. You were happily snoring away and I didn't have it in my heart to wake you. Besides, it's been so slow here lately anyway. Are you still on the floor?"

"Maaaaybe," I say, drawing out the word.

"In that case, if you haven't noticed, there's water and ibuprofen on your nightstand. We fed Gouda for you before we left, so don't believe her when she acts like she's starving. I was going to make you breakfast but Johnny thought cold pizza might be the best start to your day."

"Don't ever let me say that man isn't brilliant," I reply. "Cold pizza sounds heavenly. Give me like fifteen and I'll be down."

"Why don't you take thirty?" She laughs. "You were pretty ripe this morning when I walked into your room."

"Rude! But also yes, I probably could use a shower."

"That's my girl," she says, and I hear the bells over the front door ring. "First customer of the day, gotta go!"

She hangs up on me and I frown. The first customer of the day showing up three hours after opening is never a great sign. Gouda stomps over and sits on my chest, her tail twitching as she stares down at me.

"I know you had breakfast," I say, narrowing my eyes. She meows in response, looking put out, before hopping off me and wandering away.

I stick my phone into my pocket and head toward the kitchen. I'm just about to shove that first slice of delicious, perfect, hangover-curing leftover pizza in my mouth when my phone vibrates again. I pull it out and hit answer with a grin. "It's been five seconds, Regan, what's up?"

There's a sudden catch in the breath of the person on the line and I rip my phone from my ear, staring down at Nikki's name. *Shit.* I disconnect and it starts buzzing again. I send it to voicemail, and thankfully, it stops. I stare down at it like it's a viper about to attack, and maybe it is. It feels like it is. The voicemail alert burns through my veins as sure as any poison would.

This is bad. This is so bad. What am I going to do?

I'm struck by the sudden realization that I desperately *do* want to hear her voice.

Not her stage voice or her TikTok voice or her stupid interview voice that's always an octave higher or lower than her real one—depending on if she's trying to seem feminine and coy or serious and important. I want to hear her real voice, her lazy-mornings-in-bed, just-for-me voice. I shut my eyes like I can push that desire away that easily. Like I can shore up my willpower as long as I don't have to see the alert flashing on my screen for another second.

But I'm weak. I've always been weak when it comes to this girl.

Even if my heart is lined with more hate for her than love, I still can't stop wondering what she has to say now, after all these years.

I hit play and press the phone to my ear.

"Andy," she says, her voice barely above a whisper.

There's a hint of wonder to her tone, and warmth blooms inside me. I am instantly dragged back to the last time she said my name like that. We had just made love for the first time in a long time—most of our hookups had long ago turned to baseless fucking as our relationship deteriorated—but that night I had been crying over losing out on a role I really wanted.

She had come home with yellow orchids, not caring that they meant new beginnings when I felt like my world was ending. She never did listen when I talked about the language of flowers. She thought it was *cheesy*, could never stand how often my mother sent me books about it—or how those books pulled my attention away on our mandated set breaks.

Still, Nikki had held me that night, covering me with gentle kisses and going down on me until I forgot my own name. She could always pull orgasms from me so sweetly, like plucking a too-ripe peach from a branch and reveling in every juicy bite. I've never been with anyone so in tune with my body before. I probably never will be. That's a once-in-a-lifetime kind of thing.

We fit together like soulmates should, Nikki and me. Her bones and mine, her tongue and mine, our fingers intertwined with gasping breaths and cresting waves of pleasure—my name on her lips like a prayer, her name on mine like a gift to be cherished.

In that moment, despite all the other bullshit and drama going on, it felt like we had both remembered that we held something precious between us, something important. I might have started the night upset, but I ended it with Nikki crying and kissing my face over and over while whispering how much she loved me.

It was, unfortunately, one of the best moments of my life. I felt so loved, so safe that night . . . but moments—like relationships and life and everything else—must come to an end.

I take a deep breath, forcing myself to drag the phone away from my skin. To not let myself be undone by a single word called out across states and cell tower air. I *need* to remember what came before that, and after. To focus on all the nights spent dragging her out of bars and parties, begging her to come home with me, to not let us be another TMZ headline, to just be us for a little while—safe and cocooned in our little apartment with Gouda.

Soon after that perfect night came the reveal, a betrayal much bigger than anything she had ever done before—bigger even than the stains other people's lips left on her skin and the mean gossip rag headlines about me that I long suspected *Nikki's* team was behind.

The role.

The Oscar-winning role.

The future she ripped right out of my hands. It didn't matter that I was already feeling disillusioned with things and questioning whether I even wanted to act anymore. There was no coming back for us after she stole my role. That audition was the last gasp of hope for my Hollywood dreams—the last chance I was giving myself to prove that I was more than just Nikki's sidekick, both on set and off. Nikki knew that, and *she still took it from me.*

"Come on, Gouda," I say, grabbing my pizza and reaching for another can of cat food. "I know you already ate, but at least one of us deserves an extra-good day after this lifetime of crap we've had thrown at us."

* * *

I skip the shower—instead washing up quickly and dragging my hair into the neatest bun I can pull off with greasy hair—and head downstairs just over a half hour later. I've reblocked Nikki's number and deleted her *many* texts without opening them, but I still feel raw and exposed in a way I'd rather not. Being naked and wet and alone and sad in my shower seems like a recipe for disaster, a risk I'd rather not take.

This is me, dealing with it the best way I know how.

I step into the flower shop with Gouda trailing me, laughing when she darts forward to weave between my legs before running off to her usual perch in the sunny windows lining the front of the store.

"You gave her a second breakfast, didn't you?" Regan asks, cutting down some stems and shoving a bunch of blue hyacinths and white orchids together into some semblance of a bouquet. It looks a little chaotic, if I'm being honest.

"What's all this?" I ask, rearranging the flowers in a bid to make it at least *slightly* more cohesive. She passes me the ones she's just finished trimming and shrugs.

"Someone called and asked me to make an arrangement with every blue hyacinth and white orchid in the place. They said they'd come by in an hour or so to pick it up."

"Did they pay over the phone?" I ask, running the numbers in my head. This is going to be expensive—and huge—if they really want all of them.

"Yep, plus a big tip." She grins.

"Nice," I say, continuing to arrange the flowers as she clips them. "Whoever it is must have really screwed something up."

"Why?" Regan asks.

"Blue hyacinths are a wish for peace. Pairing them with white orchids? One of the few flowers that mean sincerity? Whoever they are, they're begging for forgiveness."

"I love how obsessed you are with flower meanings," she sighs. "Even if it does make me feel like a slacker."

"We can't all be as stunningly brilliant as I am," I tease. She nods so genuinely it makes my heart hurt. I know she means it. I know she wishes I did too.

She wrinkles her nose at me before we can get too sentimental. "Did you not shower?"

"Long story," I say, "why?"

"You have a little schmutz in your hair. Is that cat food? You know what, I don't know what it is. I don't want to, either."

"Oh my god, gross," I yelp, running to the bathroom in the back of the store and hoping she's wrong. She's not, though. I can see it in the mirror when I turn my head to the side. I don't know what it is either—dried pizza cheese, puke, both?—but it's nasty. I shove my head under the faucet, pulling out my bun and scrubbing my hair with hand soap as best as I can. Should I have run back upstairs and showered? Probably. Do I not want to be alone so bad that I'm basically bathing in the bathroom sink at my place of employment? Undoubtedly.

I come out a few minutes later, wet hair leaving damp splotches on my shirt as I use paper towels to squeeze as much water out of my hair as I can. Regan looks at me, amused, as she slides the last flower into place.

"Better?"

"Better," I say, grabbing the broom and starting to sweep up the clippings she's left beside the counter. "I can handle things if you need to head out or grab lunch or anything," I say. "Thanks for opening."

"I'm good. If I get hungry, I'll just run up and steal some of that pizza from last night. Besides, I kind of want to see this woman carrying this massive-ass bouquet out of here. She's due in any second," Regan says, checking the time on her phone.

"You didn't recognize the name?" I ask, curiosity piqued.

"They didn't leave one and I didn't recognize the voice. Maybe it's somebody from out of town taking advantage of the off-season rates?"

"Weird," I say, leaning my elbows against the counter and resting my chin on my hands.

"Very," she says, setting the flowers aside and leaning on the counter to join me. "Maybe this is her now."

I glance up and do a double take at the woman walking down the sidewalk across the street. She's dressed casually, in an oversized crewneck and jeans. A baseball cap is pulled down over her face, with her hair tucked back in a low pony. I paste on my best customer service smile . . . and then my brain finally catches up to my eyes. I'd know that walk anywhere, that *body* anywhere.

Nikki Colletti is here, in my town, about to walk into my new life.

"Oh no," I whisper, feeling warm and a little bit dizzy.

"Are you okay?" Regan asks, looking worried. "You got all pale all of a sudden."

"That's Nikki," I say, walking backward a few steps.

"No, it's not," she says, leaning forward and watching the figure waiting for a break in traffic to cross the street. "Oh my god, it almost could be, though?"

"It *is*," I say. "I have to go. I have to . . . I can't—"

"Go, go!" she says, gently turning me around. "If you really think that's her then get out of here. Hurry!"

I bolt to the tiny storage room in the back of our store and yank shut the thin curtain we use as a door. I flick off the lights just as the bells over the front door jingle. I can't help but peek out from the sliver of space where the curtain doesn't quite meet the wall.

"Hi," Nikki says, the sound of her voice making all the baby hairs on my arm stand up as my fight-or-flight response goes haywire. "I called in an order earlier. Do you know if it's ready?"

"The hyacinths and orchids, right? It's all set for you," Regan says, glancing back in my direction. I step back a little more into the shadows, trying not to let the curtain shift.

"Great," Nikki says, angling her head slightly away—just enough to not look suspicious while still making herself harder to identify. We both got good at that when we were young. I haven't had to do it in a while. A tendril of unexpected jealousy curls up my spine.

"This is beautiful," she says, eyeing the bouquet Regan has sat in front of her before casually flipping through the portfolio of past arrangements that we keep on the desk. *My portfolio.*

"Thanks," Regan says, sounding a little panicked. I'm sure she's dying to get Nikki out of the store so she can ask me what the hell is going on.

"Did you make all of these?" Nikki asks, pausing on a page I can't see. "This one's incredible."

"No," Regan says. "I own the shop, but I work with a floral

designer. Those are all her arrangements. I'm more of the meat and potatoes and she's more of the fancy stuff."

"She's very good," Nikki says, humming as she finishes flipping through. "Is this her card?"

"Yes," Regan says. "Why would you need it, though?"

"Do you ask all your customers that?" She laughs, pulling one of my cards out of the card holder and sliding it into her pocket. "I'd think you'd like repeat business."

I have never in my life been happier to know that my cards say a nice boring "Anne Lacy, Florist" instead of the Anderson "Andy" Ducharme that people from my past know me as. With any luck, she won't put it together. I'm sure by now she's forgotten my middle name is Lacy anyway.

"I do, but forgive me, you don't look like you're from around here and tourist season doesn't start for months. Business cards are expensive to print. I just want to make sure it'll go to good use."

"Oh, it definitely will," she says, scooping up the bouquet and heading for the door. She pauses, staring at Gouda lounging in the window, and I hold my breath. Nikki reaches out as if to pet her and Gouda hisses and jumps down, darting across the store and beneath the curtain I'm hiding behind. She winds her way between my legs as if to say, "See, Mom, I remember what she did. I'll hate enough for both of us until you remember why we do."

Nikki turns and looks in my direction. I know she can't really see me. I know she's probably just wondering where the cat ran off to. But I can't help but feel like she's got X-ray vision—like she's peering right through the wall, the curtain, my skin. I wipe at my eyes, I'm done crying over her, and let out a relieved breath when the bells jingle again, signaling her exit.

I rest my head against the wall just for a second, regaining my bearings before scooping Gouda into my arms and heading toward my apartment.

"Annie? You okay?" Regan calls from the desk, but I just wave her off.

I need to lie down. I need to sleep for a year. I need to find a way to rewind time. And not necessarily in that order.

Chapter Four

Emotional Support Bathtubs and Awkward Encounters

The screech of my phone alarm drags me out of bed less gently than I would have preferred. I stretch and blink blearily at the offending object, flicking it off and then rolling over to pull the blanket back over my head.

It was a late one last night, and not in a fun, get-drunk-with-your-friends-and-forget-about-the-world way. In an *oh-shit-what-have-I-done way*. It sucks.

Regan came up after closing the shop and found me sitting in the bathtub fully clothed listening to Gracie Abrams on repeat. No, not in a bubble bath, or even a regular bath, for that matter—just bone-dry with good acoustics and the scent of cleaner in the air. I don't even know why I did it, really, except once during a particularly nasty storm a few weeks after I first arrived in town, Regan insisted that interior bathrooms like mine were the safest place to shelter.

Having just left California, land of earthquakes and other

life-ruining things, this advice seemed counterintuitive, but I did it anyway and I didn't die. (No one did, but that's neither here nor there.)

Last night, I just needed a quick little "hide here in case of emergency" place to weather out the storms raging in my head. I didn't care in that moment whether that safe place came in the form of a friend or an old claw-foot tub.

Regan was freaked out when she found me in there—who could blame her—but she didn't need to be. I needed to be grounded by the cold porcelain leaching the heat out of my body; I needed to remember that the sun will rise tomorrow somehow warmer and brighter than ever before, just like I was last time I hid in there.

I blink at the soft morning light drifting in my window, relieved that the sun really did rise right on time. It's good to know that Nikki and I sharing the same zip code hasn't knocked the earth off its axis. I sigh at the sound of a garbage truck rattling its way down the road, the squeaky brakes chopping through the morning air like it's all business as usual. I suppose for them, it is. Unfair, really, when I feel like my life's flipped upside down.

I slide my legs out from under the blankets, planting my feet on the hardwood floors and trying to forget Regan's exasperated look when I admitted to her that I had indeed texted Nikki the night before. How I thought there was no way it was her number anymore and I was just chasing closure . . . and managed instead only to rip the Band-Aid off and reveal a still-gaping wound.

Gouda appears at the door as if by magic. She butts her head against my legs and purrs deeply with an expression I consider affection but understand is really just her attempt to get me moving faster. I know the second she can, she's going to herd me to her food bowl and demand breakfast. I feed her quickly, double-checking the time.

I have to open the store today and I refuse to be late two days in a row. Besides, Regan has a Small Business Association breakfast this morning that will tie her up until nearly noon. She offered to skip it but I know she loves those things. Plus, she always shoves an extra chocolate croissant or two in her bag to smuggle back for me.

Still, I take my time getting ready, unable to get out of my own way. When I finally must head downstairs, I do so with Gouda firmly scooped into my arms. Even with her soft, purring body to hide behind, I feel like I'm walking to the guillotine.

Part of me hopes that Nikki just happened to be passing through, suspects nothing, and will soon be on her way. (If she isn't already.) Part of me hopes she's here looking for me and somehow guessed right. But all of me is scared about how I'll feel in either scenario.

No matter what happens, I hope the blade is sharp and it's over quick.

Think of your happy place, think of your happy place, think of your happy place, I repeat to myself, trying to remember the various coping mechanisms Janet talked me through once upon a time. Except this flower shop *is* my happy place, and yesterday Nikki breached it—filling my beautiful garden with her weeds all over again.

Containment comes next, if the happy place fails.

I'm supposed to imagine putting bad feelings in a jar and sealing it, but I can't help giggling as I imagine Nikki trapped in a little jar that I've twisted shut. And then placed in a box. Which I then duct-taped shut. And sealed up in a safe that—oops—I can't remember the combination for.

Oh darn, did I forget to poke air holes too?

I smile, feeling a smidge better as I set my cat down and head to unlock the front door. I don't know that Janet would love my attempted mind murder, but I'd like to think she'd at least give me half credit for doing the exercises.

I flip the sign from closed to open and am about to twist the lock when someone appears on the other side of the glass, banging rapidly on the door. My hand falls as I startle backward and nearly trip over a rack of baby's breath and greenery. I catch myself from falling at the last second.

"Jesus Christ, hang on," I snap, wiping off little bits of leaves that stuck to my leggings on impact. I finally look up, instantly freezing at the sight of who's on the other side of the door.

Nikki stands there, lips slightly parted, forehead creased the way it only gets when she's thinking really hard. *Or just about to come*, my mind unhelpfully reminds me. I take a deep breath and flick the lock before walking back behind the counter. I'm doing an excellent impression of someone not falling apart, if I do say so myself. When I take my seat on the little stool near the register, it almost looks like a deliberate choice and not like I'm on the verge of passing out.

I stare down at the wood grain on the counter in front of me so hard that I'm worried it's going to be permanently burned into my retinas while I wait for the bells. The moment stretches long and then snaps, my hope that she second-guessed herself and left dissipating when they start to jingle.

I force my eyes up to meet hers as she comes to a stop in the middle of the store.

"Andy," she says, in that same breathy tone that I used to love so much.

"Don't," I say.

"You cut your hair." Her fingers twitch like she wants to touch it before she shoves them in her pockets.

"Yeah, I cut off a lot of things in the name of fresh starts," I say, giving her a pointed look. "That's really what you're leading with? 'You cut your hair'?"

She shakes her head. "I don't know why I said that. It's been five years, of course you Hi. Hello. I . . ." She trails off.

The ever-familiar blush rises to her cheeks and suddenly it's my turn to force my hands into submission. I grab the pen in front of me and start clicking it with one hand, shoving the other one between my thigh and the stool for good measure.

Nikki has come closer, right up to the counter now, and the familiar notes of her signature Tom Ford perfume crash over me. She bought her very first bottle when we were eighteen and had no idea of the horrors to come. I thought it was too complex and mature of a scent for her—I always preferred the lighter ones that reminded me of the gardens back home in Vermont—but she clung to it like it was proof she was a grown-up. It suits her well now, a fact that has a few stray butterflies confusedly stirring inside me.

Contain, contain, contain.

"Hi, hello, what the hell are you doing here?" I blink. "Actually, I don't care. How soon do you have to leave? *Can* you leave?" I correct, gritting my teeth.

She presses her lips together like she's fighting off a smile. "I mean, it kinda sounds like maybe you *do* care. At least a little?"

"What? No! Why would you say that?" I ask, feigning annoyance. "Forget I even said anything."

"Maybe I don't want to forget," Nikki says, and my eyes snap to hers—a little of my anger melting at the sincerity I find in them.

No, no way. I'm not falling for this again. She's an actress. Of course she can look sincere.

"It's good to see you, Andy," she adds, probably misinterpreting my silence as an invitation for her to go on.

"It's Anne now," I correct. "And if I had a spray bottle, I would be spraying you with it, just like I do when Gouda goes someplace she doesn't belong—like my kitchen counters."

Nikki tilts her head. "Are you saying this store is . . ."

"Like my kitchen counters, yes. Off-limits."

"And that makes me . . ."

"An asshole!" I blurt.

There she goes again, fighting a smile. "That breaks the metaphor a little bit, but fair enough. I'm not trying to . . . step all over your kitchen counters."

"Then what are you trying to do?"

"Have a conversation with you."

"Why?"

"Because you left in the middle of the night. You went dark on socials. You completely fell off the entire face of the earth!"

"I left LA," I say, rolling my eyes far more casually than I'm feeling. "Believe it or not, that's not the entire world."

"Depends on who you ask."

"Did you need something?" I cross my arms. "Because if you don't, then you're just loitering, and we have a very strict no-loitering policy here."

Nikki makes a big show of looking around the empty shop before leveling me with her gaze once again. "Busy place here. I can see why you can't afford to have people standing around."

"Oh, fuck off, Nikki."

She tenses at my words, and I wonder if she's taking the same trip down memory lane that I have been. Or maybe it's something more akin to PTSD.

Cards on the table? She definitely heard me tell her to fuck off more than was healthy toward the end of our relationship. We were toxic by then, forcing it like two opposing magnets being crammed together—except with bonus drugs and alcohol and cameras recording our worst meltdowns.

Think of the jar, I remind myself. *Contain, contain, contain.*

She clears her throat. "Actually, I do need something. Can you ship flowers?"

"Stateside, sure, but only overnight, and it's gonna cost you."

"I'm good for it." She shrugs, plunking her AmEx on the counter.

"Of course you are. I'm sure Eliza negotiated you great back-end deals after that Oscar," I scoff, feeling extra bitter. "Are you still sniping roles too, or . . . ? I swear that last period piece you did was meant for Florence Pugh."

"Pugh turned it down long before it got to me, but glad to know you've been keeping up with things," she says. "That explains how you texted me about my book announcement within hours of it going live. Do you follow my TikTok or just check it regularly?"

Shit.

"What are you doing here, Nikki?"

"Ordering flowers," she says, flipping through my portfolio.

"No, what are you doing *here*, as in *this town*."

"I needed a place to finish my book."

"Yet here you are, acting like a little stalker instead."

Nikki scrunches up her face like it's just now occurring to her how this might look from my perspective. "Wait, I was here *first*," she says and then, seeing my incredulous expression, adds, "not first-first, obviously. But before I knew *you* were here. I'm over a week into my stay already."

"You're so full of it," I say with a laugh. "There's no way!"

"You want to bet on that, Ducharme?" She pulls out her phone and starts scrolling through. "Here. Here!" She turns it toward me. "Here's the reservation email that proves it. I came here to finish the book. It felt like the right place to do it."

"What? How?" I ask in disbelief. She's actually telling the truth. She rented one of those old cabins, just like we did all those years ago—just like I did when I first came here.

She shrugs. "It's just fate or luck or *something*. I mean, this was my place too, once, when it was still ours."

"I . . ." I trail off because no. *No. I'm not doing this.*

There was a time, not even that long ago, that hearing her call this place ours would have brought me to my knees. But I'm not that person anymore—at least I'm not trying to be. I open my mouth to tell her as much, but she cuts me off.

"Whatever you're about to say, remember that *you* texted *me*.

You said you were living the dream, and I thought . . . what if? I was already here; how could I not check?"

"You're in the cabins," I say, mostly to myself.

"You know what's weird? Nothing's changed. Even that horrible painting of the sailboats is still there. I was half waiting for you to walk in my door with an armful of shells, talking about our dreams or your flowers again."

I blink and it's like the world falls away, transporting me back to the summer after our final season of *The Nikki and Andy Show*. It was a trip full of long lazy days spent lounging in the summer heat and collecting shells to line up in the windows of our little place on the shore. "Well-worn" would be an extremely forgiving way to describe the ramshackle row of cabins dotting the small stretch of Maine coast, but it was perfect for us. The ideal location to daydream about our next steps and naively convince ourselves that we would always be taking them together.

"It was never really *our* dream, was it?" I ask, digging my nails into the soft wood beneath the counter, letting the splinters ground me. "I wanted to work in the florist shop, sure, but you were never really going to become a waitress. You love attention too much. You'd do anything to keep it."

She winces, and I hope she's remembering my face when she told me she took the role I was passed over for. The role that I didn't even know she was going to audition for. Because that's the truth about Nikki. She'll say your name so sweetly while she's worshipping at the altar between your legs, but at the end of the day, she'll sell you out—over and over again if you let her. And I *did* let her, until my self-esteem was in the toilet and even Gouda was embarrassed for me.

"I need you to go," I say, wishing that my words came out sounding stronger. That I wasn't really just begging her to let me live.

"I haven't told you my flower order yet," she says, gently, as if that matters at all.

"Didn't you just get a massive bouquet yesterday?" I ask.

"Were you hiding in the back? I thought I saw that curtain move, but—"

"Shut up," I say, and this time I have no problem finding my voice. "You're not going to walk in here and make me feel small. You're not . . . I won't . . . forget it. Will you please just go back home?"

Her eyes shoot to mine at the word "home" and I clench my hands into fists because no, *this* is home, right here. There is nothing left for me on the other coast, and not even the ghost of the woman I loved standing before me can convince me otherwise.

"Andy—Anne," she corrects herself, holding up her hand like she thinks I'm going to yell at her more. "I just need some flowers."

"Yesterday you picked them up, today you want them shipped. How many pissed-off women do you have on your roster now? Enough for a team?"

"What are you talking about?" She looks offended. *Good.*

I come out from behind the counter, running my fingers along the rows of flowers lining the shop. She watches me closely and I smile. I'm taking my power back, starting *now*.

"TMZ has had a field day watching you and your . . . extracurricular friends. God knows I had a front-row seat myself when we were together. It just stands to reason . . ." I say, and she looks away.

"Right, of course," she says, glaring down at the floor. "TMZ, again."

"What do you want this order to say? You already did one that said sorry. We could do . . . 'Thank you for the screaming orgasms'? Or 'You were a great one-night stand. Hope you don't end up in the gossip blogs too'?"

"Can you really make the flowers say all that?" she asks, catching me off guard with another little laugh. I meant to insult her, not amuse her.

"Kind of. What doesn't come across from the blooms we can always add on the note."

"Excellent," she says, mischief returning to her face. "I can't wait to see what a 'Thank you for the screaming orgasms' bouquet looks like."

"Of course you would pick that one." I roll my eyes, doing my best to sort through as much of the language of flowers as I've memorized, which is, frankly, a lot.

I come by it honestly: both of my parents are botanists. I was never a science kid, though, so they taught me to appreciate their beloved buds from another angle, beauty and language. They didn't care that I didn't love plants the same way they did; they were just excited that I cared at all.

When I was staying with my aunt in LA to film, they would send me care packages full of books and pictures. I spent a lot of time on set reading them—especially when I was feeling homesick for my parents. The idea that I could tell a story with flower petals blew my mind.

Now it's the evolution that draws me in—the way meanings change over decades and centuries. After what I've been through, I can understand how a beautiful bloom can turn from a sign of hopeful romance to a funeral flower through no fault of its own.

"You have the best thinking face," Nikki says, pulling me from my head.

I ignore her, walking around the racks of flowers as I plan my attack. The dahlias catch my eyes first and I smile. I grab a few of the red—lust, desire—and the white—sympathy, sorrow. I toss in a black one for good measure, sure that the betrayal it represents will be relevant if whoever receives this bouquet has been in Nikki's orbit for any length of time.

Satisfied, I add a few sprigs of greenery here and there for aesthetics. Even if I'm making this bouquet as a giant screw-you, I want it to be pretty. Nikki eyes me carefully as I start assembling it all.

"What? Are you planning to open your own flower shop too?"

"Hmm?" she asks, clearly not listening even though her eyes are paying rapt attention.

"Why are you staring?"

"It's . . . cool," she settles on awkwardly. "You're obviously very skilled. It's fun to watch. I never thought . . ." She shakes her head and I'm glad she swallowed whatever was coming next.

I grab the shipping materials to finish up. "Where is this going?"

"Back to LA," she says, and then rattles off an address not too far from where we used to live. I wonder if she still lives there, and if she's violating her own *don't shit where you eat* rule about dating or doing business with someone hyperlocal, but I don't ask.

I turn to the register and punch in the shipping fees first, doubling the overnight charge because I know Nikki can afford it. Then I do the math on the bouquet itself—dahlias aren't that expensive, so I triple their cost to be petty.

"Two eighty-seven fifty," I say.

She arches an eyebrow. "Two hundred and eighty-seven dollars for this little bouquet?"

"And fifty cents." I smile.

"Right, and fifty cents." She flicks her credit card closer to me. "Do your worst."

I run it, hoping selfishly that it gets declined even though I know it won't. How great would it be to loudly announce *that* to her little stunned face, though. Unfortunately, it goes through just fine. Nikki has more money than god, I'm sure. She got a better cut of residuals than I did on the show, plus the whole not being robbed blind by her manager—oh, and then the Oscar probably didn't hurt.

I pass her card back and finish boxing her bouquet, mildly curious about the woman waiting on the other side of this shipment. I wonder if she knows about whoever got the first bouquet. I'll have to google the recipient later—try to figure it out over a beer or three, when I'm back to pretending that my curiosity isn't fueled by jealousy.

"Did you need anything else?" I ask, my tone dismissive.

I can't keep up the act of indifference much longer; my frayed edges are already beginning their descent from sturdy rope to useless bits of string. I need her to leave. Now.

"No, I guess not," she says, stepping back. "No loitering,

right? I have somewhere I should probably get to anyway. It was good seeing you, Anderson."

"Wish I could say the same, Nicole." I run my hand down the last bit of tape on the box. "I'll get this overnighted to your latest bang buddy and you're all set. I'm sure you can find a florist in LA for any future orders, though, right?"

Nikki bites the inside of her cheek, the skin sucking in in a way I can't believe I used to think was cute. Then she nods, just once, before heading out the door.

I flop back onto the stool to watch as she darts across the street and, strangely, heads into the church.

She was never the religious type before. *What is she up to?* Whatever it is, it's none of my business. I brace my arm against the counter, ignoring the slight tremble in my hands as I open the cash drawer and set her receipt inside—praying that she didn't just take a piece of me all over again.

Chapter Five
Shipping Charges Soothe My Soul

"Then she just willingly paid all that and left?"

Regan and I are rehashing yesterday's events yet again this morning while eating the still-delicious, but definitely slightly stale, chocolate croissants. I didn't have an appetite after Nikki left, so we voted to save them for today. Besides, Regan ate two of them fresh at the Small Business Association meeting anyway.

"I should have charged her more," I say between bites. "She barely even blinked at the price."

"We'll get her next time, tiger." Regan laughs, wiping a few stray crumbs off the side of her lips. "I'm just proud of you for holding up in the face of all that. It couldn't have been easy. You could have called me, if you needed to."

"I know, but I had it under control," I only sort of lie. "There better not be a next time, though. I told her to find a florist back in LA and leave me the hell alone."

I'm paraphrasing, but it's fine. That was what I meant, even if the words didn't really come out that aggressive. *I did my best, okay.*

"Who did you tell to leave you the hell alone?" Johnny asks, walking out of the back room with several boxes of holiday decor that Regan asked him to store at his mechanic shop across town. He has a massive garage with an attic at his place. Here, space is at an absolute premium.

We almost couldn't fit today's shipment in the little room, which means there's a giant cardboard case of flowers sitting up front still waiting to be processed. It would be an eyesore, if we actually *had* any customers come in this morning.

"Nikki," Regan and I say in unison.

"She's here? Like here-here? In town? Or just in your phone?"

"Yep, here in the flesh," I say. "She was, anyway. I'm hoping she's gone by now."

The words sound true, at least I hope they do, but the feelings beneath them are much more complicated. The truth is, I don't know what I'm hoping. Nikki leaving would be the best for both of us, probably. Certainly the best for me—but seeing her again has stirred up so much.

"Want me to slap her?" he asks cheerfully. I know he's kidding again, sort of—that was a catchphrase of a bit character on our old show, and besides, Johnny has never hit anyone in his life—but it still gets my hackles up. I don't know why I feel protective of Nikki when I said ruder things to her face yesterday. It's just . . . hard.

"You would never slap anyone, let alone a woman," Regan says.

"That's what her sidekick said in the show, *Regan*," he says, with an exaggerated scowl. "Get with the program. *I'm* the sidekick now. It's my duty to say my lines, lest I end up as big of a slacker as her former costar was! Right, Annie? You get it."

I laugh and shake my head, enjoying a nice low-key day with my friends after the dramatic events of the last forty-eight hours. Except speak of the devil and she shall appear or whatever, because Johnny has barely been gone five minutes when the bells over the door ring.

Nikki waves to me as she walks up to the counter. I start to tell her to turn back around, but Regan beats me to it.

"I thought Annie told you to get lost."

"Annie?" she asks, raising an eyebrow as she looks at me.

"Only to my friends."

"We were friends once," she says, almost sounding a little sad.

"And now you're not," Regan says, crossing her arms and blocking the aisle that I'm in so Nikki can't get any closer. "You need to leave."

I would kiss Regan for that, if I didn't think it would make things even more awkward.

"I'm a paying customer," Nikki says. "I need another order."

"This is a private business. *My* private business. I decide who can shop here."

"That's homophobic," Nikki jokes, clearly unbothered.

"It's not homophobic to tell you that you can't keep torturing your ex like this. Please go."

"Usually, people are falling all over themselves to get me in their shops. It's almost refreshing that you're trying to turn me away."

I roll my eyes and step out from behind Regan, even though I'd rather spend all day hiding there. "Cut it out, Nikki," I groan, walking toward her. "What do you want? Why are you here?"

"Like I said, I need another order. You're the best. You know I always want the best."

"Fine, then let's get it over with." I sigh, pulling out an order form and trying to ignore the fact that my heart is practically doing flips because *she said I'm the best. She said she wants me.* For two blinks, I'm a lovesick teenager instead of a woman who's been through hell . . . but then I crash back to earth. "How long are you going to do this for?" I ask.

Nikki leans against the counter. "Only as long as it takes to get you to talk to me about things."

"I don't have anything to say to you."

"You had a lot to say the other night, though. What did you text me, again? 'Fuck your book and fuck you'? That doesn't sound like someone without an opinion on things." She tilts her head, her teasing look giving way to something more serious. "Seriously, I just want to talk."

The book. I had almost forgotten about it with the shock of seeing her again. Now that I remember, the fury returns fresh. "You want my opinion? My opinion is that you don't have any right to tell my story, but I know that's never mattered to you before," I snap. "I'm not about to waste my time listening to you try to justify it. So, if you want to order, order—the money spends the same even if I hate you. But then you have to get out."

She frowns. "I'm not telling your story—I'm writing mine, Anne," she says, and that foreign name on her familiar tongue twists in my gut like a knife.

Nikki was never meant to call me that. She was never meant to know Anne even existed.

I hate this.

"*Is* there a story without Annie?" Regan asks, stepping up beside me. "Unless you're just going to talk about what happened once she stopped covering for you all the time, but then you wouldn't have done the wink, right?"

Nikki narrows her eyes as she flicks them between us. I can tell she's trying to puzzle out exactly what my relationship with Regan is. I lean a little closer to my best friend, hoping that it gives Nikki the wrong idea. I know it's awful of me, but I want her to hurt too. I want her to think that she's not the only one who has moved on. She seems so smug, so fine, after seeing me all these years later. I want her to miss me or, even better, feel like she's missed out on me.

"Do you want to order something from *us* or not?" I ask, tapping my pencil against the little order form again. A little divot appears as she scrunches her eyebrows together at the word "us."

"Y . . . yes," she says, clearly caught off guard.

Good. Make her wonder.

She stares at where Regan's shoulder presses against mine for another beat before opening my portfolio to one of my biggest arrangements. It was the backdrop for the winner's circle at a horse show I was hired to do a few months back. They paid extra for us to deliver it and set it up even though it was way, way outside of our delivery area. It's the biggest arrangement I've ever done, and the one I'm most proud of. It's also extremely *not* shippable.

Nikki taps the picture twice. "I want a statement piece like this."

"For what?"

"To send to someone important," she says, watching me, and I wonder if we're playing the same game right now.

"You can't ship something that size," I say. "It's almost three feet tall and six feet long. Regan had to help me set it up."

"Fine, a miniature version, then. I just need something loud and splashy."

"And you want this overnighted to your special someone again?" I'm fishing, and she knows it.

"No." She smiles. "This is going to someone different."

"Great," I say, wondering if all these "someone different"s know about each other.

Not my circus, not my monkeys, I remind myself. *Not for a long time.*

That thought shouldn't hurt, but it does. I pull the photo album toward me as a distraction while running through the options in my head. It's going to be tricky to keep the essence but change the finished product into something smaller and shippable. "It might take me a couple days to make this," I settle on. "I need to order in some of the flowers."

"No," she says. "I need it sooner."

"Well, I can't do it sooner. Not if you want it to be good. Tell your secret bang buddy that her gift is going to be a little late."

"Wow, you're so funny I forgot to laugh," she deadpans, quoting one of her own old catchphrases from the show. I almost wish Johnny was still here, offering to slap her.

"Don't do that."

"Do what?" she asks innocently.

"Don't come in here with your old lines and your old smirks and your old perfume—"

"My old perfume?" She looks almost hopeful. "You *do* remember?" Her fingers trail up to the side of her neck as she smiles. "I used to always dab it *right here* so you would—"

I shake my head, not giving in. "Are you trying to make this as painful as possible for me?"

"No, I . . ." Her eyes shoot to the floor. "I'm sorry, that crossed a line," she mumbles. "You can forget the design," she adds. "Just make something beautiful that can be overnighted, okay?"

"There's going to be a rush charge," Regan pipes up.

"That's fine. Ship it here, please," she says, grabbing my pen and scrawling down another LA address.

"That'll be . . . six hundred and fifty dollars," Regan says.

"For a bouquet?" Nikki scrunches up her face.

"No, for shipping and the rush charge." Regan flashes a toothy grin. "The flowers are extra."

Nikki rolls her eyes and plunks down her AmEx again, the heavy metal corner of the card digging into soft wood. I pick it up and glance between Nikki and Regan, who seem to have devolved into some kind of deranged staring contest.

Perfect. This is all totally normal and great. Nothing is wrong here at all.

"So . . . I'm just making anything I want?" I ask slowly, waving my hand between them.

"Yes," Nikki says, at the same time as Regan says, "No."

Before I can reply, the bells over the door ring again and another customer walks in—one of the little old church ladies.

She gets a bouquet of carnations once a week to bring to her husband's grave. You could practically set your watch to her.

Nikki tips her head down, pulling her hair out of her bun and letting it fall around her face. I want to tell her that Mrs. Dorian has very poor eyesight (and probably wouldn't recognize Nikki even if she didn't), but I'm enjoying how uncomfortable Nikki looks right now.

"Maybe we should wrap this up," Nikki says quietly.

"Fine by me," I say. "You being in this shop every day is going to make people talk. Even with your stupid hair and hat, people are eventually going to figure out who you are, and when they do, they're also going to recognize *me*."

She huffs out a laugh. "Nobody knows what I look like without my makeup. They accuse me of getting a nose job when my beauty advisor switches my contouring. I don't go out fresh-faced enough in LA for anyone to pick up on it."

"As much as it kills me to admit this, yes they will," I say. "You're too famous for them not to." I swipe her card and her the full $850—$650 for the rush fee and shipping, plus $200 for the flowers. I feel like a jerk, but also, Nikki just covered Regan's mortgage payment on this place for the month. "Please, you're going to cause a scene."

She sighs. "If the only way I can get you to talk to me is by buying flowers, then I'm going to be here every morning. You can get used to it or you can—"

"Wow, I see you're just as good at respecting boundaries as you were before."

"That's not . . . no," she says, stepping back like I burned her, but seriously, what did she think she was doing?

"Come on, Nikki. What's it going to take to make you go away?"

She rubs the back of her neck. "I want you to . . . I was hoping that you would . . . help me with the book."

"What?!" I shout, and then quickly switch to whispering. "What do you mean you want me to help with your book? I don't want there to *be* a book, Nikki!"

"That's literally what I wanted to talk to you about. It's not what you're thinking. Is that diner we used to go to still here? We could go there if you don't want to talk here. Just hear me out, please?"

"Anything we needed to say to each other was said a long time ago."

"That's not true. Look, I don't want to do this book if it's going to upset you, but—"

"Then don't do it, because it will," I say, turning away to, *I don't even know*, rush up to my apartment or something. I just can't look at her and her pleading eyes for another second.

"Can we please discuss this like rational people instead of you running away again? Please?"

My nostrils flare and I bite back the venom I'm ready to throw at her for implying that *I* am the irrational one in this scenario. *Me.*

"You said we shouldn't make a scene," Nikki adds.

I glance at Mrs. Dorian and then back to Nikki just in time to see her sliding her signed card slip toward me. I blow out a heavy breath. "I'm *not*."

"You're about to, though. Your nostrils are doing that thing they do when you're about to lose it. Come on, we have things to discuss either way. I know you don't owe me anything, but I would sincerely appreciate it if we could have a civil conversation like two people who used to love each other. If you'd rather go through lawyers or whatever . . . it's your call, I guess."

Used to love each other, she said. Her words slice into the softest parts of me. *Used to, used to, used to, used to.*

I feel like I'm going to throw up.

"If I meet you at that diner, you'll leave after?" I manage to choke out because I know as long as she's here, I'll never be okay. Just like I know hiring a lawyer as high caliber as whoever is repping her these days is going to be totally unaffordable.

"Tomorrow at six?" she asks softly, dodging my question.

I squeeze my eyes shut, taking a steadying breath. "Tomorrow at six."

Chapter Six
Check, Please

After three pep talks from Regan, an oddly reassuring text from my mother, two (half) joking offers of slapping from Johnny, and a nervously chugged iced coffee that I definitely didn't need and shouldn't have drunk, I find myself finally driving across town to the little diner.

Danny's Diner sits in the farthest corner of Main Street, right where the tourist shops give way to liquor stores and dingy take-out places that actually have the best food around. It feels fitting, in a way, that we meet there. It's almost exactly halfway between the flower shop and the little cabins that started it all. We're truly meeting in the middle for once... even if it still feels like Nikki is the one holding all the power.

What else is new?

Still, I can't help but think about the last time we went to Danny's together—the last time we were here, *in this town*, together. We had just come off our particularly rough fourth and final season, one that Nikki was gone for more than she was there. She had recorded most of her lines in post rather than being on set, which meant frantic last-minute script rewrites whenever she wasn't available. I had to do double the work to make up for it.

I had secretly wondered if the showrunner would recast her or write her out, but it was clear the producers wanted to keep her name attached—especially once she started to get more recognition. The fact that it meant more work for me wasn't even a footnote on the studio's list of concerns. In retrospect, my agent should have demanded bonuses or a new contract to account for all the extra hours on set—but no. He was too busy embezzling to notice, I guess.

Nikki and I had already been outed to the public by then—an unfortunate accident made in the middle of season three by a loose-lipped guest star who had assumed that, since it was a bit of an open secret on set, that meant she could talk about it in public. If ever there was a record-scratch moment at a press junket, it was when Lorna MacNeil blurted out, "It's so cute how in love they are. Dating your costar has to bring so much comfort in this crazy industry."

Cue a major uproar and both of our teams (and Lorna's) flailing around the sidelines in a panic. Nikki and I just sat there, rooted to the spot, knowing that the pin had finally been pulled, detonating the truth all over a crowd of unsuspecting TV reporters.

The headlines were relentless. Then came the protests from conservative groups saying we were trying to "brainwash the children," then the LGBTQ+ advocacy groups who wanted us to be loud and proud at all times—even on days when I just wanted to be home in my pajamas watching *Love Island* and pretending none of this was even happening.

Our publicists tried to keep us apart for a while, worried that it hurt our image, hurt the ratings, made life harder, and it did, it did. But we somehow survived it—even if our show did not. *Cosmo* even named us "cutest celebrity couple" once . . . which only ramped up the protests and headlines.

I don't think any of us were surprised when the network announced that the fourth season would be our last. I probably should have been more pissed about them cowing to conservatives, but Nikki seemed almost relieved about having one less thing to juggle, so I tried to match that energy. Besides, I was already exhausted from it all.

We came here, to this town, right after filming wrapped forever on *The Nikki and Andy Show*.

We both desperately needed a break after everything, and I hoped that the time away would *also* help us remember who we were without all the Hollywood hoopla. It worked, mostly. When Nikki wasn't taking work calls, it was downright domestic—lazy mornings spent sipping instant coffee in our room or ordering pancakes at the diner, regular afternoon jogs, plus sunsets and beach walks and learning how to do our own laundry in the little room full of machines outside the caretaker's cabin.

It wasn't a glamorous vacation, but it was real. It was perfect.

I clung to the memories of this place with a white-knuckle grip as our ship started sinking almost immediately after our return to LA—on my most desperate days, I used them to convince myself that things weren't that bad. That we couldn't have shared so much by the ocean if we weren't meant to be. That two weeks of daydreaming that she was a waitress and I was a florist made up for years of being let down.

They existed like a montage in my head, faded and overly romanticized—I swore I could still feel the surf washing over our feet as we galloped across the beach, laughing and free for the first time since our parents sent us off to set like little dolls waiting to be posed.

The shells I collected had bitten into my palms, sharp and stinging, but I didn't care. Because every time I walked up with more, Nikki acted like they were the best things she had ever seen. She would lead me inside, pressing her lips into my softest skin, and suddenly the scratchy sheets and the cold, sandy floors felt more luxurious than any of the fancy places the network had ever put us up in. It was *our place* and we had picked it *ourselves*.

I wasn't naive enough even back then to believe she would make the timeline jump with me—which is probably why the fact that she's here now is screwing with my head on every single level. It was always going to mess me up to see her again, but *here*? In *this* place? It's a level of surreal I could never have imagined.

I take a deep breath, trying to rein in my thoughts as I park my car and squint through the well-lit windows at all the people bustling around. What if I walk in and find Nikki waitressing inside, like we daydreamed about all those years ago? What would I do then, if she followed the rabbit hole all the way down?

It doesn't matter.

Those two girls on the beach—the ones who still felt like their love was something precious instead of damned—they don't exist anymore.

Now, they're just a trivia question . . . or at least I am. A footnote in every "Where are they now?" listicle, forever reduced to weighing brussels sprouts in a "last known photo," while Nikki is the bright, splashy cover image, complete with a six-page spread.

I head inside, nodding to the hostess as I make my way to the booth in the back corner. Nikki sits tucked away inside, baseball hat back on, pulled low, just like the last time we were here so many years ago. I take in the sight of her stacking tiny jelly containers into a mini pyramid, like I've seen a hundred times before—it seems no amount of media and manners training could break that particular annoying habit of hers.

Nikki stills for a moment when I slide into the booth across from her, but doesn't look up, concentrating on piling the syrup in a single tall tower instead. She makes it up to seven before I nudge the table with my knee on purpose, causing them to fall.

"Whoops," I say.

A waitress appears and sets two glasses of water down before scurrying back to the kitchen. I raise an eyebrow, confused why she didn't ask for my order, only to see a guilty expression flash across Nikki's face.

"I ordered your favorite," she says. "I hope that's all right?"

I cross my arms. "You don't know my favorite anymore."

"Are you telling me that you don't order chicken and waffles with a side of ranch and extra syrup?"

Well, apparently, she does.

"No," I lie. "I'm more of a burger girl now."

I don't even know why I said that. I didn't eat red meat then and I definitely don't eat it now. The thought of it twists my stomach, kicking up the anxiety swirling inside me to a whole new level. If I have to choke down a burger on top of everything else, I'm going to fling myself right out the window.

"If you'd like to order something else . . ." She trails off, biting her lip and tugging the laminated menu out from behind the napkin dispenser set against the wall.

I decide that making her look briefly nervous is ample punishment; no need to torture myself on top of it. "No, it's fine," I say, waving the menu away as she tries to pass it to me. "I'll cram it down for old times' sake."

"I want you to be comfortable, Andy—Annie. Anne. Sorry, I'm not trying to be a dick about your name. It's just hard for me to see you as something different."

"I am something different, though," I say. "*Someone* different. I have to be."

"Why?" she asks so genuinely it catches me off guard.

"You know why. Surely you know why." I shift in my seat, letting the awkward silence linger a bit before I add, "Anyway, I'm here. What did you want to discuss?"

"Everything," she says, looking strangely like she means it. "What have you been doing the last few years? How's *our* cat? How's your mom?"

"Rebuilding, still hates you, and . . . you know what, 'still hates you' works for my mom too."

Nikki scoffs. "Carly could never hate me! Not after I gave her my secret family fudge recipe."

"It's on the back of the Fluff container! It's hardly a secret," I say, fighting off a laugh of my own. It feels familiar, sitting across from her again, like putting on a well-worn hoodie you thought you'd lost and finding it still fits perfectly.

It shouldn't.

"What just happened?" Nikki asks, narrowing her eyes.

"What do you mean?"

"I mean I almost got a smile out of you and now your face is all pinched up like you got kicked in the stomach."

"You being here *is* a kick in the stomach, Nikki."

She winces and I grab a straw, desperate for a distraction. Wishing on knotted straw wrappers is something I've done since I was little. My mom did it religiously growing up: get your knot out and you get your wish, simple as that. Nikki always said it was goofy, but I caught her tying enough straw wrapper knots before a big audition or performance to know she didn't truly mean it.

I glance up at her now to find her studying my hands. For all the teasing, she was never shy about watching my technique. She said it was just because she loved to watch my fingers work, but . . . *come on.* I carefully loop the two ends of the wrapper together, pulling oh so gently so it doesn't tear. I leave the knot loose, glancing up to make sure she's watching, and then pull the ends of the wrapper in opposite directions, hard and fast. The knot unfurls between us, and I smile as I drop the wrapper to the table.

I get my wish. Now I just need to decide what to use it for.

Across from me, Nikki lets out a relieved sigh, like she had been holding her breath. "That has to be a good sign, right?" she asks.

"For me, yes. For you? Questionable. What if I wished you would spontaneously combust?"

"Then I guess"—she reaches forward, scooping up the pieces of the wrapper and slipping them into her pocket—"ka freakin' boom, baby."

I look away, fighting the heat inexplicably rising to my cheeks at the tenor of her voice slipping down. *I hate her, please gods, remember I hate her. Maybe remembering that forever should be my wish.*

"Nikki . . ." I say. Her mouth pulls up into a little half smile, and I know I have to shut this down. Immediately.

"What is it that you need from me? You mentioned lawyers and wanting help with your book? Let's focus on that, unless you really are just here to ruin my life."

"No," she says softly. "I don't want to ruin anything for you. I'm so proud of you."

I roll my eyes. "Could you *be* any more patronizing?"

"I'm not being patronizing," she says. "I mean it. I'm proud. Your flowers are—"

"I live in a shitty one-bedroom apartment over the place that I work, okay? In a town that's dead nine months of the year. Meanwhile, you're doing my signature wink on the set of E! wearing Versace. What's to be—"

"You seem happy, though." She cuts me off. "Not when you're around me, of course, but in general. That portfolio you have is admirable—incredible, even. You built something entirely new. I would never be brave enough to do something like that."

"It didn't feel brave, it felt necessary," I say.

"They don't have to be mutually exclusive." She shrugs. "I don't know how you did it. I can barely go out into the world without my agents and managers smoothing all the rough edges. These days, I'm more of a shy house cat hiding from people than anything else."

"Really? You want to play it like that? Because you don't seem particularly shy about writing a book about *our* life story and inviting all those people to have a peek behind the curtain."

She bites her lip as the waitress sets our plates down in front of us. Cobb salad for her, chicken and waffles for me. I reach for a syrup package at the same time she moves to pass it to me. Our fingers brushing for a split second, just long enough for me to register the heat, the softness, and then I yank my hand back.

It's wild to think that there was ever a time I sought her skin out. That those casual touches and little smiles ever kept me fed during all the long, lonely nights while she was out networking or filming. Now her skin is a flashing neon sign warning me away—poison dripping from every pore.

Keep your wits, girl. She is not for you. She wasn't then, not really, and she certainly isn't now.

I make sure her hands are back on her side of the table before pointedly reaching for the syrup again and drizzling it over my plate. Nikki watches me with big, sad eyes. It makes me feel like a little bit of a monster, *but I'm not the one who broke us.*

I notice a laptop and papers on the booth beside her and gesture toward them. "Is that the book? Let me see it."

"Really?" she asks, setting everything up on the table with a wary look.

"Yeah, might as well see how bad it's gonna hurt."

"I have a lot of reasons for wanting to write this book, Andy," she says, leaning forward to slide some papers over to me. "None of them are to hurt you."

"Anne," I correct, desperately trying not to get drunk on the way her familiar perfume mixes with the scent of her shampoo. I practically yank the papers out of her hand. She gives me a peculiar look as she drops back into her side of the booth and opens her MacBook.

"Chapter Four," it reads at the top of the page.

I swallow hard as I realize what scene she's handed me. It was our first time meeting. They called me last minute, asking for a final chemistry read. Nikki had already signed on for her role, but apparently it was still between me and one other actress for the final spot. This audition would be the deciding force.

I spent the night googling Nikki, trying to get a feel for who she was. She had done some bit parts as a kid in Hallmark movies or in soap opera flashbacks. A few commercials, like me. Small stuff in general, but bigger than mine. I'd have to bring my A game.

I needed to nail it—I was living with my aunt then in her tiny LA apartment. She was an on-set makeup artist, and it was her fault I got into acting. She took one look at me when I was born and said I was going to be a star. My parents thought it was cute at first. They would send me out to stay with her every summer and she'd get me bit parts in commercials or store ads that my parents would hang on the fridge. They were less than enthused when I moved out there permanently to make a go of it, sleeping on my aunt's couch like a real struggling actor, but we made it work.

On that day, the day I met Nikki, my mom had come to visit. She sat in the waiting room with my aunt while I walked in to meet the casting director. I was so nervous my hands were shaking. Mom and I had gotten into an argument the night before, with her saying that if I didn't get this role, then I needed to go back to Vermont with her.

It was all riding on that. My very own path diverging in the woods, and I had kicked things off with shaking hands and nausea. Maybe it was foreshadowing. A gun on the mantel set to go off when I least expected.

I sigh and skim more of the chapter—pausing to glance up at her when I get to the part where I walked in for the read. Nikki's peeking at me over the top of her laptop, biting her lip. It would be endearing if I let it. I don't.

"This isn't right," I say, setting down the papers.

Nikki looks startled. "What do you mean?"

"You wrote that I was cast and they called *you* in for a chemistry read. That's the opposite of what really happened." I shake my head. "You were cast. I was the one fighting for my life that day."

"Uh, absolutely not," she says. "Eliza was going nuts over them making me do a third audition. She thought being on *Days of Our Lives* for a week should have counted for something. I was so stressed by the time I got there. If I didn't get that role, I don't know what would have happened. My parents could *not* afford to keep me out there."

I scrunch up my face. "Okay, no, when I said I was worried you were going to tell my story, I meant, like, metaphorically. You're literally jacking *my* story in this chapter and pretending it's yours. *You* were cast, you were completely relaxed! We were only there to decide if they were going to pick me or the other girl."

"What other girl? What are you talking about?"

"The other girl who was reading for my role. They didn't say who. It could have been the Nikki and, I don't know, Clara show.

You were cast first—that's why your name came first in the show."

Nikki runs her thumb over her lip. "Huh," she says, tipping her head. "The casting director told me the same thing. They said you had been cast and it was down to me and one other girl. I wasn't relaxed at all, I was freaking out!"

I lean back in the booth, not buying it. "Why would they do that?"

"I don't know, but I'm not lying! Maybe they just liked screwing with us or maybe there really were two other girls who did a completely different read together. Maybe it could have been the Clara and Gertrude show for all we know."

I smile. "Yes, of course, because there's so many tweens and teens named Gertrude these days."

"You never know," she says, her eyes going soft as she keeps looking at me . . . and . . .

Okay, this is getting a little uncomfortable.

"What?" I finally ask, dabbing at my face with a napkin. "Do I have syrup on my face or something? Why aren't you blinking?"

"No, you're good," she says, jerking her head back to her computer like she hadn't realized she was staring.

"Nikki, if I have chicken in my teeth or something, just tell me."

"You don't," she says, flicking her eyes to mine for a second, a blush dusting across her face. "It's not that."

"Then what?" I fidget with my hair, feeling more and more insecure.

"It's just . . . you're going to be pissed."

"What?" I snap. "I'm already pissed!"

She winces, squeezing her eyes shut for a second. "It was just good to see you smile. I . . . I'm sorry. I didn't mean to make you uncomfortable." She glances at me. "You haven't looked at me like that in a really long time. It was . . . nice."

"Um," I say, my eyes already stinging at her words. The butterflies thrum and throb. *I hate her, I have to hate her.* I squeeze my eyes shut. *Contain, contain, contain. Picture a jar. Good, got it. Now I'm putting my feelings for her in the jar and sealing it shut. Excellent. There we go, deep breaths . . . shit, why are there hearts on the jar? I needed an angry jar. Oh god now I'm picturing even more hearts on it!* I open my eyes to grab my bag and then stand up. "I need to go."

"Stay, really. I'm sorry. Look, I'm typing," she says, tapping her hands along the keyboard comically loud. "Business, this is just a business meeting. See!" she says, going back to frantically typing. "I'm adding in that they lied to both of us, right now. This is good stuff. This is all it has to be between us. *This* was what I meant when I asked for your help. We don't have to talk. I take it back. Just business."

"That's not what really happened, though! They didn't tell you that!"

"They did!" she says. Her hands go still as she looks up like she's trying to remember something. "I doubt I have emails or anything that old to prove it. Do you? What was your email from back then? Do you ever check it?"

"No, why would I? I made that when I was like twelve. I have Gmail now like every other real adult."

"Okay fine, fair . . . um . . . oh. Oh! Do you remember what I said when we walked out of the audition together?"

I roll my eyes. "Yeah, because it was obnoxious. You said it should be you instead of them, like you wanted to be the one to decide if I got the role and not the producers and stuff. I thought you kind of sucked for that, but I couldn't tell if you meant it like you were gonna pick me or—"

"No! I didn't say that!" she yelps, clearly horrified. "Well, technically yes, I *did* say 'It should be me, not them,' but I didn't mean all *that*. I meant that I wanted it to be me with you, not whoever else was reading. I thought you had someone else coming in after me." She sighs. "We had done one single chemistry read, and I was already jealous at the thought of you reading with someone else. I didn't know yet what that feeling meant. I thought we would just be best friends forever," she says, laughing. "But from the second I met you, Andy—Anne—I knew I wanted it to be me by your side, not anyone else."

My mouth falls open as I struggle to find a word, any word, in the face of this revelation. It's too much. *It's too much.*

I'd like to think I'm not a coward, but I am. I throw down some cash for the bill and then rush toward the door.

"Wait, please!" Nikki gets up like she's going to follow.

"I can't do this right now," I call back, holding my hand up over my shoulder to gesture for her to stop.

Luckily, her pursuit is cut short by our waitress calling out, "Hey, you gonna pay the rest of this or what?" *Good, let the diner have a turn with her AmEx, just let me make my escape.*

I'm peeling out of the parking lot before Nikki's even out the door.

Chapter Seven
Sometimes You Just Want Your Mom

"I did meet up with Nikki," I say as soon as my mom's face pops into view. She told me my dad was at the store, probably buying more of his beloved brussels sprouts, when I texted and asked for an emergency FaceTime, so it's just me and my mom on the call.

Mom's eyes narrow as she studies my face. "Was that a good thing or a bad thing?"

Like my swollen eyes don't already give it away.

"How could it ever be a good thing?" I ask incredulously.

Why my mom doesn't hate Nikki is beyond me. It was bad enough that she *encouraged* me to go to the diner in the first place when I asked her opinion—but suggesting that this tearful phone call could imply anything good is a bridge too far.

"I wish I could give you a hug right now, sweetie. Do you want to tell me what happened today? Did you at least have a nice talk?" She gives me a little frown that's somehow both patronizing and empathetic. It just makes me feel worse.

"We barely talked. I think she just wants me to read and sign off on everything she wrote about us so she doesn't have to feel guilty."

"Maybe you should," Mom says. "All of my papers are peer reviewed. It's not that different, if you really think about it."

"Yes, it is!" I groan. "Unless your peer reviewers are the loves of your life and you have to sit next to them while they do it—but I feel like Dad would have mentioned something about that if that were the case."

"You're so dramatic." She laughs. "But it's a fair point."

"I need her to leave," I say. "Can you just come here and make her leave?"

"I'm sorry, but I have a class to teach tomorrow," she says with a little wink. "Besides, maybe you *should* talk to her more. It wouldn't be the worst thing if—"

My eyes go wide at her words. "You do remember what she did to me, right? She treated me like shit! She constantly made me look like a fool. She used me. Hell, she destroyed me! How are you still Team Nikki?"

"I'm Team Anderson, always, but she didn't 'destroy' you," my mom argues. "Breakups are hard on everyone at first, and you're doing quite well now. Please give yourself some credit. Go on, say it."

"Whatever." I pout, not loving my mom's super-logical brain. "Fine, Mom, I'm doing just great . . . or at least I was before Nikki got here. Happy now?"

"Yes, actually." My mother smiles and I sigh.

"Can we at least agree that she is slightly evil? If not for destroying my career, then for rewriting our entire history in this ridiculous memoir? She showed me a chapter today about how *she* was the one who didn't have the part when we did the chemistry read! Her! Not me! Can you believe that?"

"I don't know that she did have the part," Mom says, looking bewildered. "I think your aunt just told you that to raise the stakes. I don't remember it coming from the studio. In fact, I think they were more settled on you at the time than they were her."

"What?! Why would Aunt Judy need to raise the stakes any higher? They were already raised when you said you would bring me back home if I didn't get the part."

"Only because I couldn't afford to keep flying out, not because I didn't believe in you!" my mom says, looking scandalized. "You were so homesick! I was coming out two or three times a month just to console you. I didn't even think you *wanted* to be there anymore by that point. Every time you booked a commercial or catalog shoot you complained about the long days and too-bright lights. I honestly thought you would have been relieved to come home."

"That's not true. I might not have liked doing catalogs, but I loved filming *The Nikki and Andy Show*—well, at least until the last season or two."

My mom raises an eyebrow. "That's because you loved *Nikki*."

"I wasn't there just for Nikki . . . or Aunt Judy, for that matter. What are you talking about? I was in love with acting back then!"

"I'm not trying to upset you even more," Mom says, frowning. "I'm just pointing out that you never wanted to tell me about your great day filming, it was always about a great day *with Nikki* or about what new things you had learned from the floriculture books we sent you all the time. The show took up most of your day, but it almost felt like an afterthought when you called home."

"That's because I was being taken advantage of and didn't want to think about it once I got off set. Not to mention the fact that my agent was actively stealing from me at the time, and I was being subpoenaed! My life was chaos and when I called you, I wanted normalcy."

"That was probably true at the end, but I'm talking about the whole time. If you really want to skip to the last couple years, it never seemed to me like you were jealous of Nikki's opportunities so much as you were hurt that she wasn't giving you the attention you needed."

"Oh, so what? I'm like this horrible, possessive person now or something? You're on her side?"

"Absolutely not!" my mom says, her voice rising a few octaves. "I'm on your side, Anderson, and I love you very, very much. I just want to make sure you're not putting on some rose-colored glasses about your time out there and what it meant to you."

"Why are you acting like she didn't hurt me?!" I ask, a quiver in my voice.

"I'm not. I'm sorry if that's how it's coming off," she says, looking genuinely upset at my tears. "Maybe I'm not expressing myself clearly. You're the communicator in the family; I'm the one with her nose in a microscope and no social skills." She pauses. "I wish I could give you a hug now, Andy Bug. I'm not in any way trying to minimize your feelings. I was simply encouraging you to examine your true feelings beneath the hurt and not get them all twisted up with some Hollywood fantasy. I don't know if you would have been happy even if it had worked out with that last role. I guarantee that I've seen you smile more since your life was 'destroyed' than I did for years when you were still out in LA. That means something, honey."

I huff out a tearful laugh and wipe at my eyes. "Are you *sure* you haven't been talking to Nikki?"

"No. Not since you asked me to stop picking up her calls a couple years ago. Why?"

"She said something similar today about me smiling. That it'd been a really long time or something." I blow out a huge breath, trying to ground myself. "It was hard seeing her today."

"I know, sweetheart, but . . ." Mom trails off, looking away.

"But what?" I ask, soft and resigned, bracing myself for whatever truth bomb my literal, logical, loving mom wants to throw at me next. Because they have been truth bombs, haven't they? I wasn't happy out there. Or maybe I was sometimes, but I wasn't *peaceful*. I wasn't content like I am now.

I was antsy and stressed and unfulfilled—and now my mom's got me wondering how much of that was Nikki's fault . . . and how much I just blamed on her to avoid what was really going on.

"I don't want to upset you more, honey. It's nothing."

"No, I want to hear it. I probably need to hear it, whatever it is. You've given me a lot to think about."

Maybe I could use a little bit of mom-logic right now.

"Does that mean you're not upset with me?" she asks, looking very apologetic. "I don't ever want you to feel like I'm not on your side, Andy Bug. I'm not pushing you to do something you don't want to. I wouldn't want anyone to do that to me, and I don't want to do that to you either."

"We're good, I promise, but thanks for saying that," I reply. "Now, what were you going to tell me before you cut yourself off?"

"All right . . . if you're sure." She smiles. "I think, maybe, and again, I'm not trying to meddle or force you into anything, but *maybe* it could be good for you to hear more about her side of things. If for nothing else than closure. You left very abruptly—which I don't blame you for, at all. It was a solid choice. The most rational choice, actually."

"Why do I feel like there's a 'but' coming again?" I groan but then flash another quick smile so she knows I'm not really upset. My mom has never been very emotional, but she's always been good at advice.

"*But,*" she says with a wink, "you're both older now and hopefully wiser. You and Nikki share a lot of history, good and bad. It might benefit you both to have a chance to let go of the past and to finally say goodbye."

My breath hitches. *Closure. Final goodbyes. Letting go of the past.* They're good things. They are.

So why do I suddenly feel like I can't breathe?

"Now, that's enough seriousness for one call. Don't you think?" Mom says, waving her hand like she's swatting away all of the complicated, hard feelings I'm having. "Do you want to see the new orchid your dad put in the hothouse? Maybe it'll inspire one of your future bouquets."

I know exactly what my mother is doing right now. She's carefully pulling me back to shore the way she did every time I called her crying from LA. Giving me something happy to think about. Hugging me the best way she can when we're separated by so many hours.

"Yeah, Mom." I smile, my voice wavering. "Absolutely."

Chapter Eight
Truth or Dare But You Can't Pick Dare

It's two days of quiet before Nikki comes back—well, sort of.

It's more like two days of me waffling back and forth trying to decide how to feel. On one hand, my mom's right. Closure would be good for both of us. On the other, the one I'm *really* trying not to think about, is the realization that the thought of saying goodbye to her—*permanently*—makes me feel a little bit like one of those gutted fish they sell at the market.

Then there's the secret third thing that I'm extra, totally, extremely trying not to think about, which is that, when Nikki didn't show up the day after the diner, my heart felt like it dropped into my toes... and then proceeded to spend the entire day getting squished and splattered and stepped on inside my shoe.

It's not that I want to see her again. *I don't*. I wish she never came here. It's just that it was easier to never want to see her again when I knew I would.

"Nikki just called in an order." Regan sighs as she walks into the back room, where I'm doing inventory of all the boring day-to-day stuff we use, like floral blocks, wraps, and shipping supplies. "I'll handle the note and packaging, but—"

"You need me to actually make it," I say, acting more put out than I actually feel.

This could be a solid compromise. Maybe Nikki and I can't have each other in our lives, but maybe we can have *this*. She can call in orders and I'll send them out. A weird little grown-up version of Marco Polo where we let each other know that yes, we're still alive but no, we don't need to talk. Everything could stay superficial and out of sight and . . . yeah, I don't know. That might be even more painful than that perfectly *awful* idea of closure.

I grab the slip and study the flowers she's requested. It seems like a basic apology bouquet, with a few bonus orchids thrown in. She's liked orchids ever since she saw my dad's hothouse collection when we were on break after the first season of our show, so I'm not surprised.

I wander around the store, grabbing everything I need and then hastily assembling it all. I have to keep my head down and get to work like any other day and stop thinking about what else she's put in that memoir of hers or why she's not coming in.

Technically, nothing in my life has changed. I remind myself of that over and over and over, and hopefully—if I can at least stop yelling her name in public places, and she stops tempting fate by acting like a baseball cap and a lack of highlighter on her skin make her invisible—that can remain true, even after the book comes out.

If it can't? Well, I've been spiraling about that since I left the diner too.

Most likely scenario: I'll be looking at another move—although I'm going to have to get creative to find someplace more remote than here. The other, bigger problem is that the idea of losing Regan and Johnny hurts more than probably even leaving LA did. We've made a little family out here.

They took me in when I was at my lowest, and instead of taking advantage, which so many other people would have done, they helped me put myself back together. I'd like to think I helped them too—and I don't just mean paying extra rent. I mean sitting with Regan whenever her aging father is admitted to the hospital or making sure Johnny eats dinner when he's working extra late because he let an employee leave early for their kid's play. Again. And now, it's all in jeopardy.

I should have never sent that text. She'd already been here a week without me knowing. She probably wouldn't have come to the shop if I hadn't.

I shove the last orchid into place, completing the bouquet, and then pass it to Regan to package. Maybe the fact that Nikki called it in instead of showing up here means she already left. Maybe she's decided now, only marginally too late, to start respecting my boundaries.

I'm glad she's gone, if she is. So glad. Just extremely glad.

Two days more pass before she calls in another order. And then another two days after that she calls in again. Regan takes to answering every time the phone rings just in case it's her so I don't have to—and I pretend I don't get a stomachache trying to decide if it would be worse if they stopped.

It's funny, she technically *could* call or text me whenever she wants—I unblocked her number again—but it's only the shop phone she chooses. It's only the shop phone that I hear ringing in all my bad dreams. *Maybe she thought of the Marco Polo idea too.*

Regan helpfully offered to block her number when the new pattern became apparent, but we both know her money's good and we desperately need it. We'd be ridiculous to turn her apparently unlimited floral budget away. *Besides, it doesn't bother me that much*, I lie to myself, making yet another bouquet for some faceless person in Nikki's life.

Is it for someone she's kissed or a coworker? Are those things even mutually exclusive? They weren't when we were on set together. Are these orders a way to stay connected or to remind me that she still runs the show? What does my mom even know about closure? She dissects plants for a living.

The reality is that it doesn't matter *why* she's doing it, just that she is and that it's very good for business.

Nikki has called every other day for the past two weeks … until today. I'm pretending like I don't care about the break in pattern. That I never got used to it. That I don't feel like a toy that outlived its usefulness and was knocked into the trash—again—by this woman. But I do.

Regan is just about to flip the sign to closed, and I'm sweeping the floors and trying not to look mopey, when Nikki appears at the door. She shoves it open in a rush, nearly knocking Regan over in the process.

"Oh god, sorry!" Nikki yelps as Regan shoots her a glare. "I didn't see you there. Am I too late?"

"Too late for what?" Regan asks, rubbing her hip where she banged it against a fresh display of roses. "Too late to learn any manners? It's a possibility if you've been making a habit of running people over."

"Too late to put in today's order," Nikki says, urgently walking toward me.

I lean the broom against the wall and head behind the counter, grabbing the order slip as if she were any other client. As if my heart isn't hammering out of my chest at the sight of her, here, again. With me, again.

She's got the weekender bag that we picked out together a hundred years ago slung over her shoulder and the same leggings and hoodie she wore every time she had to fly back then. Old habits die hard and all that.

I raise an eyebrow. "Did you come straight from the airport?"

"Yes, and nobody would Uber me here, so I had to rent a car again," she huffs, dropping her bag onto the floor and blowing her bangs—new since I last saw her—out of her face.

"What's with the haircut?" I ask, studying the jagged angles. I try not to notice the way they freshly frame her delicate features—somehow making her look both sexy and adorable.

Fuck my life.

"Oh, so *now* we're allowed to ask about haircuts?" Nikki laughs and does a little twirl. "Do you hate it? Dakota Johnson dropped out of a guest spot last second. I got the call up, but they wanted to stick with the 'vibe,' whatever that means. So, bangs it is."

"They can just make you do anything? If they want bangs you have to do it?" Regan asks curiously.

I glance at her, surprised that she's choosing to engage with Nikki. We've rehashed my conversation with my mother about a thousand times these last couple weeks. Maybe it's got Regan just as confused as I am now too.

"I don't know that cutting my bangs really constitutes doing *anything* . . . but, kind of. They put out call sheets of what they're looking for and it's kind of like 'get in or get out,' ya know?" Nikki says, looking equally surprised.

"Hmm," Regan squeaks, considering it all. "That's very weird."

"Yeah, it is, but I try not to think too hard about it or I start spiraling." She giggles, like it's an inside joke we don't get. "Anyway, may I please put in another order? You wouldn't believe how much people love your work."

"Actually, I would," I say, standing up a little straighter.

Nikki studies my face and a fresh smile curls up the corner of her lips. It swiftly turns into the signature "thoughtful pout" that her agent used to make her include in all her headshot portfolios. "You know," she says, "confidence looks good on you, Ducharme."

"Is remembering to call me Anne really too hard for you? You gotta pull out the last names, Colletti?" I press, and she looks away.

"Something like that," she says, her serious tone of voice making the moment more loaded than it should be.

"You know, if you left me alone you wouldn't have to worry about what to call me."

"Now, where's the fun in that?" She winks. "So? Are you going to take my order? I've heard the employees here are real sticklers about loitering, so . . ."

I glance at Regan, who's trying hard not to laugh. Even I've noticed how happy Regan has been these last couple of weeks, how much more relaxed. Selling the starlet du jour expensive overpriced flower orders every forty-eight hours has certainly had its perks. We've pulled in nearly half a year's worth of profits in just a matter of weeks.

"Okay, what is it?" I ask, pressing my pen to the paper.

I EXPECT THE next day to be quiet, following with the pattern and all, but Nikki appears moments after I unlock the front door—waltzing in and leaning against the counter like she belongs there. I wish I could tear out the piece of me that's happy to see her and stomp it into oblivion, but alas.

"Good morning," she says a little too cheerfully . . . or maybe I'm just extra grumpy since my coffee maker refused to brew anything this morning and I was up late obsessing over how long Nikki might stay in town for this time.

I raise my eyebrow when I notice the two cups of coffee in her hands. *Maybe salvation isn't that far off after all.* I'd dance with the devil for a cup of coffee at this point. Why not?

"What's this?" I ask, gesturing to the two cups in her hands.

"Why do you hate me?" Nikki asks, the same smile stuck on her face. The same cheery tone she just wished me good morning with falling out of her mouth again, easy as breathing.

"What?" I ask, stunned by how forward she's being.

The old Nikki was the queen of beating around the bush, so desperate to avoid confrontation and uncomfortable conversations that she'd skirt around them until we both exploded, all rational forms of communication long gone out the window. Now, here, today, she's actually meeting things head-on?

Suspicious.

"Tell me why you hate me, and you get the coffee. You still like oat milk and three sugars, right?"

"Yes," I regretfully admit. It's possible that I haven't changed as much as I thought.

"Tell. Me," she says, carefully enunciating each word behind her perfectly glossed smile.

"You're blackmailing me?" I huff.

"No, I'm bribing you. There's a difference."

"Fine, keep your coffee, then." I shrug, even though I'm practically a cartoon animal sniffing the aroma so hard I risk floating toward it.

"Fair enough," she says. "I'll drink it myself."

"You hate oat milk," I remind her.

She tilts her head, eyeing me. "Not anymore. Not for years."

"Since when?"

"Since you took off and it was one of the last things I had to remind me of you. You left me a half-full carton. It was the only thing of yours you didn't take or toss. I got drunk and chugged it and then cried when it was gone. From then on, whenever I got groceries, I would replace it."

"Oh," I say awkwardly, letting her admission settle over us before I remember myself and pull out my order pad, mumbling, "Did you need more flowers?"

I'm still searching for a pen when Nikki sets the coffee down on the counter and slides it toward me. I look up, confused.

"Drink it, it's yours. I was just kidding about the 'tell me' stuff."

"No, you weren't."

"No, I wasn't." She smiles. "But I'd rather keep things light than run you off again. If you don't want to talk about that, then pick something else."

"Like what?"

"Like anything," she says, and the strangest part is that she sounds like she really means it.

"How about your order?" I ask.

She sighs, and then pulls out her phone, showing me a complicated arrangement. "Can you do something like this?"

"I'm missing a few of the flowers, but I think I can pull together something similar. Where's it going?"

She rambles off an address and I jot it down, sighing at the sight of the familiar LA zip code. The curves of the numbers feel so foreign under my pen now, but I remember when they used to belong to me too.

"Is this another 'thank you for letting me bang your brains out' arrangement?" I ask, trying to keep myself on task. Trying to remember to be snarky and cool and calm. Trying to remember not to fall apart because she's wearing that goddamn perfume again and it's taking all my willpower not to lean into her neck and—

"Glad you remember my skills in bed so *fondly*." She smirks, like she can tell exactly what I'm thinking.

I blush and shift in my seat, grabbing for one of the little note cards we write messages on and doing my best to ignore her comment. "What do you want on the card?"

She frowns and then humors me. "How about 'This week was magical. All my love, Nik.'"

A surprising jolt of jealousy twists deep and angry in my belly, writhing its way under my skin until it reaches my fingertips. I write out the words, nearly tearing the paper in the process from the force of my scribbling.

"Holding the pen a little tightly, aren't you, Ducharme?"

"It'll go out tonight," I say, effectively dismissing her.

"Perfect, thank you," she says, but she doesn't move.

"Can I . . . help you with something else?"

"I thought you'd never ask." She grins and reaches into her messenger bag, pulling out another small stack of papers. "I have another chapter for you."

"I told you I wasn't doing that at the diner," I say, even though I can practically already hear my mother's disappointed voice.

Sorry you raised a coward, Mom.

"Technically, you said, 'I can't do this right now.' I'm not even convinced that you were talking about the chapter—there was *a lot* going on at that point. Either way, it's not 'right now' anymore. It's later. Will you read it later?"

I look up at her, I mean *really* look at her. Her words are cheerful, sure, but her eyes are tired like she hasn't been sleeping and her lips are drawn tight from nerves—just like they used to get right before someone yelled "action."

I sigh. "Leave it on the counter and I'll see what I can do."

I watch the relief spread through her face before I look down at my little pad and pen. She slides the papers toward me and then steps back. "See you later, Ducharme."

I don't take a sip of the coffee until after she's left. I hope that it somehow tastes all wrong so I can throw it away.

It's frustratingly perfect.

Nikki is back again the next morning, two coffee cups in tow. She's added a giant M&M cookie that I recognize as being from the bakery down the street. I never used to eat garbage like that when we lived together, so I know this is just a guess on her part, but she's dead-on. Again.

Fuuuuck.

I accept the coffee and cookie and grab my order pen and pad. "Don't talk until I drink this. My coffee maker is still on the fritz." My pen hovers over the order sheet, but Nikki says nothing—not even after I pointedly tap it a few times. My eyebrows shoot up as I look at her. "Nikki."

She sucks her lips into her mouth and shrugs, her eyes wide.

"What are you doing?" I snap. "Stop being weird. I just told you I haven't had my coffee yet."

Her cheeks puff as she blows out a breath, leaning over the counter. "I don't know what to do right now. You told me not to talk," she says, her voice barely even a whisper—it's more like her lips are forming words as she exhales. There's hardly any sound at all.

"Oh my god." I groan. "I meant let's do the flowers first so I can wake up before you bombard me about the new chapter, okay?"

"Sure," she says, keeping her voice quiet as she quickly orders another elaborate arrangement to be shipped out to somebody in LA I've never heard of. "And for the record," she adds, "I'm actually trying extremely hard not to annoy you ... which is *why*

I wasn't making a peep. I remember what mornings were like when you didn't have any coffee. Yikes."

"I wasn't that bad," I protest, pulling together as many flowers as I can with one hand while chugging my coffee with the other.

"You told Eliza to go fuck herself once when you were still pre-caffeine. And don't get me started on all the empty mugs you would leave in our shower," she says, taking the flowers from me to free up one of my hands. Our fingers brush against each other's and I swear her breath catches.

"Okay, for one, I would have told your agent to go fuck herself at any hour of the day, caffeinated or not," I say, shoving more flowers into her hands as I move around the store. "As to your second point, I was multitasking. Coffee in the shower is underrated. Plus, if I drank while the conditioner sat for a bit, I'd be all perked up by the time I was out. You should thank me for my efficiency."

"Riiiiight," Nikki says, stretching out the word. "It was definitely fueled by your commitment to efficiency and not at all by your massive caffeine addiction and obsession with staying up too late."

"Hey!" I laugh. "I'm not the one with addiction issues."

The words fall light and teasing out of my mouth before I really register what I'm even saying. Nikki goes still beside me, and I don't blame her.

"Oh my god, I was joking, but that was too far," I say. "I'm sorry. The words just came out. I swear I'm not making light of—"

"It's okay," Nikki says, although some of the brightness has left her eyes.

"No, it isn't. I shouldn't have brought it up at all, and definitely not as joke." I groan, dropping my head back before meeting her eyes again. "The chapter?" I offer. "Want to talk about that instead?"

"Depends on if you're done with that," she says, tapping the lid of my coffee with a small smile. She's throwing me a bone—navigating us back into safer waters—and I'm not about to look a gift horse in the mouth.

"Close enough," I say, tipping the coffee cup back and chugging it. "All done. Too bad my shower's upstairs. I guess I'll just leave my empty on the counter or something."

She lets out a tiny laugh, more of an exhale than a sound. "You could just put it in the garbage."

I press my hand to my chest, gasping as I walk back to the counter. "This is recyclable, Colletti!"

Nikki blinks at me. "You really have changed if you're even recycling your own stuff now."

"I helped recycle when we lived together!" I yelp.

"Sure, sure," she says, following me back and setting the rest of the flowers on the counter. "If by 'helped recycle' you mean 'left all your cans and cardboard boxes on the counter for me to deal with,' then yes. You were an expert recycler."

I fight off a second smile, tipping my chin up proudly. "I do count that, actually," I say.

"I stand corrected."

"You do. Speaking of . . ." I pull out the pages of the manuscript from the drawer next to me, passing them back to her and then making myself busy with her order.

I glance up at her a few times as she flips through the dozen or so pages that detail our first few weeks of filming. Her eyebrows have pinched together—a look of confusion? Concern? Something else?—slipping across her face as she takes in everything I've marked as needing to be revised. She catches me the next time I look at her, our eyes meeting, and my stomach flips as I rush back to trimming the stems.

"You took out all the stuff about us," she says. Her voice is neutral, but her face is giving her away.

"You're mad."

"I'm not mad," she says. "I'm just curious."

"It wasn't accurate."

The disappointment on her face morphs back into confusion. "What do you mean it wasn't accurate?"

"You made it sound like you were obsessed with me and I was oblivious."

"I've been obsessed with you since the day we met," she says, her eyes flashing. "You *were* oblivious or at least you pretended to be."

My stomach flips again, but in an entirely new way that sends heat spooling through my veins. I swallow hard and look away. I don't know how to respond to that. I don't even know if I should. But I do know that I absolutely cannot read into her using the *present* tense. Alarm bells screech in my brain.

"I'll be right back. I have to grab the shipping stuff," I say, rushing past her. *Cowarding out again.*

She reaches out as I walk by, two of her fingers colliding with my wrist, soft and gentle but enough to stop me in my tracks. I look down at where our bodies meet. I blush remembering all the times her two fingers made me—

"Please stop running," she says.

My eyes snap to hers. "I'm not running, I'm just getting a box," I say, my voice sounding strained.

She nods, letting her hand fall away. I instantly miss the warmth.

"Come in the back with me," I say, because I'm an idiot. Because I'm confused. Because closure is the last thing I'm looking for when I'm this high on a simple touch.

Nikki follows me into the glorified closet, a new spring in her step.

"This is where the magic happens," I mumble, scanning the shipping shelves for the right size box. I grab the nearest one and spin around to face her. "And by 'the magic' I mean 'the empty boxes and vases,' of course."

Nikki crowds closer to me, so close I swear I feel her body heat through the fabric of my long-sleeved tee. She leans against the metal rack, raising her eyebrows, like she can tell how flustered I am with her in my space.

"Close quarters in here," she says, eyeing me, our bodies just a few inches apart.

I take a deep breath, trying to calm my racing heart, only to find the air tainted with the familiar smell of *Nikki*. Her perfume, sure, but also her hair spray, her bodywash, the lotion she constantly applies to her hands to keep them soft. She smells exactly the same—she smells like home.

No. No, she smells like our old apartment. Not home. Home is here. Home has to be here, I tell myself. *What the hell am I doing?*

Nikki reaches for me, like that's something we just do now. She curls her hand around a lock of my hair. "I like it shorter," she says. "Since we're allowed to talk about hair now and all." She gives it a little tug. A tiny gasp escapes my lips as I remember all the other times her hand has had my strands wrapped around it.

"Nikki..."

An iPhone alarm shatters the moment, and she pulls back. "I have to go," she says, sounding regretful about it.

I nod, not trusting my voice.

"I'll see you tomorrow, though."

She smiles at me one last time, tucking my hair back before turning away, and then I'm alone—watching her leave—haunted by her lingering scent.

Chapter Nine

Every Rose Has Its Thorn

"What's with the church?" I ask when she walks in the next morning. This time, she's brought a croissant with our coffees. It's not a chocolate one, but still. I'll give her half credit.

"What do you mean?" she asks, setting everything down.

I gesture toward the front of the shop. "This place is made of glass. I can see where you go when you leave here. I thought it was a weird one-off at first, but then you did it again yesterday."

"Can't a girl church it up sometimes?"

"I guess. I just didn't know you were religious. You were never like that before."

"There's a lot you don't know about me, Ducharme," she says, patting Gouda on the head where she's lying on the counter. Gouda promptly swats at her.

"Likewise," I say, slightly annoyed that she's dodging my question, but glad the tension from yesterday seems to have dissipated.

"Is it good?" Nikki leans forward on her elbows, a mischievous glint in her eye as she watches me take a sip of my coffee. It's perfect, as usual, even if I won't ever admit it to her.

"No," I say, taking another sip.

"You were never a good liar," she says.

Regan walks over from where she was opening a shipment of flowers, carrying dozens of roses to be stripped. We've had to increase our ordering thanks to Nikki.

"Oooh, is that from the new coffee shop?" Regan asks, looking wistfully at our cups. "I heard they have the *best* stuff. Even Johnny was raving about it, and he only drinks like Ethiopian blueberry or whatever damn snooty single-batch crap he can get his hands on."

"I love it." Nikki shrugs. "But Ducharme over here—"

"Are you ordering flowers today? Because I don't have any new pages from you, so, if not, I don't think we have anything to talk about."

"Come on, you guys obviously have stuff to talk about," Regan says, but then catches my glare. "Or not. What do I know? I . . . should go put away the rest of the flowers. Feel free to grab me a coffee next time, though. Two sugars, no cream."

I rub my temples before caving in and taking another sip of my coffee. "You don't have to bring her coffee tomorrow. Or me. Or come at all, actually."

"Did you get a new coffee maker?"

"No, why?"

"Then consider it a public service. I'm saving the town from your grumpy ass."

I snort. "The town has survived me just fine without you."

"Want to tell me about it?" she asks casually, before moving over to pretend to be interested in my portfolio again.

"About what?"

"About your life here or anything else on your mind. Your best friend seems to think we have lots to talk about."

I consider keeping up our usual non-book-related routine: take her order—if there is one—and then chase her out immediately. Unfortunately, she's been positively Pavlovian about showing up each day with treats, and now my lizard brain seems to associate her with all the little jolts of dopamine and serotonin they bring.

I could fight it more, sure, but . . . I'm not above selling out my high moral ground for some of the expensive coffee and baked goods from down the block. Plus, In Bloom kind of owes her.

Regan even implemented online ordering again—a feature she took off the website when things were slow, even though it helped us find new clients outside of the town. The idea of having it back is exciting. Exciting enough for me to humor Nikki a little, just until it feels even again.

What do I really have to lose? Besides myself, my sanity, my heart, my home . . . my brain helpfully supplies.

Yes. That. Never mind. I don't owe her anything.

I turn to Nikki, fully intending to tell her she should head out . . . but she's looking at me with her big, wide, sincerely earnest green eyes from under her frankly ridiculous Mets hat—I don't think she's ever watched baseball in her life—and it's game over.

I sigh and pick up my rose stripper, getting to work dethorning the newest additions.

"Ignoring me already?" Nikki asks, her teasing tone not quite covering up her disappointment.

"No, I'm working." I hold up the flower. "See?"

A grin breaks out across her face. "You're not kicking me out?"

"No, not until you order," I say, fighting off a grin of my own.

"What if I don't order until"—she glances at the hours on the door—"four fifty-nine?"

One minute before closing. Of course.

I huff out a breath that sounds a little too close to a laugh. "Then you're in for a long, boring day."

"I don't think so," she says, watching me run the stripper down the length of the plant. It makes quick work of all the extra leaves and thorns that come on the cheaper flowers we order.

"Suit yourself." I shrug.

"What's that from?" Nikki asks, gesturing to the fresh pink scar running up the length of one of my fingers.

"I superglued my fingers together the night you announced your book." I smile at her, like that's an extremely normal thing to say.

"Why?"

"I had cut myself earlier in the day stripping stems like this," I answer. "Didn't want to go to the hospital, so I tried to glue it closed. Ended up supergluing myself in the process. The scar would have been smaller, but I ripped off some skin trying to get the glue off before my friend came and helped."

Nikki narrows her eyes. "Why didn't you want to go to the hospital?"

"Too expensive. Plus, I didn't want to get recognized. You have to write your legal name on the forms there."

"Too expensive? Aren't you getting residuals still?" she asks, looking confused. "They run a *Nikki and Andy Show* marathon almost weekly these days."

"I do, but they're basically nothing."

"No, they aren't. My last check was for—"

"We had different agents," I remind her. "I didn't get the same deal as you. Plus, you had all those escalators hit the bigger your name got. I didn't."

She opens her mouth to say something, but I hold up my hand.

"Don't pretend you didn't know. You might have forgotten, but you definitely knew at the time. We talked about it a bunch during negotiations."

She looks at the ceiling, brows furrowed like she's thinking very hard. *Maybe she really doesn't remember.* It would be funny if it wasn't so damn sad.

"Did you ever get your money back from that asshole agent you used to have?" she asks, seemingly giving up on that line of questioning.

"No." I groan. "I have a piece of paper that says he owes me money. I guess he doesn't make much in prison, because I haven't seen a cent."

"What about the Coogan account?"

I shrug. "Still got most of that. It's what I've been living off of when things are slow here. Elton stole most of the rest."

"If I ever see your old agent again, I'm going to kill him," Nikki says.

Well, at least she remembers that.

"You'll have to break into a jail cell to do it," I huff. "The tax fraud angle really did him in. He won't be out anytime soon."

"Good," she says, looking like she means it. "What a circus it was when the news first broke. Man, the paps were living on our sidewalk trying to get a statement from you. Remember?"

"How could I forget," I say, cutting the stems a little harder. That period of my life was absolute chaos. Things were falling apart with Nikki, I had just found out what Elton did, I couldn't book a single job, but everywhere I went the news or tabloids were chasing me down anyway.

I wasn't the only one he was stealing from. I was just the only one low enough on the fame scale that people thought they could get me to talk on camera.

Nikki rubs the back of her neck. "I called your parents, you know, back when the trial started."

"I know," I say. "My mom texted me every time you called." Nikki rears back, and I raise an eyebrow. "What? You didn't think they would tell me?"

"I guess I just assumed not."

"No, they're not like that. They always told me. Well, at least until I asked them not to anymore. You know, my mom was the one who encouraged me to actually show up at the diner and look at the book."

Nikki opens her mouth and then shuts it a couple of times before suddenly getting intensely interested in the set of display bouquets on the shelf beside her. "Got it," she finally mumbles.

"You're upset I never called you back?"

She glances at me out of the corner of her eye. "I didn't say that."

"I needed space," I say, feeling inexplicably guilty.

"For five years?"

I look away, not sure how to respond. The truth is, yes, I did need it for five years, and I need it still. Or at least I thought I did before she used my appetite against me.

"Come on, what do you do over there at the church?" I ask, gesturing across the street in a desperate bid to change the subject. "I keep seeing you go in."

She smirks as she leans over the counter, like she knows what I'm doing. "What do you *think* I'm up to over there, Ducharme?"

"Torrid love affair with the local pastor?"

"She's great, but no."

"Confessing?"

"That often? You think I have that much to atone for?"

"You don't?" I snap, because *yes, yes, I do*.

"I walked right into that one." Nikki sighs. "Look, I'm not saying I didn't screw everything up or that I don't owe you a massive apology. I'm just saying I'm not the only one who did. There's a lot more to our story than you thought. You have to agree by now. I've shown you two chapters already that prove it!"

"Oh, that's rich," I say, stripping the final flower from this set and dumping it into the bucket with the others. "What about the movie?"

"Which one?" she asks.

"Do me a favor and stick your fingers out."

"Why?" she asks, doing it anyway.

I snap the rose stripper in her direction. "So I can cut one off every time you say something infuriating!" I'm kidding, of course, but her hand stays completely still, her fingers stretched in front of me like an offering.

"If it'll make you feel better."

She's joking, obviously. Right?

I shake my head and grab the next rose. "You know I wouldn't really hurt you."

"Too late." She huffs, tucking her hand back in her pocket. "Sorry," she adds, when I freeze. "I shouldn't have said that."

I almost feel guilty. *Almost.*

I cut off another thorn before meeting her eyes. "I'm sure your Oscar more than makes up for any hurt you felt from me leaving."

"It doesn't."

I suck my teeth and grab the next flower. "I guess you should have thought about that before you stole my role then," I say, even though it's not really about that.

"I'm the one who encouraged you to audition in the first place!"

"And then you stole the role."

I don't know why I'm doubling down on this. My mom is right—I *was* miserable out there by the time the part was even up for grabs. I don't know if landing it would have fixed anything. But still, it would have been nice to try. It would've given me another excuse to stay.

"I didn't—" Nikki says, and then cuts herself off. "Forget it."

"Forget what?"

"Nothing. I don't want to fight. I'm glad we're talking right now and I'd like to keep it that way," Nikki says. "Can we just rewind a little?"

"Till when?"

"Till before I pissed you off?" she says, her voice lilting up like a question.

"Hmm." I tap my chin. "How well does your time machine work? We'd have to go all the way back until . . . when? The day we met? You took my iPod and wouldn't give it back. I chased you all around set and then I seem to remember it devolving into the first of many tickle wars between us, so . . . that was probably the start of it."

Nikki lets out a little laugh, poking her tongue into her cheek as she nods. "I was trying to flirt with you, you know."

"You were terrible at it."

"It did eventually work," she points out. "Regardless, can we skip ahead a little from there? I was thinking more like five minutes ago or so."

"Okay, new question," I say. She gestures to me like "go ahead." "Are you still with Eliza?"

Eliza McCormick was Nikki's agent extraordinaire—a stage mom, cheerleader, and rabid dog all rolled into one. She couldn't stand me and didn't care one bit that when she negotiated contracts for *The Nikki and Andy Show*, her push for *more* often left me with *less*.

Eliza's favorite catchphrase was "Someone's going to get the money—it might as well be my client." She and Nikki were thick as thieves—Nikki even thanked her in her award speeches. It's why I stopped watching them.

I don't blame Eliza for my relationship with Nikki failing,

but I don't *not* blame her, either. It hurt how Nikki always put what Eliza wanted first, always ran to her for advice, always defended her when we fought. It sometimes felt like Eliza was just as much a part of the relationship as I was.

"No," Nikki says, looking away. "Not for a while."

"What?" I practically screech. "The dream team broke up? I never thought I'd see the day, especially with the way you always went to bat for her when we—"

"I moved over to someone at WME," she says, like she's talking about changing the sheets and not dropping the person Nikki always credited with getting her big break in this messed-up industry. "I've been there a few years now. It's better for me, I think. I've got a manager now too, and a PA. They keep me on a tight leash these days."

"Yet here you are, standing in my flower shop."

"Yet, here I am," she says, her voice dropping a little. "Blowing them all off for you. You don't happen to have an old iPod laying around, do you?"

Nikki leans across the counter, plucking the flower from my fingertips. I swallow hard, shifting closer in my stool and regretting ever putting this counter here between us. She tips her head to the side with a little smile, as if she knows what I'm thinking, and I squirm even more.

I grab the next stem too fast, desperate for a distraction. The tip of my finger catches on one of the loose staples that held the bundle together. "Shit," I hiss.

A tiny bead of blood wells up, and I shove it into my mouth, glaring at Nikki. *That's the thing about the past, isn't it? It's always going to make you bleed.*

"Let me see." Nikki rushes over and pulls my hand toward her. She squints as she studies the tiny wound from every angle.

"What, are you a doctor now too?" I ask, trying to distract myself from the fact that if I parted my legs, she'd basically be between them.

"I *did* have that guest spot on *Grey's Anatomy*," Nikki says, still staring down at my finger.

"You were a patient who died in your second episode," I deadpan, trying to tug my hand away. Nikki doesn't let go, so it has the opposite effect and pulls us even closer.

She looks up with a grin. "You watched."

I roll my eyes. "I've been watching *Grey's* my whole life; it was definitely not on purpose. If anything, you almost got me to quit the show entirely."

Nikki hums like she doesn't believe me but still doesn't let go of my hand.

"What do you think, Dr. Grey, will I live?"

"Probably," she says, looking down at me through her eyelashes. "You don't even need superglue this time. You just need . . ." She trails off, slowly lowering her head. "This," she whispers, before pressing her lips to my fingertip. "And this," she says, kissing it again. "See? All better."

The air between us crackles to life as I shift my legs and pull her in closer.

What am I doing? What am I doing! This is the opposite of containment! This is worse than hearts on the jar! This is both of us in the jar together!

I don't even care. The woman I loved forever, the woman who

was once so casually cruel, is kissing me all better. Is sliding her hand up the back of my neck, so gently, like I'm the only thing in the world that matters anymore. I squeeze my eyes shut, overwhelmed as the heat of her skin dances along all the places where we're pressed together.

I part my lips, expecting to feel hers on them any second, but instead she rests her forehead against mine—the way we used to do when things got tough or set ran long or one of us just needed a little grounding.

Nikki would take my hand back then, or I would take hers, and we'd find some dark corner where we could squirrel away for a little while. People assumed we were making out or feeling each other up or something else juvenile and unimportant like that. But really, she would lean into me—just like this, breathing me in like I was the air that she needed, like I was her whole sky instead of just a fleck of stardust.

On really rough days, she would curl up next to me, her head in my lap, my fingers in her hair, and I would read my flower books to her. Chapter after chapter, until she fell asleep.

Nikki lets out a shaky breath, dragging me back to the present as her free hand brushes my cheek—an act that is far, far too intimate for the middle of a floral shop on a random Tuesday in the middle of March.

I should be pushing her back. I should *want* to! I should yell at her for being so forward or crack a joke about her still wanting me—anything to try and defuse the tension. But I can't. I won't. I angle my head, brushing my nose against hers.

I'm fully intending to kiss her—half on autopilot and half

hoping that if we give in this once we can get it out of our systems. I move forward, just barely, our lips brushing once, twice, three times, feeling like a lit fuse dying to go off.

I'm just about to fully commit, when she pulls back, hard and fast. My startled eyes meet her apologetic ones as she stumbles back like I burned her.

And isn't that classic Nikki?

Everything's on her time, still, even now. When we make out, when we meet, when we forgive . . . when we have our last kiss. It's all about her.

It occurs to me for the first time that, with her money and her connections, she probably could have found me sooner, if she wanted to. But no, she came now, she chose now, when it most benefits her. *When she has a book to sell.*

"Sorry," Nikki says, leaning down to catch my eye. "I want to, but . . ."

"It's fine. Just go," I say quietly, my brain and body whiplashed from the last few minutes.

"Andy—"

"Go!" I say, more firmly.

"Can I at least explain—"

"No."

She stands up a little taller, like she's ready to fight me on this.

"Don't," I say when she opens her mouth. "I'm really tired of listening to you spin things. I need a break, okay?"

She shakes her head. "Someday, Andy, you're going to have to accept the fact that you're only sitting on half of the story. What you call 'spinning' is just me filling in the blanks."

Regan walks up, standing beside me. I had forgotten she was still in the back.

Oh god, how much did she hear? How much did she see?

"I'm sorry, Nikki," Regan says, sounding like she really means it. "If Annie wants you to go, it might be better if you did."

"Come on—"

"Get out of here, Nik. Please!" I say, my voice cracking on the last word.

She opens her mouth one last time and then shuts it, hanging her head. Regan pulls me into a hug, gesturing toward the door.

Neither of us moves until it finally clicks shut behind her.

Chapter Ten

The Miserable Business of Moving On

Nikki doesn't come in the next day.
Or the next.

An entire week goes by—one where I may or may not bike down to the cabins, only to find them all dark and empty. Literally all of them. I know because I peek in every window to be sure.

I spend the rest of my time obsessively refreshing socials to try to figure out where Nikki had gone. Still pulling off the whole "brave, healing, nonchalant" vibe to the outside world...

At least until midway through the second week, when Regan decides enough is enough and casually calls me out on it.

"She checked out that same day," Regan says, carrying over a bin of carnations that need to be delivered to the local middle school for one of their fundraisers. We've been their long-time supplier since we only charge them fifty cents a stem—they make a nice profit when they double or quadruple the price for school events.

"Hmm? Who?" I ask, as if I don't already know, while sorting all of the various colors into the vases the PTA president dropped off earlier this morning.

"Nikki Colletti," Regan says.

I freeze at the sound of Nikki's full name, out of place coming from Regan's lips. A tendril of possessiveness curls up inside my skull, like her very name belongs to me and me alone, and no. No. *I'm not going there.*

"Good," I reply, begging myself to believe it.

I have got to stop torturing myself.

"Aren't you going to ask me how I know?" Regan asks, which is how I know she's definitely seen right through me this whole time.

"How do you know?" I ask, obliging her.

"I ran into Mrs. Sanderson at the grocery store last night and decided to do a little detective work. Don't worry, I didn't use Nikki's real name," Regan says. "I just asked if there'd been any guests lately, because I know how tough the off-season can be. She said she did have a renter for cabin six, and it turns out they left the same day you guys got into that fight."

Cabin six. Nikki stayed in cabin six?

Objectively, I figured she might have—but there was no number written on the receipt she showed me, so I couldn't be sure. The confirmation that she had hits me like a tidal wave. It's one thing to abstractly imagine her sleeping in the same little cabin on the shore we once shared together, the same one I stayed in alone when I first arrived back in town—but I'm drowning in the knowledge that it's true, that up until recently she was there alone, stuck between the same sheets our bodies once met under.

I swallow hard. There's a cleaner, newer Hilton just outside of town now. I don't know why she couldn't have just stayed there. It would have stirred up less emotions for both of us, probably.

"Was she scheduled to check out that day?" I ask, even though I don't really want to know. Either she was always going to leave me again so quickly or I scared her off for good. Neither option sounds great right now.

"Interestingly," Regan says, "sort of?"

"Sort of?"

"She was supposed to check out the next morning, so she moved up her timeline, but just barely. If you were feeling bad about it, you're officially off the hook."

"Why would I feel bad about anything?" I ask, testing the waters even though the list in my head is a mile long.

"You can stop pretending, Annie," she says. "I'm your best friend. Do you honestly think I haven't noticed that you've been walking around like a kicked puppy the last couple of weeks?"

"I have not," I grumble.

"Whatever you say." Regan shrugs. "I won't pretend to know what you're going through, but that doesn't mean you have to keep it from me. I'm here for you, always."

"Thanks," I say. "Same."

"I know." She smiles, passing me more flowers to help her sort. "Now that we've established our undying loyalty to one another, you sure there's nothing you want to talk about?"

"Not really," I say. "I just . . . I should be happy she seems to actually be gone, right? I expected to be happy."

"I don't know if 'happy' is the right word . . ." Regan trails off, as if she needs to consider what she wants to say next. I set down my flower, waiting. "Nikki seemed different than what I expected from the way you've always talked about her. Nicer," Regan says. "I can see how that could be really confusing and add a hard and messy layer to an already complicated situation."

"Yeah," I say, grabbing another pink carnation to shove in with all the others. "It did."

"Hey, who knows?" Regan nudges my elbow. "Maybe she'll drop the whole book thing now. It's probably messing with her too."

"I doubt she'd drop it." I sigh.

"Why?"

"I'm sure they gave her a ton of money. She won't walk away from all that. Could you imagine?"

"I think she already has a ton of money, Annie." Regan laughs. "I mean, so do you, though."

"Not really," I scoff. "Not anymore."

"More than most, even with what you lost."

I frown, reaching my limit for talking about this stuff. It's true that my Coogan account had a decent amount left over for small-town Maine, but by Hollywood standards, that's nothing. And like I told Nikki, the odds that I ever see any of my earnings back from my felon of an ex-agent are slim to none.

"All right, subject change," she says, just in time. Regan always was creepily good at reading me.

"Thank god," I say.

"I think this is enough flowers for a chorus concert, don't you?" Regan spins the vase around for me to look over. I nod my approval, and she smiles. "Awesome, I'm going to run these over on my way home. I promised them by five. You mind locking up if I cut out a little early? Or actually, come with. I doubt anyone else will stop in tonight and we can grab dinner after."

"I'll stay and lock up just in case," I say, dodging her offer. Regan, to her credit, doesn't even try to fight me on it.

We make quick work of packing everything up into an oversized box and loading it into Regan's car. I watch her drive away for a little too long, and then shift my attention to the church across the street. The same one that Nikki always disappeared into.

I'm tempted for half a second to go inside, to try to sit where she sat and feel what she felt. If she can do it with cabin six, I don't see any reason why I can't do it at the place across the street. *Except that it's weird. And pathetic. And I need to be better than that.*

I shake my head and turn back inside. I manage to pull the door shut behind me a bit too hard, making all the bells clang. The sudden silence that envelopes the shop afterward is overwhelming, and I slide the bolt over to lock the door with a sigh.

Has it always been this quiet?

If this were a movie, I would look out the giant front windows right now and see Nikki standing there. I can almost imagine it, the hope and dread that would swirl up as she banged on the glass to be let in for some grand gesture that would make everything all better. But there's no one there. Of course there isn't.

She's gone.

She's gone.

And we were never meant to have a happy ending.

I head toward my little apartment, scooping Gouda as I go and carrying her up the stairs. She meows at me gruffly, reminding me that she does not like to be picked up but also that, since I'm doing it anyway, I owe her dinner too.

"It's coming, it's coming," I say, setting her down beside her bowls and rummaging through my cabinets to find the good cat food.

Gouda yowls at me as I fill her bowl and then there's nothing else to do. Nothing at all. I drop onto my couch, wallowing in the fact that this is my life now. This is the hardest part of it, isn't it? Of the miserable business of moving on . . . you have to *actually move on*.

Until I saw Nikki, I could just pretend I had hit pause on things. That I was *taking a breather*. But now that she's come and gone back to her glamorous life and left me here with the flowers and the rent payments, it's clear: I'm really not Andy Ducharme anymore. I'm just a woman sitting on a secondhand couch above a tiny shop in New England. Meanwhile she's still Nicolette goddamn Colletti. And Nikki Colletti has always had *better things to do* when it came to me.

Why would this be any different?

I don't know what I expected, really. Her to sit here and grovel forever? To keep begging me to talk to her even though it was my decision not to? I told her to leave, I did, so why am I so pissed she actually left? No, not pissed. *Hurt*. Why am I hurt?

This is stupid. Unless?

I flick over to my contacts, holding my breath while I stare at her name. I don't know what I was thinking: That she would somehow immediately text me? That there would be some sort of apology waiting? (Again, for what?! For finally listening to me after I accused her of ignoring my boundaries?)

The truth is, whatever she came here to find—whether it was me or just my version of events for her to sanitize in her new book—she clearly decided it wasn't worth it anymore.

That *I* wasn't worth it anymore.

"Fuck her," I say out loud, trying my best to mean it.

Gouda looks up from her bowl for a moment, startled by my sudden outburst, before going back to slurping down her food. She gags, probably from eating too fast, but I take it as tacit agreement. *See? Nikki makes Gouda sick too*, I tell myself.

Because that's the thing. I need to find my way back to anger, and if not to anger then at least to polite disinterest. I've worked so hard to heal, I can't let my feelings for Nikki—*not that I still have feelings for Nikki*—burrow their way back under my skin to fester.

Nikki is gone.

Nikki is gone but I'm still here.

My apartment isn't too quiet, it's just quiet enough. My life isn't boring, it's calm. And I *like* my secondhand couch and living in New England. It's not less than, it's just right, and I need to remember that.

I need to remember that.

I got a little turned around, sure, but anyone would have if their ex walked back into their life unexpectedly only to walk right back out, even without all the extra baggage that makes us *us*.

I put my phone down and drop my head back on the couch, letting my eyes drift shut.

It's fine. This is fine. Nikki and I have never been on the same page before; I don't know why I expected to be now. Out of sync is our thing, a forever looping roller coaster that I got off the day I started my car and pointed it east.

I'm over it.

I'm fine.

I am. I *am*.

So why does it feel so damn awful?

Chapter Eleven

Coffee Interrupted

I'm with Regan, taking a sip of my first honey lavender latte of the spring at the late-night coffee shop in town. We're discussing how to balance our flower stock against the sudden influx of online orders—that may or may not dry up at any time—when she suddenly sets her cup down and mutters, "Well, shit."

I turn around in my chair to see what she's talking about. I'm expecting to see, I don't know, Johnny doing something stupid or maybe even that one old lady who keeps complaining to the town about the pride flag we have hanging over the shop door—but instead find myself locking eyes with the very face I've been dreaming about seeing again for the last three weeks.

"Nikki?" I say, my jaw dropping open, my mantra of "hold on to the anger" flying right out the window.

Nikki stands by the door sheepishly. She's forgone her makeup as usual, her cap pulled down low, and is in a casual hoodie and leggings that if I had to guess probably cost more than my entire last year's salary.

"Sorry," she says with a little wave. "I'm not trying to ambush you. I didn't know you'd be in here. The shop was closed and I . . ." Nikki walks over and I have to crane my neck to look up at her from my café seat. I would hate being at this disadvantage—sitting while she towers over me—if she didn't look so damn sad. "I know you told me to go, and I tried, I did, but every time I sat down to work it felt wrong, knowing how upset you are with me and how differently you remember things. I almost called you a hundred times, but I figured I was blocked." She shrugs, looking utterly pathetic. "I'm not trying to stomp all over your boundaries, I swear, but if we could have a conversation . . . I want to make the book right."

"Make the book right?!" Regan yelps, her incredulity kicking her voice up an octave or two. "So you're *both* being ridiculous. Got it. Good to know."

"I'm sorry?" Nikki says, clearly confused.

"You play off being here 'for the book' about as well as Annie played off not looking like a kicked puppy after you left," she says, even making air quotes. "For a couple of actresses, neither of you are very good at pretending."

I turn to Regan with wide eyes. "What are you doing?" I whisper, looking back at Nikki in time to see her confusion morph into something lighter.

"Hopefully finally getting you two dumbasses to talk," she stage-whispers back.

"A kicked puppy?" Nikki asks, and I don't miss the flicker of hope in her face.

I narrow my eyes. "Regan's exaggerating. I was surprised you actually left, that's all," I say, afraid of what will happen if I stop this facade of aloofness I've been projecting.

"Surprised?" Nikki says, like she doesn't dare believe me.

"In my defense, you'd been acting like a fungus I couldn't get rid of. It was jarring to have you leave without a word." I shoot a look at Regan. "I was *not* acting like a kicked puppy, though, thank you very much."

"The irony." Nikki squints at me, shaking her head. "Was I supposed to stop by on the way to the airport to let you know that your wish was my command? You threw me out. You were very clear."

"You were checking out the next day anyway!" I snap. "Which you never mentioned once."

"Have you been looking into me?" Nikki tilts her head. "I'm going to have to talk to the woman who runs those cabins about privacy. It's a good thing you're not the paparazzi."

"It'll be the paparazzi soon if you keep hanging around here. Eventually your luck will run out. Especially once they realize I'm here too. Please tell me you at least haven't been flying out of LAX?" I groan.

Regan stands abruptly. "Oops! I almost forgot! I have to run this coffee over to Johnny riiiight now." She lifts up the to-go coffee we ordered with ours. "Annie, I'll catch up with you later? Good to see you, Nikki."

I open my mouth to protest, but Nikki is already sliding into the abandoned seat. I'd think she felt happy about it too, except for the way she's nervously chewing on her lip. Regan disappears out the door, leaving us to our awkward silence.

"Would you have really wanted me to come say goodbye? Honestly?" Nikki asks finally. "I thought you wanted me gone."

I look away, trying to decide the best way to handle this. The upsetting truth is that seeing Nikki here again has every nerve in my body firing simultaneously—a sudden deluge of fireworks and oxytocin floods my head and clouds my better judgment.

"Do you want a coffee?" I ask.

"If I say yes, are you going to take off when my back is turned?" She sounds genuinely concerned.

"No, but eventually the barista's going to kick us out because you'd technically be loitering and I'm almost done with mine," I say. "They don't have enough tables as it is."

"What is it with this town and its loitering policies?" Nikki smiles and taps her fingers on the table, leaning back in her chair. "Is it weird that I don't trust you?"

"It'd be weirder if you did," I say, realizing how true that is only after the words are out. She might be the one who pulled away first, but I'm the one that severed ties completely.

"Stay?" she asks quietly, and I nod. "Good girl," she adds before walking toward the register.

I'm glad she can't see the way those familiar words twist inside my head and scamper through my veins, lighting every pleasure sensor ablaze.

Did the heat just kick on in here?

It's been a long time since Nikki's said that to me—since anyone has—and the last time, the hundred last times, were in a very *different* sort of context. She looks at me from the register, a tiny smirk pulling up one corner of her lips as if she knows exactly what she's done. *Damn.*

We weren't exactly card-carrying members of the kink

community in LA—her research for a potential role being the first and only time we actually went to a dungeon party—but we also weren't afraid to push the boundaries at home. Nikki found my praise kink adorable, and I found her need to take control blissful—it was the only time I could turn my brain off and just be.

Nikki might have been a trash girlfriend outside of bed, but she was a caring, careful, incredible partner in it. It's part of why it took me so long to leave. That connection? That level of intimacy? It's a lightning strike that rarely happens twice.

She clears her throat and I startle, lost in thought, as she joins me again at the table. "Thank you," she says around her cup of black coffee.

"For what?"

"Everything," she replies. "Especially talking to me tonight. I thought you would be hurling things at my face when you saw that I came back."

"Yet you interrupted me when I had a half-full cup of coffee," I laugh. "Brave."

"Wow, that's a big turnaround for you."

"Hmmm?" I ask, taking a sip.

"Calling me brave. I think in our last fight before you left LA, you called me a 'selfish coward who wasn't worth the period stains on her panties.'"

"I probably could have worded that better." I grimace, even though I stand by what I said. It felt true, at the time.

Nikki practically snarfs her coffee out her nose at my response. It triggers a coughing fit that's frankly a little alarming until I realize it's because she's trying to laugh through it. I look away, fighting a smile as she pulls herself together.

"Oh my god," she says. "I thought you were going to say sorry or something."

The butterflies that are happily bathing in hot tubs of oxytocin in my brain quickly get to drowning. "Do you really think you're the one who deserves the apology?" I ask, my smile fading.

"Andy, Anne." She sighs. "I understand there's a lot that I don't know about what you went through during our time on the show, but there's a lot of things I was dealing with too."

"I'm sure there was," I concede. "I've gotta be real with you, though, the whole humiliating and cheating on me thing makes it kind of hard to empathize. Not to mention the Eliza situation. I might have said some mean things before I left, but I never—"

"I didn't cheat on you," says, her voice going hard. "Not once."

"Well, it was implied," I say, picking at my nails and trying to avoid making eye contact. *It's embarrassing, laying it out there like this.* "You were pretty messed up at the time. Maybe you don't remember what it was like."

"I don't care if it was implied or not. I never screwed anyone else while we were together. I know my word doesn't count for anything with you anymore. That's fair, but I promise you I didn't."

I move to interrupt her, but she doesn't let me.

"I did get wasted way, way too much on too many things, for a lot of reasons," she admits. "I was dealing with a lot of stuff, and I let people . . . They had this idea of me, you know? 'For a good time, call Nikki.' It's *why* I was invited in the first place and possibly the *only* reason."

"I let a lot of people use me in a lot of ways those nights. I do remember, Anne, what it was *really like*. I'm ashamed of what I did to you. I'm ashamed of every time you saw me on some gossip site with someone else's lips on my skin."

"How is that not cheating?" I ask.

She looks down at her coffee, spinning the cup in her hand before letting out a shuddering breath. My question hangs heavy between us but I'm content to wait her out for a response.

"I don't know," she says quietly. "Maybe I *am* just making excuses by trying to force a distinction between kissing and having sex." Nikki pierces me with her wide, honest eyes. "That's not what I want to do. I was messed up back then, and I'm not just talking about the drugs. I honestly believed that if I didn't kiss back or reciprocate the advances then I wasn't . . . at that point my body didn't even feel like my own anymore, you know? Except for when I was with you. It always felt right, being with you."

My heart pounds as I listen to her confession, every emotion swirling into the perfect storm inside my head. The tips of her fingers barely touch mine, her hand tense like she's forcing herself not to move it any closer. Her attempt at comfort lying aborted between us.

"You don't have to believe me, not yet," Nikki says. "But I'm not that person anymore. I'm not holding on to excuses either. I just . . . for whatever it's worth, I'm sorry. I've wanted to say that to you for a long time." Our eyes meet and she pulls her hand back. "That's why I came back. Regan's right, at least about me.

Pretending it's about anything else is ridiculous. If you want me to leave permanently this time, I will. You have my word. I just couldn't do it without you knowing how very, truly sorry I am for all of the pain that I caused."

"Nikki, I—"

Before I can get my thought out, the door to the coffee shop is shoved open. *Hard.* Johnny walks in with a fiery look in his eyes, as an apologetic-looking Regan scrambles in right after him.

"You just don't know when to quit, do you?" Johnny asks, storming up to our table. Nikki looks baffled by the giant man in mechanic's overalls racing toward us. "Haven't you done enough?"

"Johnny," Regan says, pulling on his arm.

Nikki looks between us. "I'm sorry, do I know you?"

"No, and you don't deserve to either," he snaps.

"Meet my *other* best friend, Johnny McFarlane," I say, wishing I could climb under the table and wait until this awkward moment passes. "He's a little protective."

"Got it," Nikki says, and then points at Regan. "So, you're the good cop in this scenario and he's the bad one? Is that what we're doing?"

"Do not bring Regan into this. While we're at it, leave Annie out of it too. You can't keep coming here and screwing up their lives whenever you get bored of counting money in your little mansion."

"*Their* lives?" Nikki says, her eyes shooting to mine. "Is Regan your partner?"

"Yes," Johnny says, at the same time as I say, "No."

Nikki looks utterly confused. "I don't—"

"Business partner," Regan pipes up awkwardly behind me. "Business partners and best friends. Nothing romantic."

Nikki turns back to Johnny. "Then you're pissed off because . . . ?"

"Because Annie and Regan are too fucking nice, and you're too fucking Hollywood. You're not going to sit here and smooth talk Annie until she consents to being mentioned in your stupid book."

"I don't actually *need* her permission to write it," Nikki says, clearly getting pissed. "Do you think Justin Timberlake signed a release for Britney Spears to put all the stuff about him in her book? That's not how it works. As long as I can prove anything I write, it doesn't matter if I have her blessing or not."

"Real nice, Nik," I say.

She looks back at me, worried. "I don't want to write anything you don't feel good about or comfortable with—that part still stands! I just need you to understand that I'm not here because of the book!"

"Sure, you're not," Johnny says, and Regan turns to respond.

"Okay, enough," I say, holding up my hands toward both Nikki and Johnny in an effort to get them to stop. "I believe you, Nikki," I say, ignoring Johnny's eye roll. "But if it was just an apology, you could have DMed or called the shop. Why did you come all the way back here?"

Her eyes soften. "Am I allowed to say I missed you?"

"No," Johnny answers for me.

I turn back to him with a sigh. "Johnny, I love you, but I can handle myself. You're going to get us kicked out of your new favorite coffee shop. Plus I really, *really* don't want to draw any more attention to the person who's sitting at this table with me than we already have. That *will* make my life harder."

Johnny pinches the bridge of his nose like he does whenever he's trying not to lose it. And I know, *I know* his heart is in the right place. My frustration dissipates in the face of his obvious internal war. Johnny has seen firsthand the devastation Nikki caused and had a front-row seat to my attempts to rebuild—to him this must look like I'm throwing my storm doors open and inviting a hurricane in for a drink.

"I know you can, Annie," he finally settles on. "I'm not trying to make things worse. I just—"

"Why don't you and Regan grab a few beers and some pizza and meet me back at my place in like thirty?" I offer. "We can hang out and decompress?"

He flicks his eyes to Nikki and then back to me. "If that's what you want to do."

I nod. "It is."

Regan links her arm firmly with his. "Come on, you're buying after all this," she says, leading him out the door with a quick wave and a mouthed apology behind his back.

Nikki watches them until the door clangs shut behind them. "Charming guy."

"I think so." I sigh. "Sorry, Johnny can be intense, but he means well. He's had a rough go of life too—I met him like the day after I got here and we did that whole found-family, bonding over past traumas thing. I was pretty messed up when I left you. I couldn't eat or sleep, I would stumble to the bar like a little zombie and . . ." I shrug, watching Nikki's fingers curl into fists on the table before she drags them back into her lap.

"I didn't know it was that bad."

"It was," I say, not bothering to hide the truth anymore. "Johnny helped me get back on my feet. He's the one who introduced me to Regan and cheered me on when I applied to work at In Bloom. They're honestly the best friends I could ever hope for."

"You sure it's friendship he's after with you? He came off a little jealous."

I laugh. "Yeah, he's wholeheartedly in love with Regan. I know that was a horrible introduction to him, but I promise he's a good guy and an even better friend."

Something flashes across her face, distrust or maybe jealousy, but just as quick as it comes, it's gone again. "Good, I'm happy that you have him, then," she says, but I can't tell if she means it.

"I should probably get going," I say. "I need to pick up my apartment and feed Gouda before everybody gets there."

"I don't suppose I could get one of those impromptu party invites?"

I laugh. "I'm pretty sure everyone in attendance is planning to shit-talk you tonight, so it might not be the best idea."

"Even you?"

"Probably," I joke, giving her a little smile so she knows I don't mean it.

"Want to know a secret? That's not really a deal-breaker. I can shit-talk myself with the best of them. I'm still in, if you'll have me." Her voice is teasing, but her eyes are sad.

My stomach clenches around the thought that she probably really means that. "Nikki . . ."

She tips her head away, running her tongue over her teeth. "It's fine, Anne," she says, my new name rolling off her tongue like a razor. "Maybe I'll see you around, yeah?"

I didn't notice it before, too caught up in my reaction to seeing her again to analyze the state of her. To anyone else, she probably looks fine, but I'm *not* anyone else. I know—*knew*—every expression, every curve of her lips, every raised eyebrow. I could always read her like a book even if she hadn't said a word. And reading her now, I can tell there's something very off.

"One drink," I blurt out before I can change my mind.

"One drink?" she asks, crinkling her forehead.

"You can come over for one drink, but then you have to go. Less than that, if you and Johnny can't pull it together."

She nods quickly, like she's worried the invitation might disappear if she doesn't acknowledge it fast enough.

"Should I meet you there or . . ." She trails off.

"You can walk with me," I say. "But let's go now. Gouda will kill me if her dinner's any later than it already is."

"Okay," she says quietly, clearing the table and carrying both of our messes over to the bins.

I shoot a text to Regan, warning her about the extra guest and praying she can help Johnny get a grip before they come over. Then I quickly try to remember anything embarrassing I might have left out in my apartment for her to see . . . but mostly, I just try really hard to ignore the tug down low in my belly—the one that's preening over the fact that Nikki cleaned up the table; that Nikki is taking care of me again, the way she used to before it all went wrong.

Chapter Twelve

The World's Worst Pizza Party

It's awkward, Nikki and me dancing around each other as I feed the cat and tidy up the apartment—things that once upon a time we used to do together in another house, in another life, in what feels like another universe. What used to be so routine, so common, now feels so stilted and strange.

Nikki stands awkwardly in the doorway, watching me move around a kitchen she's never been in before, feeding the cat she hasn't seen in half a decade.

"You can sit," I say, gesturing to the living room just a few steps away.

"Okay," she says. She takes a minute to study the bookshelf I have set up beside the couch, trailing her fingers down their spines with a little smile. "You still collect all these flower books? God, I remember in between takes that first season you would practically run for your library bag. If your nose wasn't buried in a script, it was buried in one of these books. I was practically doing backflips to get you to look up at me."

"You were not," I say, rinsing out the can and dropping it

into recycling while Gouda trills appreciatively around bites of food.

"I was!" she says. "You would put on your headphones and curl up in the bed on set like it really was your room. I would come tumbling by, desperate to get you to look up. I didn't lie in that chapter you read! I *was* obsessed with getting you to notice me and you *were* impossible. Why do you think I kept stealing your stuff?"

"I was just trying to read!" I laugh. "I needed a minute to escape and all that."

"I know. I was so jealous."

"Jealous?" I ask, arching an eyebrow.

"I wanted your eyes on *me*," she says. "I'd never wanted to be a book so bad in my life."

I meet her eyes now, the tension between us tight, tight, tight again, like a rubber band about to snap. "Nikki . . ." I say softly.

"Andy . . ." She smiles. I don't bother to correct her because in this tiny bubble, for the first time in a long time, I don't feel like being somebody else. I don't want to wear someone else's name or live their life. Seeing her in my living room somehow makes me want to both forget the past and live in it forever.

Even if only for a minute.

Nikki takes a step toward me and then another until she's crowding into my space.

"My friends will be here soon," I whisper.

"I know." Her face is so close to mine, the almost-kiss from before flashing forward into something real and tangible now. Nikki would barely have to lean forward for our lips to meet, and she seems to realize that she'll have to be the one to bridge the gap this time.

"I should have kissed you that day in the shop," she says. Her breath ghosts over mine the way it has a million times before and I never thought it would again.

I know on some level this is wrong. Too soon, too fast, too early, never again, and not now. We have so, so much to talk about, and I don't know if I even want to forgive her. If I should? If I can? If she'll even show tomorrow—but none of that matters with her Tobacco Vanille Tom Ford perfume clouding my brain and the heat of her lips just millimeters from mine. She was always so warm for me. Inviting and hot, her body made for mine as much as mine was made for hers. Who are we to deny—

The sound of footsteps on the stairs leading up to my open apartment door has me jumping away, laughing nervously. Nikki gestures to kick the door shut before dropping back against the wall, like she needs it to hold her up. She presses her fingers up to her lips with a quiet shh—as if Johnny and Regan will somehow decide we aren't home if we're quiet enough, letting us get back to where we were.

Home.

That word again. It's like ice water splashing all over my hyped-up libido. Because this is *my* home, *not hers*, and as confusing as it is to see her standing in it, that doesn't make it any less true.

"Did you get chips? I'm all out," I call down the hall, and Nikki visibly deflates.

"Of course we got chips," Johnny says, beating Regan to the top of the stairs. He's got a grocery bag full of goodies, as well as a case of the horribly cheap beer we all like so much. It's $9.99 a case on sale. You can't beat it.

Regan follows right behind him, carrying a giant pizza and some take-out boxes. "I wasn't sure if Nikki was eating or not, so I got a lot to be safe."

"Oh, I can't really indulge but thank you anyway," she says politely.

"You can't even eat a slice of pizza?" Johnny asks, barely covering his disdain. "Gotta keep the whole unrealistic body standards thing going, right? Corrupt the minds of little girls and all that?"

"I, uh, love pizza actually," Nikki says, shifting uncomfortably. "I just . . . forget it, yeah I'd love some."

"You don't *have* to," I say, hating how uncomfortable all of this is.

Johnny grins as he passes her a paper plate with the biggest, greasiest piece of the whole pie. She's barely got it in her hand before he's popped the lid off a beer and passed it along to her too.

"Oh, thanks," she says, taking it awkwardly and then heading to the couch, where Regan has already sat down with refreshments of her own.

"Be nice," I remind Johnny as soon as she's gone. She's not out of earshot—no place in my apartment really is—but it's the closest thing to privacy we're going to have without me dragging him into the bathroom.

"Why?" he asks.

"Because I'm asking you to."

"That doesn't answer my question," he says, passing me a slice.

"I don't know the answer, honestly, but seriously—this is already weird enough. Can you be civil for me for a little while? She won't be here long. Promise."

"Yeah, that's kind of her whole deal, right? Popping in to stir up drama whenever it's convenient for *her*."

"Johnny."

He holds his hands up. "Hey, I'm behaving. I even opened her beer."

"After you shamed her into eating pizza."

"It's good pizza."

"It is," Nikki interjects, holding up her half-eaten slice just in case we need proof. *So much for privacy.* "I was starving, actually," she adds. "Thanks for offering."

"Anytime, *friend*," Johnny says. He tucks his beer under his arm, shoves a slice of pizza into his mouth, and uses his free hand to drag one of my chairs away from the corner and directly across from the love seat that Regan and Nikki are sitting on. He looks like he's about to interrogate them, but then reluctantly settles back into his seat, chewing thoughtfully.

I move from the kitchen to the living room, leaning against the wall tentatively in case I need to—I don't know—leap in between them at any point. It's confusing, how I feel both overprotective of Nikki *and* ready to throw her to the wolves. How I want to keep her far, far away from my friends, while also imagining what it would be like if they all got along.

Probably best I just stay neutral. I take a swig of my beer, glancing between everyone. *As if that's even possible.*

"So, how long are you in town?" Regan asks politely, apparently happy to break the ice.

"I'm not sure." Nikki shrugs, taking another bite. "I think a little while, if it's okay with you," she asks, looking over at me. "I have a break in filming for a minute and hopefully I can stay here and keep working on the book."

"It's your life," I say, taking another swig of beer. *Since when does she care if I want her here or not?*

"Maybe, yeah. For the first time." She carries her plate into the kitchen. "Do you have any water?"

"What's wrong with the beer? Not expensive enough for your tastes?" Johnny asks.

"It's certainly more expensive than tap water, and I'm fine with that. You're going to have to try a little harder to be rude next time."

He laughs. "Don't worry, I will."

"Johnny, cut it out," I sigh. "Don't go all fake alpha asshole. Your favorite movie is *13 Going on 30*, for god's sake! You cry every time we watch *Iron Giant*. This isn't you, even if *she* doesn't know that. Either be cool or come back in an hour when she heads out."

"Yeah. She's clearly not gonna blow you, bro," Nikki says, apparently having had enough of his glaring. "So relax."

My face goes hot when she says that and her eyes widen as she notices, her head tipping forward in disbelief. She flicks her eyes to Johnny, who's now wincing like things have taken an ugly turn even for him.

"I need another beer," Regan says, throwing her napkin down.

The fact that Johnny and I slept together isn't really a sore subject or anything—like I said, we've all talked it through. Still, I'm sure it's not fun for Regan to have it randomly pop up at a pizza party that her bestie is part of her *almost, semi, kind of if you squint* boyfriend's body count.

"This guy?" Nikki seethes. "Seriously? What the hell, Andy?"

"Anne," I say, because she doesn't get to judge me for anything I did to move on from her. Not even this. "Did you think I would stay celibate forever?"

"No, but he's an absolute prick, *Anne*. You could do so much better."

"Hey," Johnny says before casually taking another swig of my beer. "At least I don't cry in the middle of going d—"

"Jesus, Johnny!" Regan shouts, looking as furious with him as I am.

Nikki sets her glass of water down and squeezes her eyes shut. When she opens them, they're wetter than I expected.

"I . . ." I stumble over my words, because how do you apologize for sharing private, intimate information with someone who was only too happy to weaponize it. "I shouldn't have told anyone about—"

"It's fine," Nikki says, rushing over to grab her bag and coat from where she draped them over the chair at my small kitchen table. "I should really get going anyway. Thank you for inviting me but this isn't . . . I'm not . . . Bye."

"Nikki," I call, but she's already bolting down the stairs, the jingling of the bells over the shop door turning to angry clanging as she pulls on it roughly in a hurry to get it unlocked.

Nobody says anything for a minute as I stare down the stairwell after her. A hint of her perfume still lingers in the hallway, and I fight the urge to breathe in deep—only resisting because I'm too angry to enjoy it.

I turn back to Johnny, ready to dress him down, but Regan beats me to it.

"What the hell is wrong with you?" she screeches at him. "You're being disgusting. Do you really think that helps anything? Anything at all?! You should be ashamed of yourself!"

He looks devastated by her scolding, as if it's just now occurred to him how far he crossed the line. "I'm so sorry," he says—I assume he means it for me, but he's still only looking at her. "I was out of line." He shifts his eyes toward me. "I'm not trying to be an asshole, Annie. I don't mean to be. I just don't want you and Regan caught in the crosshairs of all this drama."

"I know," I snap. "But that's not your decision."

"Don't you remember what it was like when you first came here? You were half dead! Regan and I practically had to force you to eat and sleep, let alone leave your apartment! The stories you told us about what your life was like before, about what she did to you . . ." He trails off, shaking his head. "But you're going to take her back?"

"No! Of course not!" I say, ignoring the way my belly flips at the idea.

I know deep down there is no universe where we work out. If there was, we would have that first time, right? But still . . . she's always been, will always be, my biggest *what if.*

What if we put each other first? What if we ran away when Hollywood got too heavy? What if I never left? What if she turned things around? What if love was enough, just this once?

"Then why does it matter if I'm nice to her or not?" he asks, interrupting my thoughts.

"Because she's a human being?" I offer.

"Human beings are not inherently worthy of respect and kindness," he says. "If we were talking about a dog or Gouda, then yes, but people? People are awful."

"*You* were awful tonight," Regan says. "The second I told you they were in the coffee shop you had to go charging over like some meathead. It was *ugly*. I hated seeing that side of you! It's *everything* I don't want in my life. Besides, you haven't seen them in the shop, John. It's not how you're picturing. It's not for us to decide how Annie gets closure!"

I pinch the bridge of my nose, trying to hold it together. "I get that you two were ground zero when I crashed here. I've never had friends who cared this much, and I'm super grateful for that, but . . ." I sigh. "I have to navigate this however I think is best. You don't have to support it or even hear about it—especially you, Johnny, if it really triggers you or something. But you *do* have to let me, even if I screw it all up. Okay? Because I have always let the both of *you*."

Regan and Johnny look at each other, probably registering for the first time that Nikki and I aren't the only two people in town being ridiculous about each other.

"You're right," Johnny says, a sad, crooked smile on his face. "I promise I'll rein it in." Regan reaches her arm behind him to rub his back gently and he looks at her like she just handed him his whole heart back. "Are we okay?" he whispers, and as much as I want to finish this group therapy session that's happening in my living room, I can't.

I owe someone an apology tonight too—if I can find her. It wasn't my story to share what happened between Nikki and me the last few times we made love—the way she cried, the way I held her, the way I knew then it was already all over. I hadn't meant to share it. It had slipped out the night of her book announcement, when we were watching an interview where she came off cocksure and braggy about her sexual prowess. I was too many beers in to think rationally, but drunk or not, it was wrong of me.

How can I argue that she can't tell our story when I've been telling it myself for years—albeit to a much smaller audience.

"I'm going to go try to find her," I say. "Would you two mind throwing the food in the fridge and letting yourselves out?"

"It's the least we could do," Regan says, giving Johnny a small smile.

"Sorry again, Annie," he says, grabbing the paper plates off the table in front of him.

"I know," I say softly. "I know."

Chapter Thirteen

Not Nearly Enough

I hop on my bike and ride down to the beach cabins, but there are no signs of life there. It occurs to me that she might not have even checked in yet, since everything about her tonight suggested she once again came straight from her flight.

At a loss for where else to look, I spend some time circling the town, trying to figure out exactly where she could have gone. I even stop by the church since it's literally across the street. I hold my breath as I tug on the massive wooden door. It's been a long time since I've stepped foot in a church . . . but it was locked. Feels fitting, honestly, that the one time I would turn to God he's unavailable.

Okay, think, Anderson.

The options are limited in this town for this time of night. I've just chucked my bike behind my house, ready to give up, when I consider one more spot she could be.

It wouldn't be ideal, but it *would* make sense.

The Spotty Dog is the closest bar to my apartment—a dive spot that the locals love and the tourists tend to run away from.

It's one of the few bars that stays fully open year-round, its bright neon signs shouting out in the windows, acting as beacons to the lost and the lonely.

It's where I came after the beach my first night here, with Gouda in her carrying case sitting on the stool right next to me. It's where I met Johnny, who came over when he realized I was alone, dying to know why I had brought a cat to a bar.

Hopefully it's where I'll find Nikki too.

I push open the heavy oak doors and scan the people inside. There are a few people I recognize, mostly regulars who hang out at Johnny's shop to talk about cars and occasionally follow him over to In Bloom to grab bouquets for their families on special occasions.

There's a bunch of guys I don't know playing pool in one corner. The stereo is blaring some weird country-pop mash-up I've never heard before and hope to never hear again. I'm about to turn and leave when I see the edge of her coat peeking out from one of the booths in the farthest back corner of the bar.

A swirl of disappointment washes over me that she ran right back to her old ways, but I stomp it down with every step I take. She's a big girl; her choices are her own. It's not up to me to drag her out or ask her to stop . . . but I do still need to apologize. I pause a few steps before her booth, hesitating. I'm not sure exactly what to say or even where to start.

"You can sit if you want," she says, startling me.

I slide into the booth, embarrassed. "How did you know I was there?"

"I could feel you," she says.

"Really?"

"No," she laughs, pointing to the mirror on the back wall of the bar, directly in her view.

"Right," I mumble. "Sorry, I was kind of glitching out for a second."

"It's okay," she says, spinning the glass of whiskey slowly in her hand.

I take a deep breath, watching the dark liquid ripple as the glass snags on the rough surface of the table.

"How many of those have you had?" I ask, trying not to sound condescending about it.

"Not enough," she answers, and I fight the little rise of anxiety that spikes up my spine. She sounds too much like the old Nikki for the first time since she's been here, and I hate it.

It's bringing everything back up—all the days when I was made to feel like drinking and drugs and industry parties were more important than me. All the nights when she would go out after every argument—or even in the middle of them. How the tabloids were all too happy to take pics of the mess we had become. The transition from Nikki being social user to substance abuser was swift and unexpected. Eliza did an excellent job of spinning it in the media to look like I was the bad guy in all of this.

They didn't go so far as to outright *say* I was driving her to drink, but they implied it.

Not to mention the countless blind items like, "Every party has its pooper: This clingy C-lister made a scene at yet *another* industry event, dragging her A-list partner out with a shout." (The only reason I even showed up to that stupid *Vogue* party was because Nikki had called me crying. It wasn't my fault that she had blacked out and forgotten that in the time it took me to drive there.)

I wonder if she's remembering the same sort of things or if her memory has done another Uno Reverse like in the chapters she's shared. I wonder if she's written all the ugly parts of her story yet. I wonder if I even want to read them.

Nikki glances over at me, but then goes back to people watching in the mirror. The men by the pool table are bickering over something, and in the back—or, well, I guess the front—a woman in a trucker hat is slowly grinding against a guy with an unfortunate beard to another song that doesn't deserve it.

"What are you doing here?" she finally asks. "I don't need a babysitter, if that's what you're worried about."

"Historically, that hasn't been true," I say, tipping my voice up at the end to lighten the words.

"Historically, you haven't been around, and I've been managing just fine."

I give her whiskey a pointed look, relief washing through me as she slides it to the side of the table away from us, rather than pounding it.

"I've been looking all over for you," I say, which seems to surprise her. "I even rode my bike down to the cabin."

"Jesus, Ducharme, it's freezing out! Don't you have a car?"

"No." I shrug. "Don't need one here. Everything's walkable, and if it's not, then I have Regan and Johnny."

She narrows her eyes. "Why were you looking for me?"

"I wanted to apologize on behalf of my friends."

"Just your friends?" she asks, biting the inside of her cheek. Her classic holding-back position, always biting something—

her cheek, her tongue, her lips. The face I've seen during a hundred arguments, the warning that if I don't let up, the next thing to come out of her mouth is going to *hurt*.

I'm tempted to feed into it, to fall back into old patterns where she pushes, or I pull, and neither of us gets anywhere good. The roller coaster that turned into a Ferris wheel that we could never get off in time.

Only I did, finally, and I'm not about to get back on.

"I'm not sorry for hooking up with him or anyone else," I say, "but I should never have told him about any . . . private things between us. That's nobody's business but our own. You were a mess back then, *we* were a mess back then, and you don't deserve to have an intimate moment like that thrown back in your face. Especially not by a man you don't know while he's acting like that. You shouldn't have been put in that position."

She seems to consider my words, letting them hang between us before she finally breaks the heavy silence. "Do you know why I cried those last few times we were together?"

"Because you were strung out and/or hungover?" I laugh awkwardly.

"Because you were fucking me like it was a goodbye."

Each one of her words pierces into my chest, niggling their way into my heart and shredding it to tatters. She's right, it was a goodbye—they all were at the end.

I had decided to leave weeks before I actually did—waiting for just the right opportunity to avoid ending up on another gossip rag or having to deal with her melting down in person. I knew I needed out, that it was best for me, probably for her too, even. We were so unhealthy back then. We *were*.

I just didn't know that she felt it too, the finality of it all. The same desperation I had to hold it in my palm, to memorize her skin in case it was the last time I got to touch her, to feel the dips and curves of her body, to lick, bite, tease, taste until it was all burned into my memory in a way that could never be scratched out, like picking at the scab until the scar became permanent.

I *wanted* it to leave a mark, and it did. *It did.*

"I'm sorry," I say again, not even sure what part I'm apologizing for anymore, but still meaning it with my whole heart. I see now that she felt it too. That it mattered to her. That saving myself, even though it was necessary, had also meant hurting her.

Nikki reaches over, brushing her fingers against mine, just barely, just in case I'm going to pull back, but I don't.

We sit there, longer than we should, not talking or moving, just letting her skin and my skin get reacquainted by centimeters. It would be funny if it wasn't so damn sad. Two emotionally constipated adults sitting at a bar, barely holding hands. Their growth stunted by childhood celebrity turned trauma queens, the oldest story in the book, just an absolute embarrassing cliché.

There's always a little truth in those things, isn't there?

Nikki takes a deep breath and I hold mine. Her pointer finger trails back and forth over my hand, and it feels like a knife cutting through all my defenses. I don't know what bomb she's about to drop on me, but I know it's coming.

"I've missed you so goddamn much," she says, her voice breaking on the words. I'm lost in the sound of her anguish. Those seven syllables crash into me like a rogue wave. I'm left drowning, kicking uselessly and gasping for air, destroyed by the intensity of her glassy stare, and I don't care if it's the whiskey that's dialing her emotions up to an eleven or not, because they're here now, finally.

No more smirks or banter. No more bravado. We are a kite in a windstorm, a cut string trailing behind us where our sense of obligation and morality used to hang, and fuck it. *Fuck it.* Let's see where we land.

I link my fingers with hers and isn't it such a shame that they still fit so perfectly? Her hand meant for mine. Her skin . . .

"Will you walk me home?" I ask.

She licks her lips slowly before leading me out of the bar, our fingers never separating for a second.

Chapter Fourteen
La Petite Mort

The trip to my apartment is short, only two blocks, but despite the cold we move slowly down the sidewalk, letting the moment linger. We walk a little too close, our quiet voices breaking the occasional stillness of this cool April night. The town is dead; there is no one to bear witness to our bad decisions this time.

I don't know what will happen when we get to my door, but I know I've missed the feeling of our hands wrapped around each other's. It's safe and warm, like stolen kisses on too-bright sets and naps in each other's trailers on the rare lazy afternoon. It feels, disgustingly, like *home*.

We stop in front of the flower shop, each of us looking at the other expectantly. The air seems much colder than it was a little while ago, what with the weight of our indecision bearing down on us. It's do or die, now, and we both know it.

"This is me," I say, and take a step back, but Nikki steps with me, her grip staying so strong on my hand that it pulls the rest of her along with it.

We tug our hands back and forth, laughing when my back hits the glass door, the little bells only a faint jingle on the other side. She presses against me, tucking her nose into my neck like she's trying to breathe me in.

And me too, me too, I feel it too.

"Are your friends still inside?"

I shake my head.

"Will you let me in?"

I shiver at her words, wondering if she's intending the double meaning or if it's my own lust-addled brain drawing a connection that isn't there.

"I don't know," I whisper. "I want to, but . . ."

"It's your call," she says, smiling into my skin. "Might be good for us."

"What, like, to get it out of our system or something?" I ask. "For an old times' sake kind of thing?"

"Something like that," she says, flicking her tongue just once against my neck before quickly replacing it with a teasing nip of her teeth, and suddenly, all of my reservations fly out the window.

I want this. I want her. One last time won't hurt anything. For old times' sake. For closure. Closure, yes! Even Regan said it was healthy. Just one last time. For . . .

"Yes," I say, spinning around in her arms to unlock the door. She continues kissing me from this new angle, her lips skimming over the back of my neck and sliding forward to press gently between my jacket collar and jaw. Cold air slips down my skin but we both know that's not what's making me shiver.

The key finally catches and the door jolts open, sending us

spilling into the store. Startled laughter falls from our lips like misspent promises of better times. She is here with me now, like she was there with me before. I feel lost and found all at once, and doubly anxious to get her upstairs.

We knock into one of the displays as I lead her backward to the stairs and the sudden scent of flowers grounds me, yanking me back into the present just as I was ready to fully surrender to the past.

Nikki seems to sense a shift in me, letting her fingers trail after mine, but respecting my space as I pull away. She waits, watching me pull off my coat and set it on the front counter before I go back to lock the shop door behind me. I head upstairs without a word, her footsteps trailing me slowly up to my apartment. I leave the door open as I walk into my place and kick off my shoes.

"Second thoughts?" she asks, hesitating in the entryway, her coat and shoes still on and ready, like she's prepared to bolt at my answer.

I look away. "I don't know what I'm doing."

"Does anyone?"

"I think, yeah," I say, looking back at her. "I hope so."

"Andy," she says, meeting my eyes. "Would you like me to leave?"

"No."

She smiles, dropping her coat behind her as she kicks off her shoes and finally, finally comes closer again. I swallow hard, thinking of all the other times in our lives and our past ones that she stalked toward me, her lithe body almost as familiar to me as my own.

"Do you know what it's like to be homesick for someone who hates you?" she asks. "To be stuck in that town without you? People throw themselves at me, but I don't want them, I never wanted them. I want *you*. It's like starving during a feast." She trails her finger down my side. "Nothing tastes as sweet as you, so why even bother?"

"I'm tired of hating you," I whisper as she slides her foot between mine. She gently kicks my legs apart before pressing me down into one of my kitchen chairs. I look up at her, waiting, always waiting. Control was not something I liked to give up in life, but something I needed, wanted, craved, to be taken from me in bed.

None of my other lovers ever really got that, not like Nikki did.

"I can make you feel something else, if you'd like to let me."

My blood goes syrupy and slow as she sinks to her knees, parting my legs even farther as I squirm under her gaze. I nod, desperate, thankful to all the gods in the universe that I wore a skirt today.

"Say it, Andy," she says. "Tell me what you need." I shift my hips toward her, and she grins, licking her lips. "With words."

"You. I need you," I say.

One last time. For old times' sake. Closure. Nothing more. It can't be anything more.

"How do you need me?" She trails her hand down my thigh, reaching the hem of my skirt and sliding it up agonizingly slowly. "*Where* do you need me?"

I should be frustrated by how easily my body and mind bend to her will. I should be annoyed. I should be a thousand other things, but right now, pheromone-drunk on her honey voice, all I can say is "Please."

She grins before rucking up my skirt the rest of the way and slipping my panties to the side. I squirm under her gaze but even from this angle I can see her hunger. "Fuck, I've missed you." She leans forward, nipping gently at my inner thigh, one well-manicured finger teasing along my folds before dipping inside, trailing the wet heat up to my clit before pulling back. I arch my hips, chasing the sensation, but she presses me back down with her free hand.

"Stay," Nikki growls, then leans back on her knees. She makes sure I'm watching before she slides her lone wet finger into her mouth and sucks it clean with a smile. "Better than I even remembered," she says. "Now open up and let me have a proper taste, doll. It's been too long."

A tiny voice whispers in my head that I should absolutely not be about to hook up with my ex on my kitchen floor, but a much louder, much more fun voice is shouting, *Oh, who the hell cares, we're just getting it out of our systems, right?*

I let my legs fall open on either side of the chair, which has the unfortunate side effect of having my panties shift back into place. Her lips fall into a pout, as she leans forward. "Now, that won't do." She reaches forward, carefully ripping them down the center. "Much better."

"Those were expensive!" I snap.

"I'll buy you twenty more pairs."

I have a split second to take offense before her tongue is there, lapping at my opening like she's dying for it, and every word, every thought, every emotion I have now or have ever had is driven out of my head by pure pleasure.

We always fit together this way, Nikki and me. Our incompatibilities were legion, but not this, never this.

Her tongue finally presses inside, and we moan together as her hand slides up to draw torturously slow patterns against my clit. I am boneless, melting, sliding in the chair in my effort to chase my high and she laughs, hot breath against tender skin, before sliding her other hand up higher, beneath my shirt and bra. She trails gentle circles around my breast until my nipple pebbles up, and then pinches it hard with her nail—just a little bit of pain with my pleasure, always, hitting just the right note that has me shuddering apart on her tongue.

"Nikki!" I cry, my muscles going taut. She slides her hand from my breast to my side, pinning me to the seat and holding me up as I ride out the aftershocks. She swaps her fingers and tongue, surprising me with soft kitten licks to my clit while she slides first one finger inside of me and then another—curling them in just the right place to send a fresh zap of pleasure coiling through my core.

"I can't," I say when she keeps going. "Nikki, I can't. It's too much, it's too much."

"One more, baby," she says, pushing up to her knees and bending me forward to kiss me proper on the lips. The angle is awkward but neither of us care. It's dirty and languid, somehow both too slow and over too soon. All the while her fingers continue to tease, tickle, press, and fuck deep inside of me. Her thumb slides back up to my overstimulated bundle of nerves and I drop my head to her shoulder, overwhelmed.

"Nikki," I whimper.

"I've got you. I've got you," she says, kissing any part of me she can reach. "You're doing so good for me. So good."

I feel it building inside me again, twisting up higher and higher—the urge to run away from her and the urge to dive deeper and never let her go—a war waging inside my head as I dig my teeth into her shoulder, riding her hand to my own release, taking it myself this time instead of it being given.

"That's it," she says. "That's it. It's okay to let go, baby. Let yourself feel me."

I come hard on her hand and feel her smile slide across my sweaty hairline, dotting me with kisses as she shifts me back. Nikki cups both sides of my face with her wicked hands, crawling up onto my lap as I fall back in the chair. She presses gentle kisses onto the corners of my eyes, letting me catch my breath before slowly peeling herself away.

"You look so beautiful like this," she says, holding out her hand to me. I take it, floating a little.

She leads me over to my couch and carefully arranges us so that I'm tucked safe against her, her heartbeat drowning out all of the thoughts in my head. It's been so long since I could just let myself feel like this—blissed out, warm, and safe. Protected for the first time in a long time.

Protected. Safe.

The thought breaks through my skull like an ice pick, my breath picking up as I struggle to breathe.

Nikki isn't that. She can't ever be that again. This has to be just a one-time thing. I can't let myself—

"Hey." Her hand stills in my hair. "You okay?"

"Yeah," I say, but my voice sounds funny even to me.

I move to slide back but she holds me in place. "Don't run again, Andy, please. Just . . . let me have this for a little while longer?"

"Let *you* have this?" I ask, and this time when I pull back, she lets me go.

"Us," she corrects, her brow furrowing. "What's happening right now? I just made love to you and now you're—"

No, no, no, no, no. I can't do this. I can't get attached. Love isn't . . . can't ever . . .

"We fucked," I say, and she winces. "We fucked in the kitchen like a couple of horny teenagers. We didn't make love. How could we make love? You don't even know what—"

"Don't lie to yourself," she says, fully sitting up now. "You can believe a lot of things about what went down between us but don't pretend I didn't love you with my whole heart as best as I goddamn could."

"Your best wasn't good enough," I say quietly.

The words hang in the air between us and then shatter all over the floor, slicing us through with good intentions and half-hearted attempts at forgiveness.

She bites the inside of her cheek, looking up and to the side, but even in the dim streetlights streaming in my window, I can see her eyes shine wet with emotions.

"I know it wasn't," she says, looking back at me. All of her bravado and confidence that came with the knowledge that she could still make my body sing falls away to expose the vulnerable woman in front of me.

I want to wrap her in my arms and hold her forever, I want to scream at her to get out, but I know neither of those reactions is fair.

The cold realization that I've let things get too far, got too carried away—that I should have never followed her out into the darkness, and never pulled her back inside my light—drenches me in ice. Tonight was a mistake, clearly, one that we're both going to have to pay for. We're not who we were, this shouldn't have happened.

I wanted closure. Instead I've reopened a wound.

It's bewildering to have the body of a stranger still feel so familiar. Because we *are* strangers now, and I need to remember that. We've lived entire lives in the years we've been apart, and the fact that she still remembered to kiss her favorite beauty mark on my thigh tonight doesn't change that at all.

Nikki was fine. I saw it myself on socials and interviews and on the screen. When the tornado of our relationship had passed, her house was still standing. It was only mine in tatters.

I don't know if I can let that go. I don't know if I *should*.

"How did you just go on with your life without me?" I ask.

"I didn't," she says, reaching for my hand, but I pull back. Nikki stares down at the space between us, ever growing as I shift to standing.

"You moved on before I ever even left."

"No, never. Is that what you think?"

"That's how you acted."

She rubs her arms with a sigh, and it looks like she's hugging herself . . . or holding herself together.

Why am I doing this? Why did I do this?

"I can go," Nikki says, slowly getting up. "If you'd like me to. I didn't mean for . . . I don't want you to regret what happened."

"Yes, I think that's a good idea," I say, even though a part of me is screaming to make her stay.

"You can call me later?" she says. "If you want to talk? I just don't want to ruin what tonight meant to—"

"Tonight can't happen again," I insist, perhaps because I mean it, but also to get a reaction. I don't know how I feel about anything anymore, everything so jumbled up and confusing. "Just to get it out of our systems, right? And now we have?"

Nikki slides on her coat and then stands in front of me. "If that's what you want." She presses a gentle kiss to my cheek, before whispering in my ear, "But for the record, Andy, so we're perfectly clear on this: I'll never get you out of my system. I wouldn't want to."

I stand rooted in place as Nikki darts down the stairs. Because she had, many times over, hadn't she?

Chapter Fifteen

Pining Is Not Just for Trees

> **Nikki:** Is it all right if I stop by the store?

> Why?

> To see you . . . ?

I stare down at Nikki's text for a few moments before sliding my phone back into the drawer by the register and shutting it with a grunt. I don't know what to do about it, so, I do nothing.

Regan is out delivering flowers to a beauty pageant and will be tied up all day for the setup, which has left me here to hold down the fort. I make myself busy sweeping and tidying up, letting myself focus on the mundane to keep my head on straight.

As if anything I do is straight.

It's been two days since Nikki and I . . . reconnected . . . at my apartment. She texted me yesterday too, although that time instead of ignoring it I gave a firm *I don't think that's a good idea.* The easiest thing would be to block her number—except no, that's a lie. That wouldn't be easy at all, judging by how many times a day I've been checking my phone to see if she's texted again.

Get her out of my system, my ass.

The jingle of the bells over the door a little while later isn't unexpected. Nor is the sound of Nikki's heels on the hardwood floor of the old shop, or the scent of her perfume that still draws me to her like that cartoon skunk. I take my time putting the broom in the closet before turning back to face her, trying very hard not to smile at the hopeful expression on Nikki's face and the two coffee cups in her hands.

Be cool, remember, she's supposed to be out of my system. That was the deal. Even if she's standing here in fuck-me lip gloss and an old hoodie of mine that I haven't seen in five years.

"Nice hoodie," I say, arching an eyebrow.

"Hey, you gave this to me fair and square before you went home on the second season break."

"Funny you just happened to pack it for this trip."

"Isn't it?" She smiles, passing me a cup. "It must have jumped in my carry-on while I wasn't looking."

"Uh-huh. And did you also already have the coffee ordered when you put on my old hoodie and asked if you could come by?" I ask, not even trying to hide the amusement in my voice.

"Hey, I gave you two full minutes to say no before ordering... I may have already been in the coffee shop, though. Just in case."

"Right." I take a sip of my coffee; it's perfect, exactly as I like it. Again. Still. I shake my head and mumble, "What are we doing?"

"It looks like you were sweeping," she offers, passing me the dustpan from where I accidentally left it sitting on one of the racks. "And I'm just bringing Cinderella her coffee."

"Funny," I say, carrying it back to storage. When I come back, I find her studying some of the plants by the window. "You hanging around town for long this time?"

"As long as it takes," she says, not looking up from the delicate petals she's tracing her fingers over. I shiver, definitely *not* imagining getting her fingers back on me.

"Takes for what?" I ask, trying to pull it together.

Nikki sighs and looks over at me. "Do you really want to talk about heavy stuff right now?" she asks. "We can, if you do, but it seems like you don't, and I'd rather just . . . be here if you'd let me."

"That's a first," I say. "Since when have you ever wanted to be anywhere you actually were?"

"Since I found you again," she answers honestly. "Since you didn't say no when I asked to come by today."

"Laying it on a little thick, don't you think?"

She takes another sip of her coffee and leans against the counter. My stomach does a little swoop at the glint in her eye. "I don't remember you *ever* having a problem with thick. In fact, I'm pretty sure that your favorite strap-on of mine was very—"

"Okay, no," I say, blushing down to my toes. "None of that."

"None of what?" she asks, batting her eyelashes innocently.

"Stop it," I laugh. "No innuendo, no talking about toys or strap-ons . . . and no sex. Again. That was a mistake."

"That's a rude way to talk about me giving you multiple orgasms," she deadpans.

"Thank you for them, they were lovely, but it can't happen again. No friends-with-benefits stuff. We needed to get it out of our systems, and we did. Officially. Period."

"Okay." She shrugs, like she doesn't even care. The pang of disappointment that whips through my body shouldn't be surprising, but it is. It's not that I want her to fight me on this, it's just that I sort of do.

"Okay?" I press, pulling out the order sheet and deciding to get a jump on tomorrow's arrangements. "You're fine with that?"

"Yes?" she says, looking at me in confusion. "Did you think I wouldn't be?"

"Historically, that was your go-to when—"

"I'm not the same person I was, Ducharme," Nikki says. "I know you aren't either. If you think having my tongue in you again is a mistake, then I respect it. Besides I'm high enough on the fact that you just called us friends."

"No, I didn't," I say, ignoring the zap of warmth shooting through me at the thought of—*stop it. Stop it. Stop it. Pull yourself together, girl.*

"Yes, you did," she says, tipping her coffee toward me. "Can't be friends with benefits if we aren't friends."

I clear my throat, trying to change the subject as I head to the corner of the store to gather the tulips I'll need for the next arrangement. "Please stop talking," I stammer out, still trying to get a grip.

"Hey," she says quietly, coming up so close behind me that her breath fans against the skin of my neck. "I want whatever you'll let me have. I hurt you, badly, in ways that I don't even know the extent of apparently, and I want to fix it, if I can. Whatever that looks like."

I pick up another tulip, realizing it might be easier for her to get this out without facing me. "Nikki, I don't . . ."

"If you tell me all you want from me is to show up every morning with coffee and then immediately leave, I'll do it. If you want to see every draft of the book to ensure I don't include anything you don't want in there, consider it done. I'll do whatever you want me to. The truth is, I didn't sell this book to hurt you, Andy, I sold it to remember you."

I turn around to face her. "What?"

"I was starting to forget things about us and I didn't want to. I didn't think I would ever see you again. The world is big, and you disappeared into it so easily," she says. "I worked really hard to turn myself into someone that I felt would be worthy of you, even though I knew you might not ever be there to see it. Now you're here, standing in front of me.

"So yes, if you tell me all I can be is your errand girl, I'll be that. If you tell me I'll never taste you again, I'll respect it. If you tell me you've moved on and don't love me anymore"—she lets out a shaky breath—"I'll deal. But I won't stop showing up for you until the day you tell me to go and mean it. Because you have me, Andy. You've always had me. You just have to decide if you want me. I can be patient while you do that."

I'm stunned by her words, nearly letting the flowers slip out of my hands. I want to soak in every word Nikki just said and believe them, but I know I can't trust them. Not yet, and maybe not ever. I need to think. I need to do whatever I'm going to do the right way this time. I need to . . . respond to her.

"Okay," I say quietly. "Friends, then, maybe. We can try." I glance at her messenger bag. "Do you have another chapter in there for me?"

She smiles. "Yeah, a fun one."

I raise my eyebrow, unconvinced.

"Remember the time they sent us to Disneyland? Season three?"

"Yes," I laugh. "I remember you being obsessed with the Dumbo ride even though you'd never seen the movie, and then hating it when we rented it that night."

"Uh-huh." She grins. "What else?"

I tap my chin. "I remember you wearing Mickey ears and calling yourself a Disney kid even though that wasn't even our network."

"Hey, anyone can be a Disney kid! It's not like I called myself a Mouseketeer! I was healing my inner child!"

"Oh, is *that* why you cried when you met Belle?"

"Oh my god, stop," she shrieks. "Is there anything less mortifying that you remember?"

I put my arm out, making grabby hands. "No, actually, but I just remembered something even more embarrassing that you did. Give me the chapter, I want to make sure they *all* make it in."

"You're lucky I lo . . . like being friends with you again," she says, blushing, as she shoves the papers into my hand.

"Guess I am," I say, grabbing my pen to scribble down every last cringey story I can think of.

*   *   *

Nikki is back the next morning, and the next. And the next.

In fact, a week of coffee delivery, light chitchat, and chapter reviewing goes by. I can't help but notice she's going a little out of order, only bringing in the funniest, happiest chapters. Each day, as soon we finish, she disappears into the church straight after.

She won't tell me what she does there, or anywhere, really, when she's not here. Still, it's nice having her around, it is, and I try hard to appreciate how careful she's being to respect my boundaries, not to push . . .

But it makes things frustratingly surface-level between us in a way they never have been. Less of a friendship and more of an acquaintanceship, and now I'm lying in bed after three rounds with my vibrator remembering when it *wasn't*.

It's late, nearly eleven. I have no idea if Nikki still keeps her night owl hours or not, but I'm pressing call on her name anyway as I curl up against my pillow.

"Hey," her sleepy voice says, drifting into my ear.

"Did I wake you?"

"It's okay." I hear the slide of her sheets as she sits up in her little cabin a mile and a half down the shore. *I wish I was there right now too.*

Those talks, those neutral, banal, surface-level chats, have somehow only made me miss her more. Maybe that was the point, maybe respecting my boundaries was just another way for her to push them, and if it was, it worked. It definitely worked.

I'm on the hook, dangling, and all she has to do is reel me in.

"Where do you go when you're not at the shop?" I ask.

"You've seen where I go."

"After the church," I say.

"I come back to the cabin and write so that I have another chapter for you the next day. Why? What's this about?"

"I missed you," I say, the torrent of words welling up inside of me and clawing their way out. I don't know what I thought I would say if she picked up, but it wasn't that, and it wasn't in such a pleading, annoyed tone either.

"I'm right here," Nikki says calmly, reassuringly, frustratingly even, and when did she become the steady one and I the violent earthquake?

"No, not now, then," I say. "Forget it, I don't know why I'm calling."

"Yes, you do."

I shake my head. She's not *wrong*.

"Whatever you want to say or ask or yell, Ducharme . . . I picked up," she says. "I'm here."

"Do you remember that last year that we were together? When you were off networking and partying all the time, and I was grinding away trying to pick up the slack? I had to get that PA job just to have a little income between auditions because my accounts kept being overdrawn and I didn't know why yet."

"Not well," she says honestly. "Everything was happening all at once and it was overwhelming. I wasn't paying attention to the things that I should have been, plus I was pretty much high or drunk all the time."

"It never once occurred to you how unfair that all was to me?" I ask, my voice quiet in the still of my apartment. "Really?"

"You never mentioned it," she answers. "Obviously I knew things were bad between us. I knew you had one foot out the door, but I thought it was more on principal. I didn't realize how unhappy you were until you left."

"Seriously?! That is so—"

"I know," she says. Her voice steady, steady, steady amidst the whiplash of my emotions. "I was horrible and self-centered and overexcited. That's what happens when you're raised on set. You grow up too fast, too selfish, and immature. I was barely into my twenties, high on praise and gifts and . . . yeah, a lot of other shit too. It was easy not to see the hard stuff," she admits. "It wasn't even that I was ignoring it. I just, there were a lot of times I couldn't look outside of myself at all. I understand how awful that must have felt. I wish there was a way to—"

"I hated you."

"Good." She sighs, as if she had been waiting for this moment and is maybe even relieved it's finally happening.

"I might hate you still."

"You should."

"Then why are you bringing me coffee every day?"

"Because you let me, and I'm hoping that means someday you *won't* hate me."

"That's pathetic." I let out a nervous laugh. "And not like you at all."

"You don't know me anymore," she says, and I can hear her smile through the phone. "I'll have you know there's little about the new me that isn't pathetic, at least when it comes to you. I meant it when I said you had me."

I roll over and shove my face in the pillow, fighting back a squeal even though I should still be upset, still be holding her accountable.

"Hey, you still there?" Her voice comes out small and tinny from where I dropped my phone.

The little voice from the back of my head says *Don't trust her*, but . . .

"Hi. Yes. Sorry. I, um, dropped the phone. But that's all very . . . nice. You're saying all the right things."

"I mean them. I want to do all the right things too, but I know it's gonna take time. You don't have to forgive the old me; you don't even have to stop hating her. I'm just asking for you to meet me as I am now and decide if I'm someone you think is worth knowing or not."

"Yeah," I say. I let the words linger between us a little longer before I add, "See you tomorrow, then?"

"See you tomorrow," she says, and I can almost picture her sleep-warmed smile as I set my phone down and burrow under the blankets.

What the hell have I gotten myself into?

Chapter Sixteen

A Give and Take

I'm sitting on the porch steps of the little cabin, two coffees in hand, when Nikki opens the door.

"Well, good morning to me," she says cheerfully from the top step. I scoot over, passing her a cup as she joins me in staring out at the ocean.

"I figured I owed you a coffee or two." I shrug, trying to play it off like I'm not just using it as an excuse to see her after our talk last night.

"I don't know, I think karma might still be tipped in your favor between the two of us."

I smile, watching a seagull swoop down into the water and emerge with a little fish. "I can't keep doing this, Nikki," I say. She freezes beside me, no doubt getting the wrong idea about the sudden revelation I had when I woke up this morning. I probably could have phrased it a little better, so I quickly add. "I can't hold on to this anger."

She tips her head, bracing herself. "Meaning . . . ?"

"Meaning maybe whatever this is can be a reboot instead of a sequel."

She grins. "A reboot, eh? You know, I just read for one of those."

I put my finger over her lips. "If it's a reboot, then you're not famous yet and we're just friends."

"Just friends?" Nikki asks. "You sure? Didn't we make out in the original, like, a week after we started filming our show? By my count, this reboot began—"

"I think we've already established you have a bad memory," I tease, even though she's right. We absolutely did make out almost immediately after we met, but what she's leaving out is that it was a dare from one of the other child actors on the set— who I think was hoping that Nikki was going to kiss *them*.

I still remember that night like it just happened. We were having "cast bonding time" at a hotel near set—the kids hanging out in one suite while our parents mingled in the other. We were all young and inexperienced, getting swept up in the excitement of being on a show. Someone had suggested we play truth or dare and Nikki, always the brave one, always the loud one, had chosen dare.

When they told her she had to kiss the cutest person in the room and Nikki kissed me? I was dangerously close to spontaneously combusting.

Sure, the rumors about us had started almost immediately after that, but somehow they didn't spread off set, letting us keep the squeaky clean, wholesome image that the network wanted. Mostly anyway. Just gals being pals and all that. We were encouraged to have sleepovers and spend time together as co-leads anyway. It was an easy cover.

They had no idea that we were falling in love. Experiencing a sexual awakening. Ruining each other for anyone else.

We didn't get to have a friendship because we were in love within minutes—a blistering, clinging, codependent kind of thing that served neither of us well. Maybe this "reboot" will be a chance to do the whole friendship part over, and do it right this time.

"No making out, then. Noted." She smirks before taking another sip. "Although, for the record, my memory is *achingly* fine in that regard."

"Wanna go for a very platonic walk on the beach?" I ask, standing up.

"Of course!" She grins. "Thank you for this very platonic coffee, by the way. It's nice to know that you remember how I take it. I assumed you deleted everything about me when you disappeared."

"I wish," I say, not realizing how it sounded until it was too late. "Sorry."

"No, you're allowed to feel how you feel. You don't have to apologize."

"So are you, though," I say, dropping my sneakers by her gate and walking barefoot in the sand. She follows suit, walking beside me as we watch the waves beat against the shore in the early morning light.

"You know how I feel," she says, raising her eyebrows.

"Not really." I shrug. "It kind of seems fake, you know?" I hold my hand up before she can protest. "I believe that you're genuine in wanting to reconnect, and I'm willing to *try* to believe that you didn't start writing this memoir with the intent to hurt anyone. My suspension of disbelief falters, though, with this nice-guy act you're doing."

"It's not an act," Nikki says.

"Come on," I groan. "It has to piss you off at least a little when I accidentally say 'I wish I could forget you'—especially after you said that you started writing your book in order to not forget *me*. Don't you get mad? Frustrated? Sad? You're freakishly steady. I don't get it. It's not you."

She pokes her tongue at the inside of her cheek and looks out into the ocean, avoiding my question, but I don't give up.

"We can't be friends if you can't be honest. Our little reboot can't only be you kissing my ass and me letting you. That's as unbalanced as we were before, just tilted the other way. I don't want that."

Nikki's eyes snap to mine. "I've spent a lot of time these last few years learning that I can't always put myself first. You used to *hate* that about me and now you're complaining that I don't do it anymore? I thought . . . I thought I was doing a good job."

"I don't want you to always be worried about doing a good job!" I say. "I want to know the real Nikki. The good, the bad, all of it. Stop being such an ass-kisser already!"

"You've never minded when I kissed your ass before. Although I guess it wasn't really kissing, as much as—"

"Okay, I set myself up for that one," I say, cutting her off before she makes me blush again.

"Yeah, you did." She nudges her shoulder against mine just as an extra-large wave sends freezing cold water splashing over our feet. We shriek and jump up, laughing as we head up the beach . . . until Nikki suddenly stops.

"What?" I ask, puzzled by the serious expression in her eyes.

She studies me for a second, her face stoic, and then pokes my arm. "You're it," she yells, racing away.

"That's not fair!" I shout, whipping up sand as I run.

She's fast, but I'm faster, and soon I've tackled her to the ground. Before we know it, we're wrestling in the sand, tickling and threatening to toss each other into the roiling ocean. It's a messy, dirty, damp affair that transports me back to the first time we came here. Back when everything felt free and safe.

This sleepy little town was such a good hiding place. It gave us a chance to regroup after finishing the series so we could plot our next steps as we transitioned from child actors to whatever came after. Flowers for me, apparently; an Oscar for her.

"What was it like hearing your name called?" I ask as we flop down on our backs to catch our breath.

"When?" she asks. There's sand in her eyebrow and I fight the urge to wipe it away, digging my fingers into my jeans to keep them still.

Friends, we're friends, I remind myself, trying and failing to not follow the trail of her tongue as it slides across her lips. *I can't kiss her.*

"Hmm?" I ask, trying to focus. "Oh, I mean, for the Oscar. What was it like being there? You must have died when they called your name."

This is the closest we've come to *really* talking about the stolen role, and we're both sort of holding our breath. Her brows furrow as she watches me. I worry for a second that she's going to hold back again—stay neutral and polite or even downplay it as if she thinks that would curry favor with me—but then her face splits into a wide smile.

"It was incredible," she says, rolling to her side to face me. "I'm there, right, and so is everybody I've looked up to in this industry for my whole life. Except while I'm looking at them, they're also looking at me. Getting nominated was enough, but hearing my name called, walking up the same steps that Jennifer Lawrence fell down?! It was surreal. It was like nothing I had ever experienced. Did you watch my speech?" she asks, and I shake my head. "Oh," she says, a hint of hurt flashing across her features. "Right, no."

"I mean, I would have, but . . ."

"Yeah, no, I get it," Nikki says softly, tucking some hair behind my ear and then quickly untucking it.

I look at her, puzzled.

"You told me stop kissing your ass, right? That means you have to get your own hair out of your face after you hurt my feelings. Rules are rules."

"Well, if it's a rule . . ." I let out a tiny laugh. "Are you very upset I didn't watch?"

"It was kind of a big moment for me." She flicks some sand off her arm. "I took my brother as my plus-one. I didn't want to share it with someone else," she says, looking toward the ocean. "Maybe someday we can watch it together?"

"Maybe," I say, unsure if I mean it. Talking about it is one thing, but seeing it? I'm not sure how it would feel—if it would hurt or give closure or both—and I don't want to think about it right now.

Because this, right here, this is nice. This I *can* do.

I prop my head up on my arm to look at her, soaking up her slow blinks and the relaxed expression on her face. I can almost feel the history spooling out into the space between our bodies—the air growing heavier with tension the longer we look at each other. *Wanting* drowns out every thought in my head until I'm nothing more than instinct and need.

My eyes trail down the curves of her body, snagging on her collarbone, the one I used to love to bite so badly. I swallow hard, my eyes drifting up to hers, finding the same heat reflected right back at me. My lips part, my body leaning just slightly, and—

Nope.

I push myself up off the ground and dust myself off. Nikki groans, dropping onto her back before propping herself up on her elbows. "Heading out?" she asks, her voice carefully neutral.

"I'm hungry," I say. "Would you like to get some platonic breakfast with me?"

"What if I made it for us instead?" she asks. "Platonically, of course."

"Of course," I say. "Platonically. Then maybe after we could... look at your next chapter?"

"We could do that," she says, her smirk turning into a full-on smile. "We could definitely do that."

"Platonically, though," I insist, pulling her up. "No more horny thoughts, and no more longing looks either, for that matter!"

"Horny thoughts? Who's having horny thoughts? You have got to get your mind out of the gutter, *friend*." She laughs and then leans closer to whisper, "I thought you were a good girl?"

Chapter Seventeen
Good Is Relative

I am sucking her tit into my mouth, platonically, at the end of our seventh "friendship date."

I've been steadily helping her with her chapters about our time on the show, fact-checking and occasionally asking her to pull something out that I want to keep as *just for us*. She's been remarkably chill overall, but I was glad when she pushed back on a couple of things—it made me feel more confident that she really was done with all the ass-kissing stuff.

We haven't gotten to the final season yet—I don't think either of us is in any rush to—but we're getting close. Today, we went to the farmers market together, in the name of avoidance. We agonized over choosing the perfect eggplant to make Nikki's famous eggplant parm.

We also got distracted by the crafts section, where someone was selling ultra-luxe robes that they had sewn themselves. Nikki saw me running my hand over them and insisted on buying one for each of us. I was tempted to protest—they were expensive—

but then I remembered she was Nikki Fucking Colletti and could definitely afford it.

The truth? I had wanted to tear her clothes off as soon as we walked in the door—the lingering looks, the trailing touches, her little innuendos throughout the day—but Nikki was steadfast and unbothered... at least at first. She immediately got to work slicing the eggplant and boiling the water, generally ignoring my attempts to get her to indulge.

We had played this game before, many times, on our first go-round, but now I couldn't tell if we were reintroducing the dynamic or if she just genuinely *was* unaffected. I'm the one who had said no making out. I'm the one who had set the boundary—how could I be disappointed that she was respecting it, yet again? Still, I was.

Frustrated in every sense of the word, I had decided to push Nikki a little further to see what happened. She was still prepping away, no doubt pulling together the best dinner I would ever have—even though I was hoping we never got to eat it. I came up behind her, hooked my chin over her shoulder and nuzzled into her neck until she finally, finally turned to kiss me.

It was gentle and unhurried, more like sliding into a comforting bath than a turbulent ocean.

"What's all this?" she asked when we finally pulled apart. "I thought you weren't ready."

"Maybe I feel like we've mastered the art of being friends and it's time to sprinkle in those benefits again." I grinned up at her then, trying to seal the deal.

She gently laughed and shook her head. "I don't want you to rush into this."

"I'm not rushing into anything. We're *friends*," I said. "I like being friends with you. I'm not ready to dive into dating or anything, but I'm not with anyone and you don't seem to be with anyone, so what's the harm in scratching that itch together? Our sexual compatibility has never been an issue, so . . ."

"Friends with benefits," she murmured. "The thing you *didn't* want to be a couple weeks ago."

"It's an evolving situation," I explained. "I'm shocked you're the one holding out against a good lay."

"I never said no. I just want to understand what's on the table."

"Hopefully me." I grinned and then ran my hand down the front of her shirt, unbuttoning as I went. Before long, the dinner we were making was forgotten and the room was a cacophony of gasps and sighs and the quiet snick of discarded clothes falling to the floor.

Now here we are, this very second, on the floor of this cabin, where I fully intend to fuck her into the rug.

The pot of boiling water bubbles over on the stove, the hissing steam nearly covering her sharp inhale when I pinch her hardened nipple between my teeth. She arches her hips up, searching for friction and finding some on my strategically positioned thigh between her legs. I lean back on my heels and flick open the button of her jeans, slipping my fingers between the fabric and her skin before shifting to yank everything off in one fell swoop.

I hook one of her legs over my shoulder, pressing tiny kisses to the inside of her ankle, relishing the way she squirms against me—so warm and vibrant and slightly ticklish. I lean forward, caging her between my arms as I capture her mouth with mine.

Nikki moans as her leg presses back into what must be a delicious stretch just shy of pain. I am suddenly grateful for all her years of yoga. She wiggles around, pressing herself back against my thigh so I can feel just how overheated and wet I've made her. I stare down at her big wide eyes, and I have to squeeze mine shut, overwhelmed by the sensations. I slide her leg back to the floor as I crawl even closer, licking into her mouth with a desperation boarding on anxiety. Nikki matches the energy but seems content to let me take the lead for now.

The urge to *kiss bite fuck consume* drags itself out of some primal place deep inside me because Nikki is here, in my hands, under my skin. *Mine. She's mine. If only for right now.*

"Hey, hey," Nikki says softly, dragging one of her hands up to the back of my neck as she studies my face. She reaches her other up to swipe a tear from the corner of my eye, and I look to the side, embarrassed. I didn't realize—

"Are you good?" she asks in a gentle voice. "We can stop."

I shake my head, not sure what to say. How do I explain that our first time back together, in my kitchen only a couple of months ago, felt like a battle, but this—this feels like coming home?

"You're not good, or you don't want to stop?" she asks carefully. "I need you to use your words, baby."

I shake my head again, feeling lost inside myself. "I'm scared of how you make me feel," I say finally, the words I've been swallowing for days suddenly out in the open. "I'm terrified of how much I want you right now. I can't . . . friends, right? We can do this and still be friends. It doesn't have to mean . . . I need you to say that we're friends."

"We're friends, Andy." Nikki shifts under me until we're both sitting awkwardly on the floor. She wraps her long legs around me as I lean back on my knees. I look away as she tucks some hair behind my ear. "What do you need? Right now, what do you want? We don't have to do this if you—"

"I want to do this." I study my hands, all the rest of my words running away. I don't even know what I want to tell her. That I need to forget? That I need to remember? That I need her to stay forever this time? That in this total reboot, all I want right now is her skin on my tongue and her hand in my hair. I need her to come with *my* name on *her* lips and *my* fingers inside of her, and then I want the same in reverse. I need to have her, in every sense. *I need, I need, I need . . .*

"Oh," she says softly, as if she can hear my thoughts, or maybe I've said them out loud, I don't even know anymore. I'm a jumble of feelings and nerve endings, more desire than common sense, and if she doesn't let me touch her soon, I might die. "Andy," she says quietly, guiding my face back to hers. She leans forward, sucking my lip into her mouth and gently biting down. The hint of pain settles me, settles us both, I think. "Are you sure?"

"Yes," I say, meaning it more than I think I've ever meant anything.

"Then go into my room and wait for me," she says. "I want you on my bed. Clothes off. We're not screwing on the floor."

"But I wanted to make you feel good," I say.

"You will." She smiles. "Now, go get ready for me while I

clean up in the kitchen. It suddenly feels like a takeout kind of night."

"But your dinner—"

"There's only one thing I feel like eating tonight," Nikki says, and I laugh when her hand drifts between my legs, the earnestness of her face in such contrast to that horrible line.

A pout crosses her face as she slowly separates us, helping me up before heading to the kitchen. I feel her eyes on me as I walk down the short hallway. The sounds of her moving around in the other room—the hiss of the boiling water quieting, the sound of pans being set in the sink—don't start until I'm safely encased in the warmth of her bedroom.

I slip my bra off and drape it over the chair in the corner, kicking off my joggers and socks before climbing on the bed. I hesitate before pulling off panties. Nikki always loved to take them off, said it felt like I was a present just for her, but *this time* she said clothes off. And I listen, because I know that this time, she's someone *new*.

I slide my hands lower, pressing at the ache between my legs and letting my eyes slip shut. I freeze at the creak of a floorboard, snapping my eyes open to see Nikki leaning against the doorframe, watching.

"Don't stop on my account," she says, pointedly tipping her head for a better view.

"Come here," I whine, reaching out to her with my free hand.

She pushes off the door and comes closer, letting me tug her down beside me and peel off the last bit of clothing keeping us apart. I wiggle until I'm pressed against her, laughing when she digs her fingers into my side and pulls me on top of her. She reaches for her lube in the bedside table—ever the prepared one—and I catch a glimpse of her favorite vibrator and the straps she used to use with me.

I tilt my head, a curious smile pulling at my lips. "Bit presumptuous, aren't you?"

Nikki follows my eyes to where the harness remains caught in the edge of the drawer and grins. "A girl can dream, right?"

I wonder if it should rankle me, the fact that she came here so prepared, as if she was expecting this to happen all along. But I can't bring myself to care, not now, while I'm perched on top of her, nearly coming undone from the sight of her in this bed. No, right now—right now it feels like a compliment.

Nerves cross her face. "I wasn't honestly expecting . . . I mean, I had hoped someday, but . . ."

"Shhh." I press my finger against her lips, not wanting to make a moment that feels so light, so joyful, so emotional into anything heavier.

Let us have this. Let us have each other, if only for now, if only forever. For as long as the universe lets us.

I grind against her pelvic bone, leaning down to kiss her as she pops open the bottle of lube and drizzles some of its contents over her fingers.

"You're so wet for me already, Andy," she says, nipping at my wrist by her head. "We probably don't even need this, do we? Because you're so good for me, always so ready."

Nikki sits up quickly and I whimper at the shift in position. She slides a hand around my neck with a determined look in her eyes as her other hand moves lower, much lower, ghosting over the skin of my belly with featherlight touches. I lean into it, chasing the sensation. *So close, I was so close, so close.* She shushes me with a kiss as her hand slides down, her palm putting just the right amount of pressure on my clit as her fingers curl inside of me.

"This is better, isn't it?" she asks and I quickly nod.

Her hand on my neck tightens, just a little, until I meet her eyes. "I want you to look at me when you come," she says, flicking her eyes down to where are bodies meet and then back up to mine. "And I want you to say my name."

"Yes," I pant, fucking into her hand as she holds my gaze.

"That's it, baby, keep going. You're doing so good for me. So good."

I nod, my mouth dropping open as my eyebrows furrow in concentration. The electricity keeps building so deep inside of me, so deliciously, that it almost hurts.

"I'm gonna come," I say. "Don't stop, don't stop."

"I won't, Andy. I want you to. Come. Now. Come for me."

Her words, her hand, her emerald eyes, she's here. She's really here. "Nikki. Nikki!" I'm a live wire snapping, sending sparks shooting through my body, arching my back until stars start to spiral in my vision.

The hand on my neck rushes behind me, catching me before I fall back. She pulls me tight against her while I ride out the waves, nuzzling into her neck. I am lost to the sensations and the smell of lilacs on her skin, chasing it with my nose and tongue like an animal reduced to its basest instincts.

"You're perfect," she says, kissing my temple before sliding her other hand from between us and wrapping me in a tight hug. I smile lazily against her neck, flicking my tongue out to taste the sweat as she shifts us back to lying down.

Nikki hums at the sensation, tugging me closer, and I swap out my tongue for my lips. I kiss her again and again as I slide lower, nibbling on her collarbone and feeling her heartbeat thundering beneath my hand.

I'm not done with you yet.

"Your heart is pounding," I whisper, resting my palm over her chest.

She drags her fingers through my hair. "It's 'cause it's happy," she says, and I grin, feeling the same, determined to show her, with my teeth and my tongue and my hands.

I will pour myself into her body until she can feel what I cannot say.

This body, I think, tugging her breast into my mouth, pulling moans from her lips as I bite and suck and squeeze . . . I once knew this body as well as I know my own. Every freckle, every mark, a map not just of her history, but of ours.

I lick at the tiny scar beneath her nipple, an unfortunate mishap with a fence when we went skinny dipping on a dare, breaking into the pool of the apartment complex next door. We were nineteen and free, and I bandaged her like we had been to war and then made love to her until she forgot it had ever even hurt.

"Andy," she sighs, like she's remembering the same thing.

I go lower, tracing the scar from when she got her appendix out, an emergency that shut down filming of our show for weeks. We were twenty then, still playing sixteen, and I had sat by her bedside holding her hand until the hospital released her.

She had looked so small in that bed. I hated it. I was so scared. But we made it through, and she got better.

She got better.

I go lower, dipping my tongue into her belly button and making her jolt, savoring the taste of the little raised dot where her piercing used to be—an act of defiance that she quickly lost once she went mainstream as an actor.

I'm about to head to my favorite spot when I see it. A jagged slice of silver across her right hip bone. My eyes narrow as I move toward it, feeling knocked off-center from the sight of something new on her body—like waking up to a fully grown tree outside your favorite bedroom window when before there was only lawn.

I trace the line with my fingers, and she pushes up to her elbow, watching me take in this new discovery.

"I was in a car accident. A bad one. They kept it out of the papers, but . . ."

A slice of panic whips through my head. I could have lost her—permanently. She was hurt and in pain and on the other side of the country *and I had no idea*. Did she wake up scared and confused and calling my name, like she did after her appendectomy? Or was someone else sitting by her hospital bed? Another lover in the place where I was meant to be?

I put my head down and suck on the scar until it bruises, until it's mine now too, instead of just hers. Nikki lets me—she even smiles at me—as if she's enjoying this reclamation as much as I am.

I feast on her skin, spurred on by that smile—sucking and nipping at anything I can, marking her and making her mine, before reaching my hand down where she wants it most. I grab for the lube, but she stops me. "No, just you," she says. "Just me."

She's so wet, so hot, so inviting. I dip my fingers inside, feeling her clench against the intrusion with a happy punched-out moan, and then I slide them up to her clit, repeating the motion until she's deliciously sloppy, grinding against my hand and making messes of us both. I want it to be phenomenal. I want her to feel it, understand it, memorize it. I want her to understand how good she makes me feel and to thank her for it.

One more nip and I drift down lower, shoving a pillow under her hips as I devour her like she's my last meal . . . or my first. Because she is, *she is*. I have been starving for her since the day I met her, just like she's been for me.

I press my tongue inside, lapping up every drop I can, not wanting any to go to waste. She grinds against my hand, my face, letting out little blissed-out noises here and there. I lay my arm across her hips, trying to pin her, but she jerks up on one arm and grabs my hand instead, lacing our fingers and reminding me that I might be eating her out but she's still the one in control.

I look up at her, our eyes locking as I lick and press and drown inside of her.

Tell me how good I am.

"That's it, right there," she says, her voice barely above a whisper, sensing my needs when I've barely thought of them myself. "Fuck, baby, you look so pretty between my legs," she says. And if I could come from words alone it would be those, it would. She wraps her fingers in my hair, tugging me harder against her, just how we both like.

Take it. Take whatever you want, I think, as she starts to unravel. Nikki clenches around me, finally coming with a shout. I keep going, the ever-obedient servant, until she shudders and slinks back against the headboard, pushing me back gently but firmly with her toes.

"Holy shit, Andy," she says. I grin, wiping my mouth with the back of my hand and then sucking my fingers clean.

Her pupils are wide, impossibly so, hiding the depths of green that I love so much. It feels heady and drunk to know that I'm the one who did that to her. I'm the one who made her come so hard there's a tremble in her breath and a glassiness to her eyes. I feel holy tonight. Royal. Me. Anderson Ducharme. *Queen of the fucking orgasm.*

Nikki reaches down to pull me up against her, letting me curl up into her body, pressing us as close as we can be. She kisses my hair, running her jaw along the top of my head, seemingly as desperate as I am for contact. I slide my leg between hers and she wraps one of hers around me. We could not be more aligned if we tried.

Nikki and I drift in and out of dozing, tracing gentle circles into each other's skin, needing the reassurance that we're both really still here. That this is true and real and really happening. I smile when her breath finally evens out—her fingers moving slowly and then stopping as she drifts off into sleep.

I did that. Me.

I shift against her, and her sleep-warm hands tense slightly like she's worried I might leave. But I won't.

I won't.

Not tonight.

Chapter Eighteen
Friends Don't Fall in Love

Regan is fiddling with the new online ordering system for the shop while I work beside her, pulling together the day's floral arrangements that we need to send out. Neither of us is saying it, but it's true that the ordering upgrades and higher-quality flowers are a near-direct result of Nikki still regularly sending flowers back to LA. Not to mention the fact that a lot of the people she's sent them to have taken it upon themselves to turn into repeat customers.

In Bloom is firmly in the black in a way it hasn't been for decades.

Thankfully, Nikki's taken to explaining who each floral arrangement is heading to lately. It's not that I'm jealous or nosy or anything, it's just that—since we've fully embraced the "benefits" side of our friends-with-benefits arrangement over the last few weeks—I've become . . . more curious. It's only natural to wonder about them, especially with the notes we put on the early ones.

Things have been pretty steady lately. Nikki and I have now

had the serious conversations about health history and been freshly tested (better late than never, I guess?). She assures me she's not screwing around with anyone else, and neither am I. We're on the same page. We scratch our itches together or not at all—and that applies even when she's had to travel a few times.

Maybe that shouldn't bring me as much relief as it does, considering our current status, which is: a complete and utter failure of banging each other out of our systems, and an even worse job at staying "platonic." But it does.

I don't know why I ever thought that would work. It's not like all we do is bang, although that is definitely one of our favorite pastimes. We're still teasing apart stuff from our time on the show when we're not tangling tongues or getting off.

Nikki continues to sidestep the biggest land mines or delete them from the manuscript entirely, though. Like last night when I went over, she gave me a chapter about when we moved into that big, beautiful apartment and she spilled hot pink paint all over the new marble floors while trying to surprise me with an accent wall. Like yes, that did happen that year, but I think the bigger issue was that she was drunk when she did it.

I pressed her a little on that before she asked me to stop. She said something like "she would add that in later when she does the rest" or whatever, and I'm not sure how to feel about that. A part of me is glad I don't have to relive all of the bad stuff while I'm buzzed out of my mind from a steady diet of good sex and a solid profit margin on the flower shop books for the first time, but . . . I don't know. Shouldn't the memoir be more than just a highlight reel?

Still, I can't deny it's been nice getting to know her again and learning all the little things that have changed about her—she really does drink oat milk, she reads a lot more, and, most surprisingly, she'd rather talk than argue when one of us is feeling down or annoyed or whatever.

Things are complicated, sure . . . but nice? I don't know. I mean, complicated is par for the course with us. I'm trying to embrace the fact that this reboot version of "complicated" is much more even and healthy than the stinging, brutal one we experienced on our first go-round.

"Three more LA orders," Regan says, shoving her shaggy hair out of her eyes and hitting print. She tears the orders out of the new ticket printer she bought last week and lines them up next to me. I'm currently making a massive orchid display for the local boaters association to raffle off for their silent auction. It's grander than most of my local orders, and I got a little thrill about pulling it together. It's nice working on something big again. We've had such an influx of smaller, shippable orders lately that this feels like a treat.

"It's wild how fast they keep coming in now that you can order online," she says. "Is everyone in LA allergic to calling or something?"

"Likely so, unless you're an agent." I laugh, adjusting some of the flowers in front of me.

"Well, you would know," she says, elbowing me.

Before I can reply that those days are long gone, Nikki walks in carrying a drink tray with four coffees on it. I raise an eyebrow as she sets it in front of me and studies the labels.

"Shouldn't you be at the airport?" I ask, because she definitely informed me last night (in between two of the best orgasms I've ever had and an appearance by our "very optimistic" favorite toy) that she had to head back to LA for a full week this time to handle some business.

I've been trying to pretend that the thought of not seeing her for so long doesn't have me as twisted up as it really does—anytime she's left lately it's been barely overnight, two days at most. Judging by the fact that she's here now, I suspect I'm not hiding my concerns as well as I thought. It's not that I think something is going to happen when she leaves, it's just . . . that I'm *worried* something will happen when she leaves.

Trust takes time to rebuild, friends or not.

Nikki shrugs. "I wanted to grab some coffee for the ride and thought I would hook you all up while I was there."

"This one's yours," she says, sliding a cup into my hand. She sets another one beside herself, and then studies the label on the third. "Do you really use five pumps of caramel?" she asks, sliding it over to Regan, who looks confused.

"How do you know that?"

"I asked the barista what you've been getting lately. I noticed it wasn't black with two sugars anymore." Nikki flicks her eyes to mine. "You said Johnny was off today, right? I figured he might be here too."

"He is," Johnny says, coming out of the back room, where Regan had put him to work building a new storage shelf. They drove an hour to Ikea yesterday to get it. With all the increased orders, we needed more places to store the various shipping materials and basic floral supplies we're going through so fast.

Johnny crosses his arms, looking down at Nikki. I think he's trying to look intimidating, but she just smiles.

"Iced decaf, soy milk, no sugar, right?" she asks, gesturing to the cup in front of her.

I look between them, silently praying he accepts the peace offering. They've been around each other a few times since that fateful night, but the reception has always been icier than the coffee sitting untouched beside me.

Johnny has been polite, just like we asked, and he did apologize for what he said that night, but I can't help but wonder if his apology was more for my and Regan's sake and not because he actually was ready to have a fresh start with Nikki. "Johnny McFarlane, Professional Grudge Holder"—he should put it on his business cards. Although the truth is, maybe if I'd held on to mine a little longer, I wouldn't be as bummed as I'm feeling right now about her leaving.

"Since when do baristas give out personal information? Doesn't that violate HIPAA or something?"

"It's coffee, not medical care, dumbass," Regan says, slapping him on his pec as she passes by to check out his progress on the shelf.

He raises an eyebrow in Nikki's direction. "How do I know it's not poisoned?"

"If it is, it wasn't by me," Nikki says, laughing. "Although I wouldn't be surprised if other people were also trying to—"

"Nikki!" I shriek, cutting her off before she can finish the rest of that sentence.

Johnny grins, seemingly pleased to see that she wouldn't immediately back down. *Maybe he enjoys their banter more than I realized.* It did seem like they were enjoying ribbing on each other the other night, when I had everybody over to watch a hockey game.

He steps forward and scoops up his coffee and straw before tactically retreating into the back room with Regan. "Thanks," he calls out, waving to her without turning around. "If I die from this, I'm going to kill you, though."

"Didn't poison it!" she calls after him before turning back to me.

A part of me thinks he's trying to give us privacy, but another, bigger part is wondering if he's jumping at the chance to get some alone time in the back room with Regan without having to worry about me interrupting. They've knocked enough things off the shelves back there while pretending to "clean up" that I—and half the town probably—have some serious suspicions about what actually goes on between them these days when no one is looking. They need to get it together already. It's long past time for them to admit their feelings.

Pot meet kettle, I think, and then quickly shove that thought away.

We haven't had to deal too much with people bothering us—Nikki is right, her lack of makeup does seem to work unsettlingly well in terms of keeping her incognito. While it probably wouldn't in LA or NYC or anyplace that people would expect a celebrity to be lurking, so far no one in this sleepy town seems to be any wiser about the Oscar winner in their midst. We'd both like to keep it that way.

"I think that went exceptionally well," Nikki says. I raise an eyebrow but she just grins. "What? He took the coffee, didn't he? That makes us best friends in my book."

"Riiiiight," I say, checking the time on my phone and frowning. "As much as I love having you around, you better get going or you'll miss your flight."

"There are worse things," she says, and then tilts her head. "Wait, did you just say you love having me around?"

She's lucky she's cute if she's going to fish like that.

"Nikki..."

"Fine, fine, I'm going, I'm going. Dinner when I get back?"

"Dinner sounds perfect. My place or yours?"

She waggles her eyebrows and I laugh at the suggestive face she makes. I resist the urge to flick some of the cut stems that litter the counter at her, pouting that she doesn't seem to have any intention of kissing me before she leaves.

"We'll figure out dinner later," she says, grabbing a lily from the rack and leaning forward to slide it into my hair. "In the meantime, keep this safe for me while I'm gone. I want it."

The way she's looking at me makes me think she's not just talking about the flower.

Our faces are so close now that I'm almost positive I'll get my kiss after all. I'm just about to close the space between us myself, when she suddenly pulls back.

"See you in a week, Ducharme."

Nikki's out the door before I can react, leaving me standing there with a flower in my hair and thoughts of her lips. Her rental car pulls away from the curb as she gives me a little wave, and yes, yes, I know the best part of leaving is coming back. I just have to trust she *will* be back.

Pull it together, Anderson.

Regan and Johnny emerge about fifteen minutes later, looking winded and flushed, with still-full coffees in their hands. A little bit of Regan's lipstick is smudged on the corner of Johnny's mouth, but I don't bother pointing it out as he waves goodbye and heads down to his own shop to tidy up a bit while it's empty.

At least someone got kissed this afternoon.

I go back to working on my arrangements, more orders filing out of the printer since we last cleared it, but I can't help but notice Regan walking over to the window. She watches him leave, staring after him the way I did Nikki—looking every bit the smitten kitten.

"Someone's down bad," I say, pointing at her with an orchid in my hand. "When are you going to stop pretending that you're not dating?"

"When are you?" She laughs, taking a sip of her coffee.

"Me?" I ask. I can't help the twinge of panic that rises up, like a rabbit caught in a snare.

This is different, I remind myself. *This is your best friend asking. This is somewhere safe. You can talk to Regan. You probably should talk to Regan about all this, actually. This isn't like when we were forced to come out about our relationship last time. Not that it's a relationship. It's a friendship. With benefits. That's all.*

It's not that I've been keeping Regan totally out of the loop. She knows how much time Nikki and I have been spending together. She also knows all about me helping her revise the book and all that. I'm sure she suspects a lot more is going on, though. I've been telling myself that I wanted to keep it just for us, me and Nikki versus the world, like old times . . . but the truth is, a part of me is scared of Regan's judgment.

Will she think this is all an epic mistake?

"Oh, come on," Regan groans. "You can pretend you two are keeping it casual all you want, but you look at each other like you want to crawl into each other's skin and stay there. It'd be creepy if it wasn't so cute."

I frown. I really didn't think we were being that obvious, especially not around other people.

"We're friends," I say, even though saying it makes my heart sink.

Regan looks at me in disbelief. "Am I supposed to pretend you didn't come to work with a hickey on your collarbone last week? Is that what we're doing? If you don't want to talk about it, that's fine, but don't pee on my leg and tell me it's raining."

I scrunch up my face. "Okay, well, that's a gross image, thank you."

She laughs and curtsies. "You're welcome. One of Johnny's clients said it the other day. We've decided to adopt it as part of our everyday vernacular."

"Speaking of things we don't talk about, you and Johnny seem to be getting pretty close . . ."

"That's because we're probably in love with each other," she says, and I nearly snort my coffee out of my nose. That's the first time I've ever heard her admit it.

"So are you together, then?"

"No." She looks away, stepping over to retrieve the fresh orders from the printer. "Not yet. I'm still working through some things on my end, but hopefully someday."

"That's great," I say, rushing over to give her a hug. Her admitting this to me is *big*.

"Okay," she says, clearing her throat. "I showed you mine, now you show me yours. What's really going on with you and Little Miss Hollywood?"

"We're friends," I say, but when Regan gives me another dubious look, I add, "with benefits."

"Really?" she asks, her voice trilling up.

"Yep, but that's it. That *is* the whole story. Glorified coworkers who bone and like to hang out," I offer up, wishing I could really believe it. *Needing* to really believe it for my own sake. "We're working on the book and getting reacquainted slowly."

"So slowly that you have to bang about it?"

"The chemistry between us was never an issue." I laugh. "It was a natural progression."

"A natural progression to start hooking up with your ex?" She leans against the counter. "And there's no feelings involved beyond being friendly, casual acquaintances?"

"Basically," I say, not realizing how much of a lie that feels like until I say it out loud.

She frowns, looking worried. "Annie, you look at her like she hangs the moon. You've been moping about her leaving all morning."

"So? Friends can miss each other," I grumble.

"*Sooo*," Regan says, dragging the word out. "I thought you had it under control, but I gotta say, you pretending you're 'coworkers who bone' has me worried. It's one thing to lie to me about having feelings, but are you lying to yourself too? If you really want to be friends with benefits, go with god, she's hot as hell, but if there's more to it—and from the outside, it looks like there is—then you're doing each other a huge disservice by not being open about it."

I look out the window and sigh. None of this is news to me, obviously. I've been wrestling with my feelings since even before we started up the friends-with-benefits thing, and while Nikki's been up-front about the potential for more, I haven't been. Not to Nikki, not to Regan—maybe not even fully to myself.

"What do you mean, 'it looks like there's more'?" I ask, sliding the arrangement over to begin work on the next one.

"Nothing really. Just happiness looks good on you. You're very cute together and it seems like you genuinely care for one another. I can understand why you fell in love with her twice, and I can't believe I'm saying this, but—"

"I'm not in love with her again," I say, wrapping a tulip bouquet so tight with twine that I accidentally crease a stem. I cut the wrapper off in a huff, pulling the flower back out to trim it.

"Are you positive about that?" Regan asks, sipping her coffee.

No. Yes. No.

I sigh. "I missed having her in my life, Regan," I say. "We're building a kind of friendship while I help her fact-check the book. We have a lot of chemistry, yeah, and that's probably what you're picking up on. It's . . . confusing but it's not love. I won't let it be. Like I said, we're glorified coworkers who bone. That's all we can be. The sex is amazing and the friendship is fun, but I could never *really* give her my heart and she knows that. We both know that."

Stop lying, my heart screams.

"Okay," Regan says, studying my face. "If you say so. Just be careful with yourself, you know?"

"Yes, Mom," I say, trying to lighten the mood—which reminds me. I really should call home again. I've been texting them Nikki updates, but Mom and Dad are definitely due for an extended FaceTime.

"Ugh, gross, 'Mom' is the last thing I ever want to be," she laughs, flinging a paper towel at me before getting back to work.

I turn Regan's words over in my head as I rearrange some of the flower displays and freshen up others. Regan's not wrong; happiness does look good on me. I love living here, and I love the little flower shop. I love that working with flowers has given me a way to reconnect with my family on a whole new level, bringing us even closer. I've built a good life, with good friends, and a new career I'm proud of—and now I've even wrangled a way to get my sex life back on track.

I'm not hiding. I'm not. I'm not taking the easy way out. I'm getting shit done.

Besides, even if I wanted something more than friends with benefits, and I *don't*—Nikki and I wouldn't stand a chance together with us living on opposite coasts, leading *very* opposite lives. It wouldn't be fair to either one of us to ask the other to stay.

Nikki would never be happy here, not forever, and my life on the West Coast is a door that needs to stay shut. No matter how much it hurts to watch Nikki head to the airport alone, it's necessary. I have to keep that in perspective.

Someday soon, Nikki will get called to film and be gone. That's the truth. We'll go from friends with benefits to friends who occasionally text, and after a while maybe not even that. If there's something I've been avoiding, it's not the idea that I'm in love with her, it's that this reboot has a hard stop and always has.

Maybe it's good we'll have this week apart—a little practice for when, *not if*, she's gone for good. We're friends. Friends. And friends don't fall in love.

Liar.

Chapter Nineteen

Sometimes Lies Are Better

Nikki texts me as soon as her plane lands, before she's even disembarked. Her enthusiasm is adorable and—whether I want it to be or not—extremely contagious. Despite my reaffirmed plan to keep my heart under lock and key and be realistic about this little reunion, I'm smiling nonstop while I spend the next hour that it will take her to drive from the airport stress cleaning my apartment in an effort to run out the clock.

When the alarm on my phone dings to let me know it's time to head over and meet her, I hop on my bike and pedal to her cabin like some sort of lovesick teen. Not that I'm lovesick.

Not anymore. Not in nearly a decade.

I've been wrestling all week with how I feel and what I want. Regan being able to see right through me didn't help matters. I know that Nikki and I are more than just friends with benefits—and definitely more than the crudely put "coworkers who bone" that I've been insisting we are. I'm almost positive Nikki can tell how I feel too. That doesn't mean that's right or that we should give in. It also doesn't mean that there's any kind of future here beyond however long Nikki's escape from LA lasts this time.

That doesn't mean I want it to stop, which is probably why I'm peddling so hard.

It's all so confusing. In the beginning, all I wanted was revenge, then it was free coffee and orgasms and to make sure she wasn't shit-talking me in the book. How that morphed into an actual friendship and companionship, I have no idea. But now I've just spent an entire week missing someone I never wanted to need again.

I need to reestablish boundaries. I can do this. I can. I have to.

I take the last turn, finally bringing the tiny cottages into view. Most of them are dark—thanks, slow season—but cabin six is lit up brightly like a lighthouse in the storm. Nikki beat me here.

I slow down, taking deep breaths as I pedal closer, until I finally come to a stop outside. I take my time leaning my bike against the dingy clapboard—trying to be chill and rational and relaxed and generally the opposite of all the feelings that are welling up inside of me right now.

But then Nikki is there, flinging open the front door, her hair wet from a hastily done shower—no makeup, no pretense, just pure *her*—and every thought I have goes out the window. It doesn't matter what I think I should want, or think I should do, not when her name is thundering in my chest like a heartbeat.

She races down the rickety steps, pulling me into a tight hug. "Damn, I missed you," she says, and then her lips are on mine.

The kiss is a frantic, desperate thing—teeth and tongues clashing, swallowing my laughter as I relish in her unbridled enthusiasm. We're standing in her doorway kissing like a couple of fools on the beach, and in this moment, I'm forgetting again why I ever thought this could be a bad idea.

"Hi," she says, smiling, when we finally break apart.

"Hi, yourself," I say softly. I peek behind her through the cabin door, spying a bag of takeout on the small table by the kitchenette. "Is that going to get cold?"

Nikki shakes her head. "I really need to work on my kissing skills if you're thinking about food right now."

I'm about to protest that her kissing skills are just fine, more than fine, fan-fucking-tastic actually, when my stomach grumbles, betraying just how hungry I really am. I've been too excited to see her today to eat anything much, the anticipation and nerves combining in a way that left my stomach unsettled and my brain buzzing.

"Oh," she says, tangling her hand with mine and leading me over to the table. "Baby, you're starving! Sorry, let's eat." She gestures for me to sit as she moves about the room, pulling out plates and silverware and carrying it all over to the table. It's awfully domestic, and I know that should give me pause, but . . .

Nikki's about to settle in across from me when I give the laptop poking out of one of her bags by the door a pointed look. "Were you working on the flight?"

She looks sheepish. "Yeah, my agent has kind of been on me for not getting it done. I've already had to get an extension, and I rewrote most of what I had done before I first came out here. She's worried my editor is going to be upset about some of the stuff I'm changing in it."

"What do you mean? We've been working on it all along—how fast do they want it done?"

"We've been working on *some* of it," she says, and I know what she means. *The good parts—the happy ones.* "Plus, the more time we spend together the more bitter I get about how things went down. The tone of the piece has changed quite a bit from the proposal."

I pull open the bags of food, waiting for her to elaborate on her own, but when she doesn't, I decide to do a little prying. "Bitter about . . . ?"

"When I started this book, I just wanted a place to get everything out of my head and to make sure I didn't forget any of the happy times. It was almost like a way to honor and remember our past and how things really were. I also thought it might clear up some misconceptions people had. It turns out I was the one with all the misconceptions.

"Things were a lot more messed up for a lot longer than I realized. I'm mad that I—that *we*—had to go through so much at such a young age. My editor bought a book pitched as a fun and occasionally scandalous accounting of things, and now it's turning into a condemnation of the whole industry—or at least of the people who were around me in the early years."

"Well, I always hated Eliza, so if you want to condemn her, I fully support you." I'm half kidding, but Nikki frowns anyway.

"Seems a little like kicking her when she's down, given that she hasn't done much since I fired her." Nikki shrugs. "Even if she did bring it on herself."

Nikki's so casual about it, like she's not talking about how she tossed her biggest ride or die to the curb, and it's kind of messing with my head. Nikki and Eliza were . . . well, frankly, they were already totally enmeshed with each other by the time I met them. It only got worse as Nikki's star began to rise. In the beginning Eliza was simply an adviser and advocate, but as time went on Nikki became almost *dependent* on her. She wouldn't even go on vacation without making sure Eliza approved, let alone anything else.

Whenever I would try to question it a little, Nikki would always just say she owed Eliza because Eliza helped her get her start in the industry and that Eliza believed in her when no one else did.

I guess we had very different interpretations of what that meant back then.

Nikki felt like Eliza had plucked her out of obscurity and given her a chance. All I saw was a star fucker overstepping her bounds. To me, it looked like Eliza hung her shingle on a rising actor who didn't have as much familial oversight as I did—Nikki's parents were more worried about bragging rights than actually keeping their daughter safe. It made for an easy mark. Eliza was all too happy to become Nikki's de facto parent and manager, on top of being her agent. She was involved in every single tiny detail of Nikki's career and life, at a level I never saw with anyone's else's agent—certainly not mine.

I was jealous. My agent always made me feel like he didn't have time for me. I could barely even get a call back. But there was Eliza, practically holding Nikki's hand to cross the street. Nikki even jokingly referred to Eliza as her "agent-mom."

At first, I thought it was a little weird, but mostly fine. But the more Eliza interjected herself into Nikki's life outside of work—the more she intruded in *our* relationship—the more I found myself hating her. I can't even remember how many fights I had with Nikki over Eliza's meddling. Especially when all the stories came out about us dating, effectively outing us to the world. Eliza advised Nikki not to be photographed with me anymore, as if we could put that particular genie back in the bottle. She was worried it would impact Nikki's "marketability" and "scare off shareholders at the network."

Meanwhile, my agent was MIA and my parents wanted me to make a statement confirming things—own our queerness on our own terms—which, while I didn't love that I was being forced into the position, was what I really wanted to do.

In the end, Nikki and I landed somewhere in between, meaning no formal statements were made but also there was no hiding away and pretending we didn't know each other either. *Let people talk; neither confirm nor deny* became the strategy.

And talk they did.

It was awful for a minute, having not just our feelings for each other but our whole sexuality put on display for the public to shred—the amount of people who thought we were doing it for publicity was staggering. I was glad to have Nikki by my side during that time, both on and off camera. I thought it was a sign that she was gaining independence . . . but of course it wasn't. Eliza was right back to meddling in our business on every other front and keeping Nikki under her thumb. Which is why I'm *still* so shocked that Nikki actually fired her.

"How long has it been since you parted ways?"

"Hmm." Nikki pauses, thinking. "Maybe four and a half years? Give or take."

Not long after I left, then.

"You want to talk about it more? Or do I have to wait for the book?" I tease.

"It just wasn't working for me anymore." She pulls open one of the boxes of fried rice, spilling some onto her plate and avoiding eye contact. "That's all."

"You sure about that?" I probably shouldn't be pushing the issue, but I can't help myself. Eliza was such a sore spot between us right up until the day I left LA. How could things have changed so quickly once I was gone?

"I didn't trust her advice anymore, that's it," she says. "I had to let her go."

"Her advice about what?" I ask.

"How about this, since you like questions so much tonight," Nikki asks, the barest hint of irritation in her voice. "What was it like when you first got here? Was it strange being away from all the LA bullshit?"

I look at her for a moment, deciding if I really want to let her dodge my question and if I really want to answer hers. Regan's words about how Nikki and I are clearly more than just friends echo through my head. If I share what she's asking for, it will feel suspiciously like reinforcing that. Those early days were *hard*. I was raw, I was a mess, and the worst part was that all I wanted to do was turn my car around and crawl right back into the bed Nikki and I shared, self-respect be damned.

I reach for one of the take-out boxes, weighing my options as I pour food onto my plate. I glance over at her laptop again, taking the coward's way out.

If she can do it, so can I.

"What were you writing about while you were gone?" I ask, changing the subject.

I catch a quiet "Thought so" under Nikki's breath before she shovels another forkful of rice into her mouth. I think she's going to drop it completely for a second, but—

"That, kind of. You leaving, me wondering where you went and if you were okay." She looks up just in time to see the smile slide right off my face. "This week away dredged up a lot of memories. I know it's not the same as now, obviously—we FaceTimed all week and things are solid—but stepping into my empty bedroom the other day after being with you so much . . . it brought me right back to coming home and finding out I was the only one who lived there anymore."

"Right," I say, wondering how I managed to get myself out of one minefield just to immediately land in another. We've been avoiding anything to do with me leaving or what happened after. I didn't realize that she was ready to work on that, let alone already has been all week. Sure, a part of me is curious to see how she's laid it all out for her future readers, but the other part of me has been steadily dreading this moment since she handed me that first chapter.

The spiral I thought I had staved off on my ride over comes roaring back to life.

What are we doing? What am I doing? I shouldn't—

"I understand if you don't want to talk about that right now. Seriously, it's fine. I just didn't want to lie." Nikki gives me a tight smile that almost morphs into a grimace before brushing her fingers against mine briefly—there and then gone in a blink. I wonder who that was supposed to comfort: me or her?

Maybe the lie would have been better.

I sit sharply in my seat, not sure how to get from one sentence to the next, because where do you even start? Me leaving was the culmination of so many things—her partying, our fighting, all the drama and chaos of finding out my agent had been stealing from me while hers had been trying to push me out of the picture all along. The resentment, the hurt, the jealousy... I was clawing my way up the mountain and losing ground while she was on a private plane to the top.

The show, I think, *the last season—the other elephant in the room we've been avoiding. That's what really set us down the path to ruin.*

That last season, when Nikki was away more than she was on set, was the knife in my back. Everything that came after was just us waiting for me to finally, *finally* bleed out.

Even our time here all those years ago, that little mini vacation to bridge the gap between the end of what we knew and everything that still lay ahead, was little more than a Band-Aid. A temporary fix. We dug our fingers into each other's skin, desperately holding on to the relationship for a few more years after that, even though we probably should have walked away long before we did.

If we're being honest, I think we both knew it too.

And if we're being *really* honest, I think a case could be made that we're doing that again right now.

I watch her eat, my earlier hunger completely dissipating in the face of this conversation. A part of me wants to flip out. To yell at her. To sneer, "What could you possibly say about me leaving? You left long before I did, you just kept coming home at night pretending you hadn't!"

But instead, I simply ask, "And what's your take on all of that?"

Nikki hesitates and then sets down her fork. She looks as if she's bracing for something much worse than a brief conversation about our shared history. The entire mood has shifted now. Everything that made this feel like a happy homecoming flies out the window as her eyes slide up to mine. *This* is the work. *This* is the war.

And good. Good. Maybe we need to rip that Band-Aid off for us to heal—for us to move forward in whatever form that takes.

Closure. Closure. Maybe that's all we have left for each other. Maybe that's all we deserve.

"Do you really want to talk about this right now?" she asks quietly.

"We probably should, if you're behind on your work," I say, already hating the next lie sitting on my tongue. "This isn't like . . . you shouldn't put important things off for me. You can keep writing while I'm here. It's not like this is a formal date or anything. Like we said, we're friends—"

"Friends with benefits," Nikki finishes for me. "How long are we going to keep telling ourselves that? You have to feel it too. You—"

"As long as you're in town, probably, because it's all we can ever be." I pretend the disappointed look on her face doesn't hurt. *Reestablish boundaries. Protect your heart.* "This is what I meant before when I said I needed your honesty. It can't just be the good stuff! We can't build a friendship on highlight reels."

"How real do you want me to get?" Nikki asks, looking sad.

"More than you have been." I shrug. "But maybe a little less 'real' than whatever you're thinking about saying right now. Let's ease into it together, all right?"

She hesitates for a few moments, squeezing her eyes shut and exhaling sharply before reaching for her bag. "All right, Ducharme," she says. "We can do that."

God, why is this so hard?

"If you really want to talk about why I left, I think we need to start earlier than you coming home to find out," I say. "Catch me up on the stuff you were doing on your own. Did you write about the last season yet?"

"Only some," she says, opening the laptop with a tiny shake in her hands.

"Which part of it?" I ask while she clicks around.

"I'm writing about when we had that guest director come in, that actor's daughter who did the second episode. The one who took me to my first *real* Hollywood party."

"That woman was hitting on you that whole week and you refused to see it," I grumble into my rice.

"I didn't care. I was in love with *you*, remember?" she says, like that matters. "Besides, all of our producers were at that party too. I wouldn't have gone otherwise."

"Wouldn't you have?"

Nikki sighs. "I guess that's fair, given everything that happened, but no, I wouldn't have gone if the producers didn't suggest it would be a good career move. I wasn't interested in that director at all. I was head over heels for you and only you."

"If you say so." I force myself to take another bite of my dinner, hoping she can't see how worked up this all has made me. While that whole season is an incredibly touchy subject, the industry party at the start of filming, the one I specifically was *not* invited to, was the turning point.

The very first cut.

"I thought I was doing something good for *us*," Nikki explains. "That if I made connections, that meant you'd have the connections too."

I shake my head. "That's not how it works."

"I know that *now*," she huffs. "But back then I had everyone in my ear telling me different things. You didn't want me to go since you couldn't but the producers kept saying how important networking could be. Even Eliza showed up excitedly that night with designer dresses for me, talking about how good this party would be for both of our careers."

"Fuck Eliza," I growl. "I remember everything about that night, you know? How me and Gouda sat on the couch together while I cried into her fur. How you came home drunk and smelling like other people for the first time . . . it was weird! I felt like you had been abducted by aliens and then sent back to Earth. You went on and on about how beautiful the mansion was, how much I would have loved it, and then you called our apartment a 'comparative shithole' before passing out with all your clothes still on. I had to figure out how to get you into bed all on my own. I did it, though, not even realizing I was going to be doing it almost nightly for the next few years.

"I remember lying there next to you—the booze on your breath, the faint smell of cigars and money and perfume. You were someone else already, someone I didn't know."

"I wasn't."

"You can't pretend that night didn't change you."

"It was one party!" Nikki groans. "It was the first time I completely let loose. It was good for me after working so hard on the show for so long. I—"

"Wait," I say, scrunching up my face. "Did you write it in the book like it was a fun anecdote? You did, didn't you?"

"It *is* a fun anecdote!" she says. "It was my first true industry party."

I roll my eyes. "First of a thousand."

"Yes," she says. "Yes, I got incredibly carried away with the party scene, I take full ownership of that. That first time, though, that's not a bad memory. Nothing happened that night except I met a few famous people and did shots by a pool in a house so huge I could never even have dreamed of it. It made me realize how much bigger this career could be for me."

"For you." I nod. "It's not a bad memory *for you*. I was the one sitting home alone wondering why I wasn't good enough to even be your plus-one and if you were screwing that guest director in a random bathroom or not."

"You never told me that!" she says, looking shocked. "Why would you have even thought that? We were good. We were solid. None of the other stuff had even happened yet."

"It's hard to feel solid when your partner chooses a party over you. The one that your producers are at. For the show we were *both* on. How did you not see how differently they treated us? You were always made to feel like the next big thing, and I was always treated like I should be grateful for being there at all. Do you know how that felt?!" I'm ranting now but I can't stop. "No, how could you? Because you were too busy being young and hot and rich and snorting drugs off famous actors while I was home feeding our cat and running lines because I *always* had the early calls. I always had to be on set first thing. I—"

"Maybe I didn't want to be home back then! Maybe I didn't want to be feeding the cat and acting like somebody's wife! I was barely twenty! I was a baby!"

"So was I!" I shout.

"Don't act like I never invited you to those things once I was allowed to," Nikki says quietly, as if she's trying to balance my loudness. "Half the time you turned me down."

"Are you talking about the network Christmas party? Because that's the only one you wanted me at and I was *already* invited to it! Or wait, do you mean the *Vogue* party when you called me blackout drunk and then forgot?" I shake my head. "Even if you did invite me, which you *didn't*, I was doing twelve-hour days on set by then to cover for you always being gone! I was up at like five in the morning! Then you got that recurring role on *The Flash* on top of it and were around even less!"

"We got a new apartment with that money! I paid the mortgage that entire year and never asked you for a penny! You can't be pissed that I didn't do things exactly the right way when I was taking care of *both* of us."

"Exactly the right way?! You were going out every freaking night! When you did bother to show up on set, you were hungover! I don't even think you were sober that entire last month we lived together! And Eliza was right there, cheering you on and trying to convince you that I was holding you back. You want to talk about when I left? Why don't we talk about that last fight where I begged you, I *begged* you, to get help—to stop listening to Eliza—and you defended her! Do you even remember that?"

"Not really, no," Nikki says, swallowing hard as she slumps back in her seat.

"You told me to make sure I knew what I was doing because if I kept trying to make you choose between me and Eliza, I wouldn't like the answer."

"No!" she says, looking at me as stunned as if I just slapped her. "If I said that, I didn't mean it. I would never mean that. I was so screwed up by then. I hadn't slept in days when we had that fight and I—"

"You still said it, though, Nik. Doesn't matter if you meant it, because you thought it and you said it."

"I . . . I'm sorry," she says, and we both go quiet for a minute. "I hate that I said that to you and I hate that I hurt you and I hate that I don't even really remember doing it," she says, finally, her entire body painted freshly pink from shame. "I'm so damn sorry, Andy."

Any validation or vengeance I have from finally unloading all of that pales in the face of how gutted she looks right now. I needed to say it, or I wanted to say it—I don't even know anymore—but it didn't have to be like this. It didn't have to be angry and loud and awful . . . did it?

"I'm sorry too," I say. "I shouldn't have exploded on you like this."

"No, it's . . . fine. It answers some things." She pinches at her eyes as if she can hold the tears back with her fingertips. "Excuse me for a second," she says, nearly knocking over her chair in her rush to the bathroom. The sound of running water picks up behind the now closed door.

The first thing I realize as I stare at the door is that I'm a jerk who handled this so, so wrong. And the second is that I would do *anything* to fix that. To just be Nikki and "Ducharme" again, eating Chinese food and laughing over something ridiculous.

It needed to be said, sure, but not in anger, not with the intent to hurt.

I start reboxing the food, at a loss for what else to do. I'm just putting it all in the fridge when the bathroom door opens.

Nikki watches me, looking pitiful. "Are you leaving?"

"No," I say, moving closer until we're face-to-face. "But do you mind if we table all the heavy stuff for the night? I . . . I just want to be happy you're back right now. Is that okay? I know I'm the one who brought it up in the first place, but . . ."

"Yeah," she says softly, sadly, brushing my hair back. "Yeah, we can do that. You already put the food away, though, so . . . how?"

"I'm not hungry anymore," I say, pulling her into my arms until she tucks her head against my neck. She smells like fortune cookies and her favorite perfume, and I press a gentle kiss behind her ear. And then another. And another. Until we're both nipping, kissing, biting, panting—desperate to forget what just happened and remind ourselves that we're here, grown now. We're not those screwed-up children playing at adulthood.

Her hand trails down to my thigh and I laugh against her skin. "Think we just figured out how."

"I want to . . . god, I want to. But do you think we should?" Nikki asks, dropping her forehead against my shoulder. Her fingers squeeze tighter against my thigh before trailing to my center, the pressure delightful even through the denim of my jeans.

"I don't want to think right now," I gasp. "Let's not think . . . please? Let's get out of our heads. It'll feel so good. You always make me feel so good."

Nikki leans back, watching me as I slowly slide my hands under her shirt and unsnap her bra.

What were we so upset about again?

She bites her lip and pulls back. I think, for a second, that I've lost her now, just like I lost her then, but then she's pressing me against the nearest wall as she flicks open the button on my jeans and slides her hand inside.

And yeah, yeah, sometimes the lie is better.

Chapter Twenty
Come Together to Fall Apart

I made her come twice.

That shouldn't feel like such an accomplishment, but making Miss One and Done fall apart *twice* feels important. Heavy. Like I'm reclaiming her body the way we're reclaiming our history, our friendship, our futures. Like we're setting the train back on the tracks after our dinner argument derailed us.

I crawl up the bed and nuzzle in beside her, wrapping myself around her body like a vine, one leg draped lazily over hers as I run my hand down her side. My fingers catch on that same new-old scar and the familiar pang rises back up in me, the homesickness for the years we were apart. Familiar thoughts cascade through my head, reminding me that this is more than just sex and companionship, no matter how I try to tell myself it isn't.

I made her come twice.

I'm drawing lines in her skin with the pads of my fingers, leaning over to kiss anything I can reach as she drags her nails across my scalp in slow-motion circles that leave me even more blissed-out and relaxed than I already am.

"I love your hands," I sigh, twisting my head to press a kiss to her sternum. She laughs, digging in her nails, just a little, in a way that leaves me arching my head against her like a cat.

"At least you love something about me," she teases. "I'll get you to forgive me yet, Andy, even if it's one good lay at a time."

My hand stills when she says that, my brow furrowing as I soak in her words.

Suddenly the hand on my neck feels suffocating, the pleasing scratch of her nails turning to needles. Because we're not *falling* into old patterns, no. We're already there. This *is* the old pattern.

How many times back then did we use sex to distract ourselves from the bigger issues? How many times did we rely on sex instead of communication to get us through?

Constantly, and now we're doing it again.

"Andy?" Nikki says, her voice full of quiet confusion when I grab the blanket and sit up on the edge of the bed.

"I need a shower," I say, crossing the room and shutting the bathroom door behind me. I turn the water up as hot as it goes, trying to wash her off me as best as I can with some generic brand of cabin soap. If I use her body wash—if I smell her right now—I'll probably explode.

I can't think, can't breathe, can't even *trust myself* right now, when I'm fuck-drunk and lovesick. The hazy butterflies in my belly roil around and I feel nauseous.

Is this a panic attack? I haven't had one of those since LA.

I guess all the avoidant orgasms aren't the only pattern rearing back up.

"Baby, what's wrong?" Nikki asks, slowly pulling back the shower curtain.

I startle, so wrapped up in my own head that I didn't even hear her come in.

Nikki frowns and steps into the tub, pulling me against her in a gentle hug. She only lets go for a second, just long enough to adjust the spray to cover both of us, before she's back. I let her hold me, too exhausted and spun out to do anything else but bury my head against her warm skin. The water makes every bit of her feel slippery and new and *how?* How is this my life? How is it that the one person I most want comfort from is also the one person I should probably *not* be around right now?

"I need you to talk to me, Andy," Nikki says, tipping my chin up so I look at her.

I take a shaky breath, meeting her eyes with such sorrow because I know what I'm about to say is likely going to ruin everything. How could it not?

"We're doing it again."

She looks at me with pained confusion and my heart cracks open.

"Old patterns really do die hard, Nik." I step away from her, shoving back some of my hair that's become plastered to my face.

"What does that mean exactly?"

"Do you remember when we were fighting all the time? When it got really bad between us?" I ask.

Nikki gives me a sad smile. "Yes, of course I do. I'd rather think about the making up, though."

I think she means for that to be an out, a way to steer this back into safer waters with a little joke, but instead it's just proving my point.

"That's the thing, though. We didn't really make up, did we?

We'd fight till we were exhausted and then we'd screw until we convinced ourselves everything was fine again. We used sex as a distraction, and we're doing it again tonight."

"No, we aren't."

"We are!" I insist. "It's the first time we've really talked about what happened to us, like *really talked about it*, and then . . . and now . . ."

"That's not why we had sex! At least it isn't for me."

Nikki reaches for me again, but I shake my head. "It's exactly the reason! We bickered and then we landed in bed and suddenly we didn't care what we were even bickering about! You're winning me over one orgasm at time, you are, you said it yourself! It's the same way you kept me on the hook, kept me home for you, back then. It's what you do."

"It was a joke, Andy!" she says, stepping out of the tub. "Jesus Christ! You're the one who initiated it tonight!"

"For the wrong reason!" I shout.

"You don't mean that," she says, going still.

I shrug, terrified that if I open my mouth the dam will break, and I'll be the girl in the tub sobbing about Nikki. Again.

She looks at me, stunned, and then grabs a towel off the rack and storms out of the room. I give her a second to cool down and then roughly twist the water off, quickly wrapping myself in one of the big fluffy robes that we brought home from the farmers market a few weeks back.

My heart falls to the floor when I find Nikki already mostly dressed, rushing around the room to find where each article of clothing landed in our haste to tear them off each other.

"What are you doing?" I ask.

"I need to take a walk. I need to clear my head. I'm . . . you should go home too."

"You're acting frantic. You're worrying me—"

She scoffs at me, finally finding her missing shirt and tugging it over her head, hiding her final expanse of skin from me. "I have to go, Andy," she says, sounding like she's on the verge of tears, and no. No. That's not how this is supposed to go.

"Nikki—"

"Don't 'Nikki' me," she says, pulling on her socks and hopping on one foot as she does. "I'm not going to stand here and get dumped in my birthday suit."

"Dumped?" I say, the word shattering like glass in my mouth. Because being dumped implies a relationship and a relationship implies commitment and—

"Wow," she says, the same realization seeming to hit her. "Now who's pretending not to notice. You can tell yourself whatever you want, Andy: that we were friends with benefits, that the chemistry was good, that we're just screwing each other out of our systems—"

"That's not fair!" I yelp.

"You keep telling yourself whatever you need to sleep at night, whether it's the truth or not." Nikki drags her fingers through her hair. "Maybe I deserve this, maybe I do for what I did to you in the past, but I don't have to stand here and listen to it. I don't have to be an active participant."

I reach out for her, but she pulls away. "No, you know I don't . . . it was more than that for me too," I plead. "If it wasn't, I wouldn't be so freaked out right now about falling into old habits. I want us to be something more, but I don't know if we *should*. I can't afford to get lost in you again," I say. "I can't be the person chasing you *anymore*. I can't go back to who I was!"

"Be honest, Andy, for once in your life!" Nikki shouts. "It's not *you* doing the chasing! It hasn't been since the day you ran out on me! You've flipped the script entirely," she says, tears welling in her eyes. "I got it, though, at first. I did. I was happy to chase you, I was happy to wait, but I can't keep . . . If you want to run—run. But just do it already. This back-and-forth is killing me! It was easier when you hated me. At least I knew where I stood!"

"You're writing a book!" I yell back. "How am I supposed to trust anything you're doing when I know you're writing a book! For all I know, this, us, now, is just more content."

"Fuck the book!" she says. "Fuck you too, if you really believe that. I don't know how to prove myself to you any more than I already have! If you had told me to get lost forever after we finally talked for real, I would have respected it. But you didn't. You let me keep crawling on broken glass with my stupid little cups of coffee to try to prove my love for you, and you know what? I didn't even mind. I would have done it forever. Because you are the good thing that got away for me. You *are*." Her shoulders slump, her breath coming in ragged pants as she struggles to hold herself together. "I've had to do a lot of work to become someone who I was proud of. I've had to put a lot of effort into changing for the better. You don't owe me another chance, you don't, but don't sit there and act like I haven't done the work.

"Tonight wasn't falling back into an old pattern. Not for me anyway. It was a gentle way to reconnect after a difficult conversation and a week away. I've been daydreaming about you since

I left. I wasn't trying to distract you from anything! Anything! I missed you and I missed being in bed with you." She squeezes her hands together and sighs. "You know, I was actually happy that our conversation didn't ruin our night. I thought it showed *growth* that we could set things aside for more appropriate times—because god knows that's not at ten p.m. after a seven-hour flight on three hours of sleep. I had no ulterior motive for going to bed with you. None. It hurts me that you think I did and it devastates me that you—"

"It wasn't intentional. I just think we fell back into it when things got hard tonight," I say. "Growth would be resolving the issue and finishing the talk. We—"

"There's always going to be more to talk about! We're going to be healing forever. *I'm* going to be healing forever. There are things you don't know and I'm positive there are things I don't know—but tonight, I just wanted to hold you after being gone. I wanted to kiss you and be in *this* moment, now, instead of the past. Of course we were always going to talk about things more! It was never meant to be a one-time conversation! I get that you're scared but—"

"How do I know that? How do I trust that?" I cry, wiping at my eyes. "You don't get it. I *missed* you. I missed you so much it scared me! And I don't just mean this week, I mean the first time you left after coming back here and the second and . . . and . . . I can't let myself get so wrapped up in you that I forget who I am again! I can't! I can't go through that."

"I would never, ever want that. Is that how you feel? Now?" she asks, looking stricken. "If I've done anything to make you feel like that, Anderson, I don't—"

And then it hits me . . . *She hasn't. She really hasn't.*

"What if it's me?" I ask, our eyes locking. "What if I don't know how to love you any other way but full throttle? What if I keep forgetting where you end and I begin? Do you know what it feels like to love someone that much? Do you?!"

"Yes, I do," she breathes, looking at me with such pain in her eyes that I nearly fall to my knees.

"It's not how it's supposed to be."

"Why not?"

"I don't know, it's just not. Other people don't feel like that. Other people just . . ."

Nikki hangs her head, taking a heaving breath before asking, "Are you sure?"

"I'm not sure about anything! That's the problem!"

"You're not," she says—a statement, not a question. Nikki nods to herself, wiping at her eyes. "You should get dressed, Anderson. You should go home."

I cross the room, shakily pulling on my clothes while she stares down at the carpet. I drop the robe onto her bed beside her towel, pulling on my clothes with a growing panic in my belly.

"I don't want to leave," I say.

"But?" She looks up at me and I feel like I'm going to be sick. I want to hug her, hold her, take everything back, even though I know I shouldn't.

You can do this. You need to do this.

I take a deep breath. "But you're right. I should go home and you should go back to LA. We need to take a break. You need to finish the book on your own terms, without me telling you how to feel about it, and I have more orders than I can count, plus a wedding expo in a couple weeks I really should already be prepping for."

"That's it?" Nikki asks. "You're running again?"

"No, I'm not, but I can't keep hurting you like this. I can't keep jerking you around. I've been there, remember, I know how bad it feels," I say softly, sadly. "I don't want to keep blaming you and I don't want to keep worrying that every time you leave you're never coming back."

"But you do."

"I want to be with you so bad I can't stand it . . . But I don't know if I trust it and I don't know if I ever will. That's not fair to either one of us." I let out a shaky breath. "I don't know what to do here, Nikki. I'm terrified of how much I still love—"

"Please," she says, resigned. "Please don't say you love me while you're telling me all the reasons you wish you didn't."

I shut my eyes, letting the tears fall in earnest now. "Nikki—"

"I'm sure there's a flight back tomorrow. I'll be on it. I won't bother you anymore."

My stomach free-falls to the floor. I've lost her, again, and the fact that it was my choice, on my terms, doesn't make it any easier at all.

Chapter Twenty-One
Sad Songs on Repeat

I don't get out of bed for two days.

On the third day, Johnny shows up to drag me out of it and throw me into the shower, but it hurts, how every place has a memory of her, even there. How I wanted space but now that I have it, all I want is to give it back. There's a desperate, clawing sensation in my chest these days, like my heart is trying to extract itself all on its own, like it would have rather left with her than sit here with me for another second.

I can relate.

There's a place set at my table with a cup of tea and some food when I get out of the shower. I rubbed my skin raw with the hot water; the sensation is making me feel even more fragile and exposed. Johnny sits in the other chair, hands folded in front of him, concern pulling down his normally jovial cheeks. I slide into the empty seat across from him, pushing my food around instead of eating it.

"I can't believe she did this again," he says, and I look up, startled.

I haven't really explained what happened beyond texting Regan "she left, it's over," which resulted in Regan rushing right over. I told her she didn't have to—she's been on babysitting duty with me way too much—but she insisted. She said I've been covering so many of her shifts lately that it's the least she could do. Before I could even protest, she added, "Besides, friends don't keep score. They just show up," and I knew the argument was lost.

I was grateful for the company, like I'm grateful for Johnny's now, but I wasn't ready to talk about it. I'm still not, if I'm being honest. But while Johnny's anger is refreshing, or at least better than the pity or misery I've been draped in for the last couple of days, it feels disingenuous to let him keep blaming her. I broke my own heart—and maybe hers too. It's time to own up to it.

"She didn't," I croak out, my voice scratchy and tired from disuse. It's not just the talking; it's that I haven't done *anything* really, besides lie in bed and watch all the TikToks that I shouldn't, and stare at all her Insta posts that I shouldn't.

The morning that she left, she posted a single image—a picture of the ocean taken from her cabin door. The little rickety steps are in view, as are the tracks from my bike, my pathetic footsteps wedged into the sand beside it.

There was no caption.

Most of the comments were random fans commenting "pretty" or "where is this?" but there was one, from a woman named Julia, that simply said "come home."

Come home.

The jealousy roiled up inside of me at the sight of those words. Who was this woman? How did she know Nikki? The truth, I realized in that moment, is that her life is probably full of people I don't know—friends, (ex) lovers, her team—all of them strangers. She's probably not sitting around with our old friends and neighbors any more than I am here. No, she's living her whole new life at her whole other *home*, one I've never been a part of and now never will be.

I can't be jealous, and I certainly can't be mad. She offered me her hand and I bit it.

This is on me.

"You don't have to defend her," Johnny sighs, leaning back in his chair. "I was never her biggest fan."

Right. Time to fess up.

"She really didn't, though," I say, taking a sip of the tea and then clearing my throat. "This one is all on me."

"None of this is your fault," Johnny says, reaching forward to cover my hand, looking more sympathetic and gentler than I have any right for him to. "I don't care what she said or how she tried to convince you otherwise. Nikki waltzed in here, got what she wanted from you for her book, and then took off to leave you with the consequences. It's okay, though, Annie. You've done this before; you can do it again. You're way stronger now than you were last time."

And it's weird, isn't it, how Annie—the name I've embraced so fully these last few years—suddenly sounds so wrong. *Call me Andy*, I said, the first day I met Nikki all the way back on that casting call looking for "teen girls between the ages of fifteen and nineteen with a wholesome look."

Now here I am, with neither name fitting.

"I sent her away," I finally force out. "Nikki didn't want to go."

"Of course you—wait, what?"

I push the eggs around on my plate some more, wishing I could bring myself to eat so I'd have an excuse not to answer him. I take a deep breath instead. "I made her leave. I told her we were falling into old patterns and that I didn't trust her. I'm a coward, though. I don't even think it was about that. I was just scared of what would happen if we took the leap and it didn't work out again. I couldn't stop worrying about it. I pulled the rug out from under us just to be first."

He looks at me, confused, so I tell him the whole sordid story start to finish. I tell him how, even though I put her through the wringer, she kept showing up for me day after day—how it was beautiful, it was brilliant, it was *terrifying*.

He listens intently, only getting up once to grab a Diet Coke and then resting his elbows on the table, and when I finally finish, when I tell him how I slept with her to escape my feelings and then accused her of being the one doing it, he sucks a breath through his teeth so hard I hang my head in shame.

We're quiet for a bit after that as he twirls his soda in slow circles on the table. I can't help but wonder if he's thinking about me right now, or about him and Regan.

"You're sure Nikki hasn't tried to contact you or guilt-trip you, or manipulate you in any way, since you asked her to leave for good?" he finally asks.

"Nope," I answer, my lip starting to tremble. "I haven't heard a peep."

"Annie," he says. "Did you do this to yourself this time?"

"Yep," I say, my breath hitching as the tears come again.

Johnny's around the table in seconds, wrapping me in a hug

that's strong and warm and loving . . . but it's all wrong. It's too big, it's too firm. His hands too rough and large. I cry harder as I pull away, too lost in my own grief to even allow the comfort.

"I don't blame you for any of this," he says, finally giving up the pretense that I'm going to eat and dragging us both over to the couch instead. "You shouldn't blame yourself either."

"How can I not?" I ask.

"Because she hurt you, very badly, and there's no timeline for healing from that. You don't have to forgive her, ever. Even if you love her still, or again, or whatever the hell this is between you. If you don't ever want to see her again, you'll get through this just like you got through it last time. You don't have to do it alone. You're my best friend, and my other best friend's best friend." He smiles. "I've got you, whatever you want to do."

"That's the problem. I don't know what I want."

He sighs, squeezing my shoulder. "You don't have to know. No one has to! That's the beauty of life, right? We're all just swirling around the sun on this rock, completely winging it."

"What if I made a mistake?"

"Then congrats, you're human. You can try to fix it or not. It's up to you."

"What if I take too long trying to figure out what I want, and she gets sick of waiting?"

He shrugs with a laugh. "Some people are worth waiting for. Trust me, I know. If she's not around by the time you figure your head out, then that's an answer in itself."

I look up at his sad smile, thinking about how long he's been waiting on Regan. As long as I've known him. Probably much longer than that. She had sworn off dating altogether by the time I met her, thanks to a string of bad relationships, but Johnny has been there, patiently proving to her that there are good men left in the world, loving her, never pushing—living his life and letting her set the pace as they take slow but steady steps toward each other.

A part of me still can't help but wonder, though, if he was the one who hurt Regan in the first place, if the damage he was undoing was inflicted by his hand, like it is with me and Nikki, would it still work between them? Would it ever be enough?

I've made a lot of mistakes with this reunion; I know I have. But I also know that I can't give in to my desperation for her to come back, at least not yet. I need to figure out what *I* want—for my future and all the people I want in it—now that she's made her case abundantly clear. I need to sort my head out first, or it isn't fair to either one of us. Nikki hurt us first, yes, but I'm hurting us now—that has to stop, either way. I have the space I wanted again, but this time, I need to *use* it. I need to heal, really heal.

"I don't know where to start with figuring this out," I say, hugging a pillow to my chest.

Johnny gives me another sad smile. "It's okay to decide to stand still for a minute, if you need to, as long as it's not forever. You've built a great life here. You don't need her to be a part of it unless *you decide* there's a place for her here and *you* want her to fill it. Look, I respect her for backing off and realizing you needed time—that says a lot for her character. But she still kind of sucks for what she did before, and for the record, I'm still happy to slap her if that helps at all."

I laugh despite everything, hugging the pillow a little tighter. "I might be the one who deserves to be slapped."

"Nope, that's where you're wrong," he says, popping his "p" for emphasis, before looking down at his watch. "Shit, I lost track of time and there's a carburetor calling my name down at the shop. Want me to toss those eggs in the microwave for a second before I go?"

"God no, gross, microwaved eggs?" I shudder.

"I could whip up some more?"

"No," I giggle. He would honestly remake my whole breakfast if I let him. Regan and I are lucky to have him. "I'll make some for myself, though, don't worry."

"Promise?"

"I promise," I say. "Now go, before your carburetor takes off without you."

"That's not how that works," he says with a laugh, giving me another hug before heading out the door. "Make. Your. Eggs."

I nod and then wave him off, making a show of going into the fridge and grabbing eggs to demonstrate how serious I am.

I've got this. I know I do, especially with Regan and Johnny here with me.

Even if I don't quite know what *this* is yet.

Chapter Twenty-Two

Say It with Flowers

I have been standing still for over a month.

Not literally, of course. If we're talking literally, then I have pretty much run myself ragged. I have survived the bridal expo—in which I had an arrangement of mine take first place in a floral contest. Then my favorite client and her farrier wife announced they were hosting a last-minute wedding and a horse show on back-to-back weekends out of state—very nearly ordering me out of the whole store.

Plus, I've even had a bunch of virtual sessions with Janet, my old therapist from back in LA. She was shockingly happy to put me back on her regular schedule, even from across the continent. We have a lot to work through, but I'm starting to figure it out, or at least finding better ways to cope.

And that's all on top of the myriad of online orders we've been getting—most of which are still from people in LA who must have gotten word from all of the people Nikki sent flowers to that I do good work.

I can hear the ticket printer spitting more out even now.

I can't help but wonder what Nikki's doing out in L.A. Is she back with whoever she sent the first batch of flowers to? Is that the woman who commented "come home" on the Insta Nikki has never updated since?

That thought slingshots around in my stomach, turning it sour and making me push my iced coffee farther away. Even drinking coffee makes me miss her. *Everything makes me miss her, if I'm being honest.*

Regan has been supportive but not prying over the last few weeks, and Johnny left things how he left things. He's not one to be sappy on the regular, so it's mostly been business as usual. Janet has been helping me untangle my feelings without judgment—helping me make sure I'm not clinging to the idea of Nikki because of old wounds, revenge, or even nostalgia. She's been annoyingly neutral when I ask her point-blank if she thinks Nikki and I should be together, instead redirecting me to a discussion of what healthy romantic boundaries might look like in that scenario.

Overall, it's been . . . not bad, actually.

You know, except for the gaping hole in my chest where my heart used to be.

It's taken me a long time—and some extra therapy sessions—to work up the courage to text Nikki, but last night I finally did.

> I wish I really knew you.

It wasn't *exactly* the conversation starter Janet and I discussed—that was more along the lines of something like,

"I've been doing a lot of work on myself lately and I would love to have a conversation with you if you're open to it." But . . . "I wish I really knew you" was what came out when I tried.

Nikki didn't reply, which is one of the outcomes I was prepared for. She doesn't owe me a response, just like I don't owe her a second chance. No one is in the other's debt, no one should be keeping score.

It's all very healthy in theory.

With the benefit of time away, a clear head, and an expensive therapist, I've realized that I don't know the new Nikki, not really. Looking back at our time together here, I can't help but feel like she was so wrapped up in things about me and making *me* comfortable that I never learned enough about her, or at least about the things she went through and how she spent the years we were apart. If we're really going to do this right, we need to be there for each other. Equally.

Of course, none of that matters if she doesn't reply.

"Annie," Regan says, walking toward me with another order slip in her hand. "How many arrangements do you have left to do today?"

"Please, no more new orders," I say, dramatically throwing my hand over my forehead until Regan laughs. "I'm wrapping up my last one and then I need to be done for the day. My hands are killing me, and I still have ten more to do in the morning. We might need to shut it down if they keep coming. I'm happy to call people and explain that new orders can't go out until I finish this wedding order."

"It's not for you to make, it's . . . well . . . it's *for* you. I just didn't want to show you if you still need to focus."

"What do you mean *for me*? You can't just say that and not show me."

"No, finish up. It can wait."

"It absolutely can't. You can't tease me like that," I say, making grabby fingers. "Hand it over."

She grimaces and sets the slip down beside me on the counter. "I wasn't sure if I should just toss it in the trash or what, but that's not my call. I would want to see it if I were you, even just to throw it out yourself."

I stop fussing with the arrangement long enough to stare down at the paper. My forehead crinkles. It's an odd mix of flowers, not really cohesive at all in appearance ... but in meaning? There are purple hyacinths for regret and sincerity, white tulips for forgiveness and respect, pink camellias to symbolize longing ... but then, confusingly, there's morning glory, which signifies unrequited love, and . . . zinnias? For friendship, I think? I'm scrambling in my head to remember all of them. Finally, at the bottom of the list, they request a lone black rose—that's a rough one. It can mean death or goodbye.

Goodbye. My heart stutters in my chest. *I know who this is from.*

Nikki's name is emblazoned across the top of the order slip, because of course it is, my name just below it in the "ship to" section: Anne Lacy. Not Andy. Not even Ducharme. It feels like a punch to the gut, an unexpected finality, and I take a few steps back, sitting down on the little wooden stool beside me.

Goodbye? I guess I got a response to my text after all.

I almost crumple it, completely ready to stagger upstairs and let myself have a good cry instead of finishing this final arrangement. Regan was right; I should have waited. Or I should have let her throw it away. Nikki is moving on, and she's using this bouquet to tell me.

It feels cruel, even though I know that probably isn't her intent. But then my eyes drift lower, to the message she wanted to have printed on the card.

"Check your email one last time, if you really wish you knew me."

"I . . ." I trail off, staring down at the sheet.

"Yeah," Regan says, biting her lip. "I can finish this up if you want to . . ."

"Yes, yeah, sure," I answer, stumbling off my seat and heading up the stairs to my apartment. I feel out of it, like I'm wrapped in gauze, everything suddenly feeling a little fuzzy and constricting.

Goodbye, the flowers said. *One last time*, the note said.

I feel sweaty sick and hot all over because no, no, this isn't what I wanted at all and every step up the stairs makes me feel even surer of that. I've been punishing her for what another her in another life did to a version of me that doesn't exist anymore. If we have any prayer of rekindling any sort of relationship—romantic or platonic—I need to make peace with that.

Young Nikki was nothing like the one who's been here, and neither am I.

Driving her away before I realized that was a mistake.

A stupid mistake that I'm going to regret probably for the rest of my life now that she's sent me the closure I don't want via the petals of a very black rose. I should call her. No. I should read the email. Or wait, should I call her *as* I read the email? No, probably not.

I take a deep breath, mentally buckling up as I walk over to where my old MacBook is collecting dust in the corner of the room. Regan borrows it sometimes when she's doing accounting stuff, but otherwise it's just a glorified paperweight. I don't have many emails to check anymore, outside of the store account. I've barely checked my own account since I came here.

Actually . . . *have* I checked since I came here? Maybe? Probably not, though. I have little use for email in my new life, now that I'm not anxiously awaiting to hear back about contracts and callbacks and emails from my agent at all hours of the night.

I fire it up and wait patiently for it to load, stumbling twice over my Wi-Fi password when it doesn't automatically connect. I pull up my email, holding my breath as the screen pops up, and then . . .

Nothing.

There's nothing.

Just random spam and newsletters I should have unsubscribed from years ago. My heart free-falls to the floor as I look back at the wrinkled note in my hand.

Check your email one last time.

And then I remember the old one.

The one I had when I was a teen, back when Nikki and I first met. An amalgamation of my interests when I created it at the tender age of seven: PrincessKitty and my birthday on a Yahoo account.

Nikki had even brought it up once when we were lying in bed

a few weeks ago. She was teasing me for my old username and asked if I ever checked it anymore . . . but of course I didn't. It was a hundred years old. I had migrated to Gmail long before I even left LA. Why would I check that one? Unless . . .

I swallow hard and click over to log in to the old account, my fingers stuttering over the old password: the name of my childhood fish and the number I had in the tank that day (BertandBeth2, naturally). The log-in page circles for a minute and then loads.

There's a mess of unread messages, some spam, some not, but on the very top is Nikki's email, dated from this afternoon and labeled "one last time."

Except . . . that's not the only email from her.

I scan down, startled to realize that she's been emailing me this whole time. I click over to the search bar and type in her name, my eyebrows shooting to the ceiling as I realize there are pages and pages of results. I click to the last page, my eyes welling up with the desperation in the subject headings, beginning the day after I first left her.

> **Subject**: where are you
> **Subject**: please andy i cant do this without you
> **Subject**: do you even check this

The hurt, then the anger, then the sadness. The resignation as the weeks ticked by. I'm confused at first—*why here, why this*—and then I realize the answer: I had blocked her on everything else. This was the only thing I didn't think to block her on, because I barely even remembered it existed.

I click forward again and again, my eyes scanning the screen. She wrote daily at first, and then weekly, and then monthly and then less often. Short, quick updates on her life; long, rambling missives. The first night she ever slept alone in our house. The day she was getting ready for the Oscars. The morning after the car crash. A catalog of her life without me.

> "Went on a date tonight, wish it was you. Fucking sucked."
>
> "What's that peanut butter you used to love? I can't remember and it's gutting me."
>
> "Will we ever talk again?"
>
> "I saw the grocery store picture. you were adorable. Since when do you eat brussels sprouts?"
>
> "Is there a word for the emptiness you feel when you know you're dead to someone but they aren't dead to you? If not there should be."
>
> "not gonna have access to email for a while, but it's okay. It's good."
>
> "I should stop sending these but I can't"
>
> "If we ever meet again, ill do it right."

I wipe my eyes. I could torture myself all night reading these—this diary of hers that she has splayed open for me. Proof of her dedication. Proof of her trying to move on.

I click back to the newest page of results, letting my mouse hover over the one labeled "one last time."

The message is short and to the point.

> Attached is the complete latest draft. I hope you will take a look. I wish you knew me too. I wish we had a different ending.
>
> Love always,
> Nikki

I open the manuscript, and I begin to read.

Chapter Twenty-Three
It Was the Best of Times, It Was the Worst of Times . . .

I have long considered my life as belonging to two separate people. But that was easy—that was letting myself off the hook. It was only when I began to reconnect with my past that I realized if I truly want to be whole, if I truly want to make amends for the fuckery of that past, I have to honor the disaster that I was, and own up to all of my mistakes. Rehab and years of therapy and recovery programs helped me to see that, but a clandestine trip to the beach in the middle of nowhere solidified it.

 It was there, watching the same piercing blue waves that I stared at a lifetime ago, that I finally understood what I was meant to do. That this was the answer to why I was still on earth, a question I asked myself a hundred times when I was younger, messier, and deeply in pain . . .

Nikki is honest in these early chapters, brutally honest. Here, finally, are all of her secrets spilling out across the page the way they've spilled out across our lives—the truth about things we never said, things we tried like hell to ignore. Some of it is horrifying: the drugs she was fed, the things that were done to her, the way Hollywood sank its hooks into her skin and hung her from the rafters to bleed—which she handled with such good humor that to the rest of us she simply looked like she was floating.

It breaks my heart in new and fresh ways, leaves me aching for a time machine, a way to crawl back to way back when, to a time when I was blinded by bitterness—content to be angry at her, to blame her, instead of acknowledging that *she* was a victim too, just in a very different way. Nikki was drowning. She was drowning and I was jealous.

No. That's a lie. An excuse. And I'm done hiding behind them.

The truth that I've come to know is that it was never about parties and stolen roles or asshole agents or the Oscar she won or any of the other ten million things I've told myself and others were the reasons I left. The truth was: we were young and dumb, with too much money and not enough common sense. Our relationship was beautiful, deep, but rotten to the core. Our love became just another drug, and the codependency would have eventually killed us both. I think I knew on some level that I had to find a reason to hate her in order to leave, and I had to leave in order to save myself.

My eyes blur with tears and I paw them away, adjusting the screen of my laptop so I can keep reading. Nikki doesn't pull punches in the memoir. Not one . . . except when it comes to me.

She dances around the topic of us, a mighty feat considering how much of her story is *our story*.

She even cheekily writes directly to readers at one point.

```
I know what some of you are here for, most of you
even, and I'm sorry to disappoint. My relationship
with Anderson was made public far too young and
far too early, while we were both grappling not
just with typical adolescent questions of sexuality
but also with what it means to be a queer kid in
Hollywood, where every move you make good or bad
is going to be splashed across TMZ. Her story is
her story, and perhaps someday she will bless us
all with sharing it, but I've screwed up more than
enough in my life to fill this book. It's time to
let that particular sleeping dog lie.

    Besides, in the great words of Russell Crowe in
Gladiator (2000), "Are you not entertained?" Surely
you're at least a little interested in my story too,
since you've paid $35 for a hardcover. (Or are you
reading on an e-reader so no one knows?)

    (Am I a secret just for you?)

    (You get it, then, why I won't talk about her.)
```

I wonder what her fans and readers will think when they read this. When they see, read, hear her protecting me—offering herself up to be picked apart while shielding me from the masses. It's the exact opposite of what she did when we were younger, and the exact opposite of what I thought she was doing with this book—what she said it would be when we first started talking again.

Nikki met me—the new me—and she listened, and she changed it. I scroll ahead, shocked to realize that she cut out even the anecdotes I approved—the ones we worked on together. This isn't what I expected at all. This is a memory book turned confessional—an apology and an explanation all at once.

I should have trusted her.

I brace myself and scroll to the next chapter. It starts with a shockingly detailed description of her cocaine addiction, and I stop. A new realization washes over me. I don't want to hear about this in a book. I want to hear it from Nikki, with her face in front of mine, preferably while holding her hand. I want to trace comforting words on her skin while she tells me all the things I ever wanted to know, and then return the favor.

I want her here with me.

I want her.

Not in the twisted, needy, codependent way of our youth, but in the gentle, quiet-cups-of-coffee way. The laughing-at-the-farmers-market way. The we've-seen-enough-war-to-make-our-own-peace way.

A knock on my apartment door has me up and rushing to open it, hoping against hope that somehow Nikki instinctively understood this and came back. That she said "forget one last chance, have another," even though I told her I needed space. Even though I told her I was confused.

I fling it open, my hopeful expression giving way to disappointment when I see Regan on the other side.

"Hello to you too," she teases. "Don't look so glad to see me."

"Sorry," I say, holding the door open and ushering her inside. "I am. I just—"

"Hoped I was someone slightly more famous?"

"Slightly?" I smile.

"Well, my flower shop is getting lots of traction with the LA crowd," she says, fanning herself. "At the very least, I'm fame-adjacent because of you."

"Because of Nikki," I correct, and she gives me a look. "Okay, fine, because of me *and* Nikki," I amend.

"Much better." She smiles. "Remember, it wouldn't matter how much Nikki hyped you up if your arrangements were garbage."

"I know, I know, I'm just . . . going through it right now."

"I figured. I closed up for the night and wanted to check in before I left. That flower order was kind of heavy. A black rose? Ouch."

"It's the book."

"Hmm?" she asks, grabbing us each a Diet Coke from the fridge and following me out to the living room.

"The email she wanted me to check. She sent me the whole manuscript."

"Oh my god," Regan says, cracking open her can.

I follow her lead, letting the crispy fizz of the bubbles rattle around my skull, grateful to feel something else, if only for a second.

"Are you going to read it?" she asks, when the silence stretches on uncomfortably long.

I blink myself out of my head and shrug. "I read some of it already—the first few chapters or so. She really did keep me out of it and she owned up to everything that was going on back then—the drugs, how she never showed up to set . . . all of it."

"Wow," Regan says quietly. I'm sure she's thinking the same thing as me—Nikki really *is* one of the good ones.

"I don't want to read any more."

"You don't have to," Regan says. "It's okay to be done, Annie. It is. Even with all of this."

"Wait, I thought you liked her?"

"I do. The woman who I met isn't like the girl you described all these years. That doesn't mean anything, though! It doesn't mean you *need* her or *owe* her. That's all I'm saying. There's a reason second-chance romances are usually best kept for books. It's hard in real life. It's complicated and painful. If you don't want to read her story, then just stop. Let her go for good."

"No, but that's not why. I want to know everything, I do, but I want to hear it *from her*. I don't want to read it in a book meant for a million other people and I don't want it written out in small, digestible chapters that have probably passed through a dozen other people's hands. I want her to tell me herself. I want to—"

"Then call her!" Regan laughs, like it's just that easy. "I said you didn't *need* her, not that you can't try to make it work if you *want* her. The ball is in your court. It's been there."

"I don't know," I say, looking away. "I lost so much of myself on our first go-round. I have hardly anything left to spare. If we didn't work out now, when we're both finally in a place to make a real attempt . . . I don't—"

"What if you get it back?"

I scrunch up my face. "What do you mean?"

"What if you never lose more? What if you get back what you lost instead?"

"What if I don't, though?" I ask. "That's the problem."

"You're right, what if you don't?" she says nonchalantly, studying her nails. "Better to just sit here and watch her Tik-Toks over and over and pine for the rest of your life. Solid plan. Sounds much better than taking a chance on the person you love."

"You're one to talk!" I snort. "You've been pining for Johnny for years and you're not willing to take a risk because of one bad relation—"

"We're together."

"What?"

"Come on, Annie. You can't pretend you haven't seen us sneak off to the back room. Plus, when's the last time you came over and he wasn't there? We practically live together at this point. I'm sure you've noticed."

"I mean, I did, but I just thought it was more of your, you know, weird dynamic. Why didn't you say anything? I'm so happy for you two! It's been a long time coming. I can't believe you didn't tell me," I say, smacking her arm.

"Telling our other best friend that we finally got it together right when she's falling apart over a relationship felt obnoxious. We've already been waiting so long for each other—a little longer to go public wouldn't kill us."

"I would have been happy for you," I say. "I am happy for you!"

"All right, then we should have told you. I'm sorry. We just didn't want you to make you feel worse than you already did."

"No," I say, jumping up to give her a hug. "I would never! I'm so happy for you, honestly! But what changed? What happened? You've been dancing around each other for years!"

"You and Nikki happened," she says softly, studying my face like she's waiting for a reaction.

"Uh, what?" I ask, dropping back to the couch.

"You inspired us."

"You were inspired to finally date the man who's obviously your soulmate by watching me and Nikki fall apart?"

"No, I was inspired to make the move because I saw how much hurt was caused when neither of you did. I realized that I was letting my past hold me back from something good, and from where I'm sitting, it looked like you two were doing the same." Regan holds up her hand before I can reply. "You have your reasons, and they are incredibly valid. I'm not going to pretend that it's not different—the person who screwed me up wasn't Johnny. That makes it a hundred times easier, because I just had to let go of my own past, not *ours*. I did hurt him, though, with my indecision, and we've had a lot of talks about that. Still, I'm not gonna pretend to know what it's like for you and her. But I do know that when you ripped open your door a little while ago, it wasn't me you wanted on the other side of it."

"Fair enough," I say, running my hands down my face.

At least one good thing has come out of this train wreck.

"Annie, if you're going to move through the world happy and fulfilled without her, I am all for it. I don't care how many perfect coffees she brought me," Regan says, laughing. "All I know is that, either way, just like me and Johnny, you need to put the past behind you—whether that's with *or* without her. You can't just stagnate. It's holding you back from your future, which, judging by the amount of orders we get now, is gonna be really friggin' great. You've built something incredible and I feel lucky to be a part of it. You are so far from the woman you were when you first got here—I hope you realize that."

"I was trying not to cry tonight," I say, tearing up as she gets up to hug me.

"I'm so proud of you, Annie, not just for everything you've accomplished at the flower shop, but for leaving LA in the first place and for these boundaries you're trying to set. But are you *happy*? Are you whole? That's what matters now. Not what happened before. I love Annie Lacy, but I wouldn't mind getting to know Andy Ducharme better too. If you'd want that."

I wipe at my eyes, nodding. "I know," I say. "No, I know." I rub my eyes with my palm again, wiping up the tears that just won't stop coming. "I'm done running, Regan. From her and from myself. It doesn't work! It's ridiculous!"

"It is." She smiles. "I know because I did it too and it was such a stupendous waste of time."

"Yeah," I say, taking a deep breath as I look down at my phone. "I'm going to make some changes around here, and I'm going to start with a phone call."

"Good, but Andy?" she says, and my head snaps up. It's the first time she's ever called me that. I expect it to feel strange, but it doesn't. It feels *right*.

I smile at her. "Yeah?" I ask, and she grins back, clearly happy with how using that name landed.

"Just know that no matter what happens next—no matter what—Johnny and I will always be there for you, for better or for worse. You're stuck with us."

I groan, pretending to be put out, even though I wouldn't have it any other way. "Forever? Maybe I should have thought this through."

Regan laughs, tossing a pillow at me before she heads to the door. "Guess next time you'll scope out the riffraff before committing to a new town."

"Hopefully there won't be a next time," I sigh, glancing down at my phone.

"Something tells me you'll be just fine."

Chapter Twenty-Four
Love and Hand Dryers

I wait for Regan to leave before I make the call.

Well, that plus about another hour spent wearing down the hardwood floors in my apartment, trying to decide what the perfect thing to say to Nikki would be. Which isn't to suggest that I figured it out—it's more like that was how long it took me to realize there really *wasn't* going to be a perfect thing to say.

There is no magic word to undo the hurt we've put on each other, and sweeping things under the rug won't help either. We need to have an honest talk about what we both want and what we both need—and if that includes each other, which, god, I hope it does, then about how we would make that work too.

There's a chance I've blown it. There's a chance she has too. But we won't know until we try, until we sit down and finally have that brutally honest conversation I've been running from. No more spinning out inside my head, no more predicting the future or trying to guess if she's being sincere. It's time to woman up and be real with each other, as terrifying as that sounds.

I punch in her number and hold the phone to my ear with shaking hands, each ring making my heart beat faster and faster, until I feel like I'm on the verge of a heart attack. I don't know what I'll do if she doesn't pick up.

"Andy?" she says.

Oh my god, she picked up.

"Nikki?" I say over the din in my ear. It's loud where she is. It's so loud. "Hi."

"Hi," she says. She sounds relieved to hear from me, and the voices behind her become more garbled, replaced by the sound of hand dryers and flushing toilets.

Did she duck into a bathroom?

"Where are you?" I ask, even though that's not the point. I'm scrambling for words, the relief of our connection, even across cell towers and countless miles, turning my thoughts into slick, slippery things that keep falling from my hands as I try to grab onto them.

"Sorry, what? You keep breaking up. I'm at the airport right now. I have to fly to Florida to shoot a commercial. Everybody and their mother is in the Centurion Club tonight for some reason. I can barely hear you. I'm so sorry. Is everything okay?"

"If you're busy, I can—"

"No!" she says quickly. "No! I'm not! I'm so glad you called. I take it you got my email?"

"Yeah, and not just the one, Nikki," I say, and the words sound a little watery, a little more on edge than I mean to sound.

Be cool. Be chill. You've got this.

"Did you read any of the book?" she presses, when I don't say anything else.

"A little," I say. "I really didn't want to keep going, if I'm being honest with you."

"Of course. Yeah, you don't have to," she rushes to say. "I just thought you might want to after I got your text. I'm sorry for bothering you." Nikki sounds disappointed, and my heart splinters.

I'm screwing this up already.

"No, it's not that. I want to know how it ends, I do . . . but I realized as I was reading it that I'd rather you tell me, when you feel ready. I don't want to read—" Another hand dryer clicks on, making it impossible to hear anything.

"Huh?" she says into the phone. "I'm sorry, I can't really hear you."

"I said I want to hear it from you!" I shout.

"Sorry, hang on," she says, and then her voice goes a little muffled, like she has her hand covering her cell. "Can you guys stop with the hand dryers for five seconds? Please! No. No! I'm not signing anything for you, you can see that I'm on the phone. I don't care if you post that I'm an asshole. *I think you're an asshole.* Great. Don't watch it, then. Plenty of other people will! Look, I'm trying to talk to my girlfriend here, can you just—"

The words "my girlfriend" punch the air right out of me.

Is that how she sees me. Now? Still? After all this time? After everything?

"Sorry," she says, the room going suspiciously quiet around her. "What were you saying?"

"Your girlfriend?" I stammer out.

"No, I didn't . . . I don't know why I said that. It slipped out. I don't think that's what we . . . you've been very clear with me."

"It's okay," I say softly, hoping that she can still hear me, but more than that, hoping she can *feel* me. "I don't mind."

"Oh," she says, seeming surprised. "You don't?"

"No," I say, backpedaling a little in case she still tries to take it back. "I mean, it slipped out, right? So . . ."

"Right, yeah," she says, that deflated tone seeping back into her voice, and this is stupid, this is so stupid.

I'm dancing around things again, losing my nerve, doing the exact opposite of what I said I would. Maybe *this* is the pattern I really need to break—not Nikki, but my inability to speak up. To say what *I* need to say, for myself.

"I miss you," I blurt out. "I don't want to learn about your life from a book, Nikki. I want to hear it from you first—straight from your lips. I want to know how it ends—"

The hand dryers start up again. "I swear to god," Nikki groans as they again drown out any hope of us talking. I would laugh if she didn't sound so upset. "This is what I get for flying commercial. Hold on a sec, let me see if there's one of those sleep pod rental places here. I think I saw one a few gates back. I'll have to fight through the crowds, but I'd rather not have this conversation in the bathroom. Can you just stay on the line?"

I smile, relieved that she's seemingly just as anxious to talk to me as I am to talk to her.

"No, I get it. Don't leave the club," I say, remembering what a pain that was even back when we were only marginally famous. I can't imagine the stir she would cause wandering around out there with the general public now.

As much as I hate delaying this for even a second, I know what we need to do. A conversation this important deserves both of our full attention . . . plus, I can still hear the person grumbling about how ungrateful Nikki is for not signing her autograph in the background.

"Why don't you just call me when you get to Florida? We'll talk then, when we won't be interrupted."

"I really would rather not wait," she says.

"I know, me neither, but it's okay. I'm not going anywhere," I say, and for the first time that really feels true. The urge to run has fully dissipated in the face of potentially losing her again, forever this time.

"But I . . ." She sighs at the sound of more toilets flushing and doors banging. "Okay, maybe you're right. Promise me you'll pick up, though. I don't know what I'll do if you don't."

"I promise. I'll pick up."

"Swear on Gouda," Nikki says, and I laugh.

"I swear on Gouda that I will pick up when you call."

"Okay, then I believe you," she says. "We start boarding soon and then the flight is, like, five hours or so? I don't suppose you want to text me what you have to say? If ever there was a case for using in-flight Wi-Fi, it would be this."

"No, it's a conversation we should have face-to-face—or, well, ear-to-ear, I guess."

"This is going to be the longest five hours of my life. You know that, right? I'll call you as soon as I can."

"I'll be waiting." I smile, hoping she can hear it in my voice.

"You better be," she says in a fake stern voice before we disconnect.

I stand there uselessly for a bit, feeling adrift in my emotions. I wish she didn't have to go . . . but if someone turned on that hand dryer one more time, I think we would both have lost our minds. It's better this way, I know that objectively. If we're doing this right, and god I hope we are this time, then we shouldn't have to rush. An hour, or five, shouldn't make or break anything if it's as real as it feels.

I sigh and get to work stress-cleaning my apartment. What else do you do when only three hundred minutes—plus boarding and unboarding time, and all that other stuff I'm trying not to think about—are all that separates you from telling the person you love that you want to give it another try? There's a soothing element to cleaning things up and setting them right.

Maybe it's a metaphor, or maybe it's just how nice it feels to have a clean apartment, but either way, it helps.

Five hours come and go, as I'm elbow deep in the tub with Scrubbing Bubbles or scraping schmutz off my cooktop with a razor. The sixth hits while I'm dusting every inch of the house. I even pull out the step stool to get the blades of the ceiling fan. The seventh hour has me utterly exhausted, struggling to stay awake while I vacuum my one small area rug over and over—running out of both chores and excuses. It's after midnight and she still hasn't called.

Her plane was delayed. She's stuck on the tarmac. There's an odd amount of traffic in Florida on a Tuesday night and she doesn't want to call me when the driver is around. Her hotel room was double-booked and she's frantically talking to the manager.

Every nightmare travel scenario becomes less and less plausible the longer she goes without so much as a text. My heart sinks as I watch the numbers on the clock slide over to twelve thirty, then twelve forty-five. Maybe she's not calling this time.

Maybe this is what I get for ghosting her once and chasing her out the second time. It doesn't seem right, but what else could it be?

Finally resigned to the fact that she's not calling, I fall into bed, burrowing into the blankets, and slowly, sadly, drift off to sleep.

MY ALARM IS going off.

That's the first thought in my skull as I jolt awake. The second is that I definitely did not set an alarm. The third is *What the hell? Why is it still dark out?*

The grating sound begins again, urgent and shrill, and this time, I'm awake enough to realize that it's the doorbell downstairs. We had it installed to ring in my apartment in case any deliveries came at off hours. We missed a UPS delivery once, and by the time the driver had come back the next day, the flowers were wilted from spending extra time in a too-hot truck in the summer heat. It set us back *months* in our budget. Thus the doorbell, more like a firehouse bell, currently going off in my living room.

It's probably those kids who hang out around the gas station down the block all night. They've done it before. I glance at my phone to see it's nearly two a.m., prime time for ding-dong-ditch. I wait to see if they stop, but instead it rings again in quick succession.

I grab the baseball bat I keep next to my bed, along with my phone, which I pre-dial to 911, and head downstairs. I don't want them to get annoyed that I'm not playing along with their little scheme and break a window or something instead. We're just finally firmly in the black now; we don't need any unexpected surprises like that.

I tiptoe down the steps and unlock the door at the bottom, sliding through the floral racks, which seem spookier under the moonlight. I contemplate turning on the heavy fluorescent lights, but the idea of me being lit up in the floral equivalent of a glass fishbowl while whoever is outside gets to stay in the cover of darkness manages to creep me out even more.

I stick to the shadows instead, as whoever is ringing the doorbell continues their urgent pressing of the button outside. I can kind of see someone moving out there. It looks like it's just one person, not that it doesn't mean the other kids aren't hanging out of sight, ready to, I don't know, laugh at me? Rob me? Anything feels possible at this time of night.

My grip tightens on my baseball bat as I jump out in front of the still-locked glass front door, hoping the sight of a disheveled woman wielding a bat is enough to scare away whoever's at the door so I can finally get some rest. God knows I could never actually hit anybody with this.

"Get the hell out of here or I'll call 911," I yell at the person on the other side of the glass. I can barely make them out, thanks to the rain and darkness, but I can tell they're startled.

Good.

"Andy? It's me, Nikki," she shouts through the door. She moves closer to the glass, and oh my god.

Oh my god.

I have never run to unlock a door so fast in my entire life. My fingers fumble with the latch and I only half undo it, tugging the door prematurely. The half-open bolt catches and slams it back shut. I flick the light on before quickly flipping the lock the rest of the way, anxious to see her face. I'm happy, so happy, to see her, but now that there's light falling on us both, I can tell Nikki looks serious on the other side.

I pull the door open and step back, gesturing for her to come in out of the rain. She's dripping across the floor, but I don't even care. *Damn, I want to kiss her right now, but I don't know if she wants it.* It's entirely possible that my decision is far too little, far too late—but Nikki came here. She flew here instead of to her commercial. That has to mean something.

I swallow hard, wishing I had just the right words to make everything better. "Nikki, I—"

"It's up to you," she says, cutting me off before I've barely gotten a word in. "It's *always* been up to you, Andy."

"I don't . . . what is?" I ask, because it feels very much like at this moment, things are up to *her*.

"You said you wanted to know how the story ends. It's . . . that's for you to decide, Andy. You know how I feel about you. How I've felt forever, really," Nikki says. "I wanted you when we were teens, and I wanted you when I was twenty, and I want you still. I can't imagine a world in which I *don't* want you. I know I ruined things the first time, and whether we want to say 'we met too young' or blame it on Hollywood, where most relationships are doomed from the start, or the drugs, or the fact that your cat hates me"—she pauses, watching Gouda wind between my legs, her sleepy eyes growing sharper as she notices Nikki is the cause of the commotion—"the truth is, I've made a hundred bad decisions, I've made a hundred mistakes, but loving you was never one of them."

"Holy shit," I breathe, because whatever speech I thought I had in my head won't come close to topping hers.

She smiles, stepping even closer. "Is that a good holy shit, or . . . ?"

"How did you even get here? I thought you had a shoot tomorrow," I say, my brain struggling to catch up to the fact that this is really happening.

"I'll always come running when you call."

"Nikki, that's . . ."

"Too far?" She winces. "I just—"

My lips are on hers in an instant, my fingers tangling in her wet hair as I pull her even closer. I cover her in frantic, loving kisses, desperate to show her everything that I was too afraid to tell her before.

And Nikki's there, all parted lips and matching energy, as she brings one of her hands up to hold my face. Her warm tongue is a sharp, heady contrast to the coolness of her skin and lips—she's trembling or shivering, I can't tell, and it doesn't matter anyway, because our mouths are meeting like long-lost lovers and the thumb of her other hand is sliding over the bit of bare skin between my sleep shirt and sweats.

This moment . . . it's *everything*. It's the whole world, the universe, the big bang, and all I could ever want or need, right here in this shop, surrounded by flowers in bloom.

Nikki pulls back, still smiling, and then rests her forehead against mine. She presses our hands together as she squeezes her eyes shut and I follow suit, content to just be breathing in each other's air. And god, it would be so easy to fall into bed with her right now.

Do it right this time.

I sigh, scraping the last of my willpower from the depths of my soul and taking a step back, just a little, careful to never let her hand fall.

"I'm so glad you're here and there's nothing I'd rather do than keep kissing you forever," I say. Nikki breaks out into a grin that's so bright I have to look away or I'll lose my nerve to say the rest of it. "But we need to talk."

She nods, her tired eyes going serious and strained and damn if I don't just want to jump right back into kissing her, to chase that lightness and laughter right down the rabbit hole and see where we end up.

But if we're doing this, if we're *really* doing this, then we owe each other this conversation—cards on the table, truth out in the open—real, honest vulnerability on both our parts. It's the only way.

I know it's going to be just as hard for me as it is for her. I know that I'll hear things that I won't like, and she probably will too. I know it's going to be a lot, and nothing will be solved within minutes, but I believe we can build something from the scraps.

I squeeze her hand, giving her another soft smile. "You with me?" I ask as I lock the door and lead her up the stairs to my apartment.

"I'm with you," she says.

Chapter Twenty-Five
Lies Aren't Better After All

We're sitting on the couch with two mugs of steaming tea between us. Nikki changed into some borrowed clothes of mine while I put hers in my dryer. I'm trying not to get too distracted by the sight of her in my hoodie, but it's sending strange and delicious thoughts spiraling through my head. There's just something about her tucked up on my couch, in my tiny sleep shorts and oversized hoodie, that has my primal brain howling at the moon to make her officially mine.

I think we'll get there.

No, I know we will. She showed up for me, she keeps showing up for me, and if we're going to have a real chance, I need to not just trust that but also do the same for her. It's time we get our lives together, for real, as equals who love each other, instead of desperate apologists and angry has-beens.

Nikki stirs the sugar into her tea and takes a deep breath. "Is there anywhere in particular you want me to begin?"

I consider the options, latching on to the most glaring thing I saw before I closed the document. "Your book says you're sober."

"I am," she says seriously.

"You had a beer that time you came over here."

"No, I held a beer that was forced on me by your friend. I never took a sip."

"What about at the bar? The whiskey. You said—"

"Didn't drink that either," she says, looking me right in the eyes. I can tell she's taking this seriously. "You asked me how much I had to drink and I said, 'Not enough,' because that night, having none didn't feel like enough. I didn't give in, though. I never took a sip. I only ordered it to prove to myself that I could. I wanted to feel like I had a choice, since things with you felt very out of control that night."

"That seems very dangerous."

"It was, and very stupid. I called my sponsor the next morning to tell them what happened and went to an extra meeting that afternoon."

"Meetings? Are you in AA?"

"I don't think you're supposed to ask that," she says with a laugh. "The second 'A' does stand for 'anonymous,' you know, but since I'm the one who brought it up: yes, for years now. I did inpatient for a while—the good old 'exhaustion' rumor. Then I did a long-term outpatient day treatment and progressed from there. I've been going to meetings pretty regularly ever since."

I tilt my head, suddenly putting it all together. "All those visits to the church across the street."

"Did you think I got really into religion or something?" She smiles. "I guess I did a little, but not all organized like that and definitely *not* that one. No, there's a women's meeting there three days a week and a general meeting the rest. I've been going whenever I'm in town. I wanted to make sure that I didn't fall off the wagon and I also wanted to make sure I wasn't just trading addictions."

"What do you mean?"

"You're very . . . enticing," she admits. "I wanted a place to process my thoughts and make sure I wasn't trading one addiction for another or having sex with you instead of dealing with my emotions."

My breath catches, snagging on her verbalizing what has been my biggest fear this whole time. "Were you?" I ask quietly.

"No," Nikki says, shaking her head. "Which is why it hurt so bad when you accused me of it." She looks away. "The first time we were together was impulsive, I admit it. I did some soul searching and some extra meetings after that, and I really think that I went in with my eyes open the rest of the time I was here.

"I think *you* may have been, though, but I was willing to give you the benefit of the doubt and see how it all played out. Was it a little pathetic of me? Yes. Was it me falling back into my old codependent routine? No. I don't think so. I had a lot of discussions with my sponsor and my therapist about it, and while they weren't exactly thrilled with how everything was going down, we talked through all the possible outcomes and *why* I was willing to take that risk," she says, waving her hand. "Believe it or not, I had a couple boundaries. We just didn't hit them until that last night."

"What were they?" I ask, thinking over all the time we spent together these last few months.

"If I felt bad after being intimate with you, instead of good, was the biggest one. My care team felt like that would be a red flag that we shouldn't ignore, and I never did until that night. If you were cruel to me was another one—not angry, I did things to deserve that, but actually cruel for the sake of being cruel."

"You thought I would do that to you?" I ask, frowning at the realization that she was making an even bigger leap sticking around here than I realized.

"I thought you were very upset with me," she says, "and that I caught you out of the blue. I didn't know what to expect."

"Was there anything else?" I ask, nervous about the answer.

"I had one other big one," she says. "If I thought we were hurting each other instead of healing, then I needed to leave for good. My therapist's advice was to 'be curious.' It's one of his favorite sayings whenever I get anxious about anything. 'Don't get upset, don't try to predict, just be curious.'" She laughs, lowering her voice in an apparent impression of him. "'Watch what happens and adjust accordingly instead of wasting your energy worrying about something you have no control over.'"

"It's that easy for you to do?"

"God no." Nikki laughs. "But the plan was, whether you remembered you were in love with me or we got closure instead, I was going to 'be curious' and see how it all shook out," she says, taking in my raised eyebrow. "Hey, I'm not saying I didn't have an agenda! I was hoping it would go a certain way, but I also recognized that there could be beauty in an ending between us—a real one this time. We left things in such an ugly way that first time. If the only thing that came out of seeing you again was a period at the end of our sentence instead of an angry exclamation point, I think it still would have been worth it."

"Wow," I say, and I mean it. "That is . . . really, really, healthy."

"I'm trying. I still screw things up a lot, though, don't worry," she says and then bites her lip. "What else do you want to know?"

I take a deep breath. "I was kind of wondering if you really didn't know I was here when you decided to come to town and finish the book."

"I'll swear on whatever you need me to. I had no idea you were here. That part was just fate or luck or whatever you want to call it." She smiles. "I rented the cabin to write the book . . . but you're right in that it wasn't the *only* reason I came. This place felt like the closest I could be to you, since I had no idea where in the world you actually were. There's this thing when you can't make actual amends to the people you've hurt—you're supposed to find other ways to kind of balance things and make peace with them. That's the other reason I was here."

"How were you going to do that?"

"I was going to see what the town needed and donate it— maybe a little garden or green space? I didn't have a great plan." She shrugs. "I just knew I wanted it to be here, anonymously, and involve flowers or plants somehow. I was still working up the courage to go talk to the town planner about it. Doing that felt so *final*—I wasn't quite ready—and then you texted."

I nod, trying to process everything Nikki just said. She was going to let me go, put her apology out into the universe, with flowers. Here. I might've walked by them a hundred times and never known. Nikki could have come and left while I sat here still trying to hate her because I was too scared to admit that I made mistakes too.

"We might need two anonymous gardens, actually," I say,

giving her a sad smile. She quirks her eyebrows up in a silent question.

"It feels a little ridiculous. You were doing all this work on yourself the whole time, while I was hiding here, mad about a stolen role because I was too much of a coward to admit that some of it was my fault too. Not to mention that ghosting you after everything we'd been through was probably not the best way to extract myself from the situation. I called Janet, by the way, my old therapist. I've been working with her a few times a week since you left this last time—it sounds like we've been talking about a lot of the same things as you have."

"That's good." Nikki shifts in her seat, sucking in her lips as she sets her mug down.

"I really am sorry for how I left," I say, and she shakes her head. "It was probably the most traumatizing way to handle it for both of us."

"No, you had to. I don't blame you for—"

I hold up my hand, cutting her off. "I had to leave, yes, but I didn't have to pack up in the middle of the night without a goodbye. We had been together for years and I didn't even leave a note. I picked so many fights and lied to myself that the stolen role was the straw that broke the camel's back." I swallow hard. "But the truth is, I think I just wanted to be done anyway. Not only that, but by the time I left I was so messed up and bitter, I think I wanted *you* to be scared for *me* the way I spent so many nights being scared for you. I wanted you to hurt, and that's . . . It's not the right way to go about things. I don't regret leaving, I can't be sorry about that, but I am horrifically sorry for the way I chose to do it."

"Thank you," she says, meeting my eyes so I can see the sincerity in them. "I know that was hard to say and it means a lot." She scratches the back of her neck, hesitating. "There's something else I should probably clear up, though, before we go any further."

"Oh god," I say, jokingly bracing myself to try to lighten the mood. "Okay, I'm ready."

Nikki gives me a small smile. "Okay, so, I . . . I don't really know where to start with this." She shakes her head. "I guess I'll just say it. I never stole your role. I wouldn't have done that to you, not even back then. That's not part of the flower garden at all. Well, I might owe you one for my dishonesty, actually, but not for the role itself."

I rear back from her words. I guess, of all the things I thought she would apologize for, I figured the stolen role would be the easiest. The least of a land mine.

Apparently, I was wrong.

"What do you mean? What dishonesty?" I ask, bracing myself for real this time for whatever's coming next.

"Okay," she says, leaning forward to take my hand. "Okay, so . . ."

I resist the urge to pull away. "So . . . ?"

"The truth is," she says, "my agent had already sent in my headshots and an old audition tape to the casting director by the time you started talking about wanting it. I had no idea Eliza had done that. I never went behind your back to secretly audition, if that's what you've been thinking this whole time. My excitement and encouragement for you was real.

"When my *former* agent called and told me they wanted me

for the role, I was horrified. I told Eliza that you were going for it too and deserved it way more than I did. She said if I didn't take it they were going to move on to read with the next person they had scouted. They weren't even going to call you for an audition! I told them I wouldn't come in for a formal read unless they gave you one too. I thought if they heard you, if I could just get you in front of them . . ."

I swear all of the air just got sucked out of the room. I open and shut my mouth uselessly, trying to make sense of it all. Of all the things I thought she might say, it wasn't ever that.

"Nikki, what the hell!" I practically whisper, my voice running off to wherever the oxygen went. "Why didn't you tell me any of this was going on? Why did you make it seem like—"

"How could I tell you? You were over the moon when they called you in! You were brilliant and had worked so hard prepping for it. I really thought they'd give it to you, and I'd never have to tell you that you almost didn't get a call. I really, honestly, thought that role was made for you."

My head suddenly feels like it weighs a hundred pounds. I slide my hand out from under Nikki's and sink into the couch, needing its support. "Why didn't you tell me even after it was clear I wasn't getting it?"

"Because I got drunk about it instead and decided it would be kinder to let you think I stole the role from you. I didn't want you to feel like you weren't good enough or had another failed audition—instead it could just be about me letting you down again. Like I always did by then. I was trying to protect you in a really, really convoluted way." She sighs.

"You could have not taken the role either," I point out, incredulous that this is the explanation she's going for. "How did you not see that *that* would have been kinder than pretending to steal it!"

"I was also supporting both of us at the time, if you recall," she says, sitting up a little straighter. "You were already suing your old manager and dealing with—"

"You had a higher percentage of residuals coming in and you were paid significantly better than I was on *The Nikki and Andy Show*! How can you even pretend that money was—"

"It was going up my nose or down my throat faster than it was coming in, Anderson! You don't know how bad it was. I kept it from you."

"Not *that* much. I would have noticed if it were *that much*."

"No, you wouldn't have. I'm an actress, remember?" Nikki shakes her head sadly. "There were so many parties," she says, her voice cracking. "At first, producers, actors, people I looked up to, would feed the drugs to me like it was candy. They were all doing the same to each other, but I was the belle of the ball for a little while there. I was shiny and new, and people more important than me wanted to talk over lines or buy me endless top-shelf drinks and . . . other things.

"I was just trying to keep up. I had to impress everyone, or they'd move on to the next new face, and I'd have blown my chances—or so I thought. That was very expensive. I don't know if you understood how badly I didn't want to be Nikki from *The Nikki and Andy Show* anymore. I wanted people to see that I was sophisticated and important and *worthy*. I wanted people to think I had things under control. I nearly went broke doing it."

"Nikki..."

"Eventually, it wasn't just expensive to show off to all my 'new friends,' it was expensive to stay steady. It took a lot of work and a lot of drugs to find that fine line between being productive and sloppy. I got pretty good at it, though."

I look at her with huge eyes. "I knew there was a disconnect between us then and you weren't home very much, but this doesn't make sense to me. You were in trouble, for sure, but not to that—"

"You thought I didn't want you at those parties because I was keeping them for myself, but really, I didn't want you around those people. I especially didn't want you to see *me* around those people. I am *deeply* ashamed of the things that I did, even though I've been working hard for years to make peace with it. I think I'm most ashamed that I hid that from you when you'd been nothing but loving and helpful and kind. I took away your agency at every turn by keeping it from you.

"The only explanation I have is that something broke in me back then and a lot of people took advantage of it. If you want to hear every sad, sordid story, I will tell you, just maybe when I'm not six thousand miles away from my therapist." She laughs bitterly. "Is that okay?"

I reach forward and grab her hand again, trying to wrap my head around how bad it actually was. I was so distracted with everything going on with my agent—the interviews with the IRS and the police, balancing court prep with auditions, having the paps hounding me on the way to my PA job, looking for a reaction. It was chaos.

I know it's not my fault, and that Nikki's not saying it is, but I can't help but feel like I should have paid more attention instead of alternating between getting angry and trying to cover it up. I knew she was struggling and partying too much, but . . . "I wish I tried to help you more before I left."

"No," she says, squeezing my hand. "It wouldn't have mattered. How many times did you show up at the bars back then when I didn't come home? How many fights did we have over what you thought was just me drinking too much?"

"A billion? Conservatively?" I say.

"A billion," she says. "You leaving was the best thing you could have done for both of us. I know it's horrible to say Oscar night was my rock bottom—especially after telling you how awesome it was, but—"

"Oscar night? Really?"

"Coming home alone again to our empty apartment after such an important night . . . sitting on the couch wasted with *no one* there? I was living in hell, and I was tired of it. I checked in to my first rehab the next day. Admittedly, it took a few tries before sobriety stuck and it's a forever kind of process but . . . yeah."

"This explains so much. I can't believe I didn't get it, not really."

"I lied to you so that you wouldn't. My greatest performance ever," she huffs. "You couldn't have prevented it, even if you did really 'get it.' You couldn't have saved me. I had to do it for myself—just like you did when you left—and I wasn't ready then. You know, when you left, a part of me wanted to die, but the other part was relieved that you had escaped."

"I ran away. I hid."

Her fingers tap my hand. "Sure, but then you built a life."

"Then I built a life." I smile. "I did. A good one too, for the most part."

"You always were so brave, Andy. I was so jealous of you. I still am."

"You're jealous of *me*?" I laugh. "Which one of us has the Oscar again? The millions of dollars?"

"Which one of has the friends who would practically murder for her? The cool job they love? The cat who lets you pet her?" She smiles, looking at Gouda, who stops licking herself long enough on the floor beside me to hiss in Nikki's direction. I can't help but laugh at the timing.

"Don't feel bad for me, though," Nikki says. "I don't. I'm not proud of what I did, but I'm proud that I came out of it on the other side and that I'm doing the work to stay there."

"And here I just thought you were a selfish asshole," I sniffle.

"I was." She grins, catching one of my tears with the pad of her thumb. "I'm trying not to be anymore."

"You overshot simply not being an asshole," I say, wrapping my arms around her and pulling her closer. I need to feel her body warm and strong beneath my arms. I need to feel her breathing and healthy and alive. I think of how many other child actors Hollywood chewed up and spit out, and how few of us ever make it to the other side healthy and sober. "You're pretty great these days."

Nikki laughs into my hair. "So are you."

"I'm sorry that all happened and I'm sorry for the things you went through that you're not ready to share with me yet. I hope you know, whatever it was, you didn't deserve that either."

"I do. I've had of lot of therapy. Like, a lot." She laughs, wiping at her own eyes. "It helped."

I take a deep breath. "Now what?"

"What do you mean?" she asks, hesitant.

"I mean, what do people typically do after the love of their life comes back and you finally do the whole no-bullshit vulnerable honesty thing? Do you get pizza, or . . . ?" I ask.

Her anxiety seems to melt away at my words and she tugs me down on top of her on the couch. I wiggle around until my ear is over her heart, relishing the steady beat. Strong. Alive. And somehow still loving me.

"The love of your life, eh?" Nikki says, kissing the top of my head. I hear the smile in her voice, and it's contagious.

I reach up and flick her arm. "It's a figure of speech."

"Are you sure that's all it is?" she asks, her voice lilting up even more.

I laugh into her chest, reaching my hand along her body and . . . wedging my finger into the spot on her side where she's most ticklish.

Nikki shrieks and tries to buck me off. "'Are you sure that's all it is?'" I say, mimicking her voice. "I'm being sweet and you're out here fishing for compliments, Colletti?"

"Oh, that's how it's going to be, *Ducharme?*" she asks, grabbing the back of my knee and tickling.

We're fully wrestling now, falling off the couch with big belly laughs, and I'm suddenly so, so glad it's the middle of the night and no one is downstairs. I pin Nikki beneath me, holding her hands down with my own and shooting her an exaggerated glare.

Both of us are out of breath, but her eyes track me, heavy-lidded and needing sleep. She licks her lips, and the energy in the room changes as we both seem to realize the position we've landed in. I lean down to kiss her, but she presses her hand to my chest, effectively stopping me.

"Not yet," she says, and I jolt back, surprised.

"Sorry, I—I . . ." I trail off, not sure how to finish that sentence. I climb off her and grab both our mugs off the table, carrying them to the kitchen just for something to do. I'm embarrassed and awkward and—

"Andy," she says, coming up behind me at the sink. She hooks her chin over my shoulder and slides her arms around my waist, letting one hand dip lower and lower.

"What are you—"

"Don't think I don't want you," she breathes into my ear, making me shiver when her fingers press between my legs. "I want you, in my bed, for hours, Anderson Ducharme."

I spin around in her arms, letting her press me against the counter. "And we aren't kissing right now because?"

Nikki laughs and bends to nip her way down my neck before trailing her tongue back up to my ear. She sucks my lobe into her mouth, making my toes curl as I shift my hips forward. Just when I'm about to tear her clothes off, she pulls back, looking just as gone as I feel.

"Why the hell did you stop *again*?" I whine.

She's breathing heavily, looking like it physically pains her to pull herself off me as she steps away. "Believe me, it's taking all my willpower," she says. "I promised myself that I wasn't coming here just to fall back into bed with you. We need to do it right this time. That probably doesn't mean hooking up on our first date."

"How many first dates can we have?" I hang my head back and groan before looking back at her with a pout.

She arches her eyebrows at me, waiting.

I sigh. "You're right, I know you're right. Doesn't mean I have to like it." I turn back to the sink, letting the tap run cold and flicking some water at my face.

Down, girl.

Nikki comes to my side, looking amused as she passes me a dish towel to dry off with. "Better?"

"No," I laugh. "But it's as good as I'm going to get. It's late. You can take the couch," I say, heading to the closet and pulling out the spare blankets and pillows.

"Are you sure you'd like me to stay? I can go down to the cabins. I never did turn in my key."

"I want you to stay, Nikki," I reply, shoving the blankets and pillow into her arms. "But I'm going to bed before I combust. I'll see you in the morning."

"See you in the morning." She laughs, smacking my ass with her pillow.

I'VE BEEN LYING in this bed for five agonizing minutes. My sleep pants are still sticking between my legs where she touched me— the evidence of my arousal painfully evident. I'm tossing and turning, listening to Nikki getting settled on the couch, when a devious idea fills my head.

Just because we're taking this slow doesn't mean I can't have a little fun on my own.

I reach into my nightstand and pull out my lube and favorite vibrator. It's the best of the best, an award-winning toy that, once positioned *just* right, feels like it's sucking my soul right out from between my legs.

The only drawback? It's loud. Incredibly loud. Normally I hate that, but tonight . . . ?

I turn it on and let the familiar buzz drift through my apartment. I've barely got it between my legs before Nikki calls out, "Hey, Andy, whatcha doing in there?"

"Two guesses," I call back with a giggle.

She's never seen this vibrator—it came long after her—but maybe someday they'll meet. Not tonight, though. Tonight is all about the tease.

"What happened to taking it slow?" Nikki asks. Her voice sounds a little closer now.

"Oh, I plan to take it nice and slow with myself tonight," I sigh, feeling the orgasm already building. I let out a moan, half because I need to and half because I want her to hear.

"Andy," she says, her voice strained. "You're killing me."

She's at my door now. Good.

The thought of Nikki listening, separated from me by only a few inches of fake wood, is enough to push me right over the edge. I come with a gasp, so keyed up and oversensitive that I practically throw my vibrator out of the bed.

There's a sound at my door that sounds suspiciously like her head banging against it, and I laugh. "Good night, Nikki," I call out.

"Good night, Andy," she grumbles.

For the first time in a long time, I can't wait for tomorrow.

Chapter Twenty-Six

Rise and Shine

I wake up slowly, my excitement about getting to see Nikki sleeping on my couch tempered by my healthy fear that maybe everything yesterday was just a dream. I'm terrified to open my eyes and find out none of it ever happened.

I hold my breath, listening for any sound of life beyond the purr of my cat. My ears strain so hard I swear I can feel them *trying* to hear, but it's shockingly silent on the other side of my door.

Or at least it was.

All of a sudden there's an explosion of noise that sounds suspiciously like all my pots and pans toppling over and spilling across my kitchen floor. I know that sound well. Gouda jumps, claws digging into me, and I wince. If Nikki was trying to be quiet, my precariously-shoved-in-the-cabinet pans blew it for her.

"Shit," Nikki says from the other room.

Gouda pins her ears back and hops off the bed, apparently deciding that she doesn't care if she hates Nikki, as long as Nikki has fingers that can open cans.

I smile and let the cat out of my room before making quick work of my morning routine. I throw on a hoodie, nearly tripping over my vibrator that's still on the floor where I tossed it—*I have to remember to clean that later*—and then search for a fresh pair of sleep shorts. Once I'm reasonably put together, I stumble out into the living room, where I instantly melt at the sight of Nikki crouching on the floor of my kitchen—still in my pajamas—trying to wrestle the pans back into the cabinet.

"Morning," I say, and she turns around slowly, giving me a bashful smile.

"You weren't supposed to be up yet," she says, standing up and into my hug. "I wanted to surprise you with breakfast in bed."

"You should have thought of that before you threw my pans everywhere," I tease. "Besides, I didn't mind getting up. I'm just glad this wasn't all a dream."

"The fact that you said 'dream' instead of 'nightmare' feels like progress," Nikki says, looking very cute.

I kiss that look right off her face and then turn to survey the mess. "Let me help." I wiggle most of the pots and pans back into place within a minute or so and then pass her my favorite nonstick.

"How did you get those put away so fast?" she asks, utterly flabbergasted.

"Magic." I shrug. "I have to do it every time I eat. I've gotten good at judging angles."

"You know if you put them away properly every time this wouldn't happen."

"Where's the fun in that?" I ask, pushing myself up to sit on the counter as she scrambles the eggs for our breakfast. There's a fresh loaf of sourdough beside my stove—our favorite lazy weekend breakfast when we lived together. Nikki must have snuck out to the bakery while I was sleeping.

I'm just about to insist she let me take over spatula duty—taking care of each other equally, remember—when I spy a terribly made arrangement of flowers on my table. I almost make a joke that she should have just ordered from me instead of whatever awful grocery store florist made this abomination, when I realize that they *are* the flowers that she ordered from me. The exact ones that came with the note to check my email—even the lone black rose. The vase looks suspiciously like the ones we stock at the store too.

I hop down to inspect them closer. *These are definitely from In Bloom.*

"What's all this?" I ask, and she turns toward me with a smile.

"I know it's not exactly on your level, and yes, I *do* realize that they look terrible together now that I see them—what do you always say, 'It's important to have a cohesive arrangement'? Well, these are not that." She laughs. "I couldn't help but notice you never made them and I wanted to fix that. It wasn't cheap, you know. Regan triples her prices for me."

"I didn't really think about them anymore after I saw the whole 'check your email' thing," I say. "But thank you. No one ever buys a florist flowers, let alone makes them for her."

"We should change that." Nikki smiles. "Except maybe I shouldn't be the one in charge of pulling them all together."

"You *definitely* should not be the one in charge of pulling them all together," I say as I drop into a kitchen chair and kick my legs up onto another one. I don't miss the way her eyes travel up my long legs all the way to my teeny, tiny sleep shorts and then snag. A blush rises to her cheeks that turns me on more than I want to admit.

"My eyes are up here," I say, and she somehow blushes even harder before going back to stirring the eggs.

"I didn't mean to stare," Nikki says.

"It's okay, you can. In fact, I encourage it."

"Yeah?" she asks, glancing at me. She pulls the pan of eggs off the burner and turns to look at me. "Good, because I'm a little in love with you. If you can't tell."

"Only a little?"

"Maybe a teeny bit more than that," she says. "But I deducted points for the way you keep your cookware."

I roll my eyes. "Well, hopefully it will even out, because I just *gave* you bonus points for using the language of flowers to woo me. Although I could have done without the black rose."

"Why?" she asks, looking genuinely confused.

"Death? Goodbye? You scared the hell out of me with that."

"No, it means 'the end,' I googled it. It was a pun because I finished the—oh my god, I didn't even think how else that could be interpreted."

"I had a full-on existential crisis over that rose and it was a *pun?*"

"Whoops." She winces. "Add another plant to the apology garden, because I am so sorry."

"Yeah, I'm definitely in charge of flower picking from now on."

"Agreed. You know, speaking of flowers," Nikki says, leaning against the counter. "That big bouquet I ordered the first day I was here, the one Regan put together for me before I even knew for sure I had gotten the location right? That was for you too. I was going to do this whole cathartic releasing into the ocean thing if I misunderstood your text and you weren't actually here. Sounds cheesy, but . . ."

I scrunch my eyebrows together, remembering how grand it was. "Wait, did you study the meaning of flowers before you even came here?"

"Maybe." She bites the inside of her cheek, glancing at me before pulling some plates down and scraping equal amounts of eggs onto each one. "I have another confession to make too."

"I might need coffee before we do that," I say, the words slipping out as my body tenses up.

"No, no, you'll like this one."

"Okay," I say, dropping back into my seat. "Hit me."

"None of those early bouquets I ordered were ever for anyone I slept with. I haven't really been with anyone since I got clean, no matter what TMZ says. Most of those 'girlfriends' at the beginning were my sober-living coaches. Even my first order wasn't to any one-night stand or whatever you accused me of. There haven't been any. Not for years."

"Who did they go to, then?" I ask, scandalized. "Oh my god, I was obnoxious and raunchy in the first few!"

"My agent, a couple friends, my sponsor, Julia. Pretty much anyone I could pre-warn about a tag that said 'thanks for the screaming orgasms' without getting sued for sexual harassment got one."

My ears go hot and start to ring. "Wow. I guess we're about to find out if you officially *can* die of embarrassment."

"Don't go dying anytime soon, because you've been blowing

up on the left coast after all that. Your style is fresh and unique. Everyone who's seen them has been flipping out."

"That explains all the LA orders. I just assumed that your exes had good taste."

Nikki laughs and joins me at the table with both of our plates. I hop up and grab us each seltzer water and some napkins. *Equal partnership.*

"I have a confession of my own," I say. "Or more of an idea, rather."

"I'm listening," she says, tilting her head.

"Last night I was thinking about ways we could get to know each other again and reconnect."

"Oh, is *that* what you call what you were doing last night?" she teases.

"After the whole vibrator thing!" I squeak. "I meant after!"

"Right, right, *after*," she says. "What did you come up with during your post-orgasm glow?"

"It's a little outside the box." I wince. "It's probably going to be a huge pain in the ass for you, and if you want to say no, it's fine. Seriously, it's fine."

"Immediately yes," she says, sliding some eggs delicately into her mouth.

"You don't even know what I'm going to say!"

"You're telling me that you have an idea that could bring us closer. I don't care what it is. If it means skydiving naked, I'm ordering a parachute after the breakfast dishes. I'm in, Andy."

"It's not naked skydiving. Sorry to disappoint," I say, taking a bite of toast.

"Still," she says. "I'm sure I'll be into it, whatever it is."

I should probably be afraid of her devotion—in my past life I would have been, but right now, here, with everything we've been through—it feels so damn right. So natural. Especially since I feel exactly the same way about her.

"I want us to cowrite the book—a total do-over, from scratch. You'd hear my stories, I'd hear yours. We could do alternating chapters for the years we were apart or something—make it truly *our* story and write our *own* ending."

Nikki sets her drink down and meets my eyes. "That's going to ruin the whole anonymity thing you have going on here. You'd be back in the spotlight, especially if it did the numbers they're hoping for. People would recognize you, for real this time."

"It's time to ruin it. I'm sick of pretending to be Anne Lacy and acting like Andy doesn't exist. I want to be both. I *can* be both. I'm not giving up the shop or doing flowers, but there's space enough for my past and my future. I get that now."

She grabs the side of my chair and slides me toward her. "A few weeks ago, you didn't know what you wanted, and now you want to tell the whole world—in writing—that we're lovers?"

"Too soon?" I giggle.

"No," Nikki says, kissing me.

"Is that a yes?"

"Yes, I'll marry you," she says, pulling back to pepper my face with kisses. "Or did you mean the book? Either way yes, my answer is yes."

"Good." I laugh. "We should celebrate my new book deal, then."

"What do you have in mind?"

"It's not our last first date anymore," I say, letting my hand drift up her thigh to the edge of her sleep shorts.

"No, it's not," she says, her legs falling open to invite me in.

I slide my hand under the fabric, just a little. "Are you sure this is okay?" I ask. I wait for her to consider my question and add, "We don't have to, if you're not feeling good about it yet. Being here with you is enough, it really is. I promise."

"God, I love you for asking that." She presses her hand over mine. "But it's more than okay, Andy. It's goddamn *divine*."

I smile, leaning forward for another kiss.

"Your phone is buzzing," I grumble into the pillow.

Nikki shifts, kissing the back of my neck before rolling off me to grab her phone. "Oh no, it's my assistant."

"Take it," I say, rolling over. "Seriously, take it. If we're going to make this work, we have to make the real world work too. Which means, sadly, we both have jobs."

She looks unconvinced, letting voicemail make the decision for us. "I'm scared," she says with a sad little laugh.

"Of what?"

"That if I leave our little bubble something will happen—like you'll change your mind or disappear on me again."

"We have to trust each other," I say, lacing our fingers together and kissing her hand. "We have to build fresh. You can't keep thinking I'm going to disappear, and I can't keep thinking you're going to hurt me. It's going to take time, but we have to believe in *us*."

"Yeah," she says, looking down at me. "I do. I trust us."

"Good," I say, sitting up to kiss her nose. "Now call your assistant back."

Nikki nods and pulls up the number. Her PA starts talking

before Nikki even gets a chance to say hi. "Yeah, okay," Nikki says, looking at me. "If that's the only flight out, I can make it." She looks sad about it, so I give her a reassuring thumbs-up.

This is part of it.

This has to be part of it.

Nikki is going to have to leave for work, and I'm going to stay here and handle my business too. We have to be willing to join our lives without holding each other back or we're dead in the water before we've even begun.

"I'll be there this afternoon, on time," she says, grabbing my thumb and bringing it to her lips for a kiss. "No, I still have my rental. I can drop if off at Logan. Okay. Yeah. Yes. I'll see you there." She clicks off and tosses her phone on the carpet.

"How long do we have?" I ask, as she presses me back down into the sheets.

"Long enough to get my mouth back on you, if you're not still too sensitive?"

"I think that's doable," I giggle.

"Promise me you won't whip out that vibrator the second I'm gone?" Nikki asks, nipping at my breast. "I'll be back in two days, and I want you ready for me."

"You're mean," I pout.

"That's not what you said when I was—"

"Shut up," I laugh. "I love you."

"I love you too." She grins and dives back under the covers.

And if she barely made it to her plane on time, running down the platform just before they closed the door, well, her assistant never needs to know.

Epilogue

Two Years Later

Strike a Pose

I'm arranging a bunch of lilies into a crystal vase for a gorgeous wedding arrangement when Regan rushes into the store, tightly gripping the latest issue of *Vogue*.

I roll my eyes.

I sent her to the grocery store on a fake errand in the hope of getting rid of some of her nervous energy—or at least keep it from spilling over onto me while I still have work to do.

As they say, no good deed goes unpunished.

"Look what I got," Regan chirps in a little singsong voice. If she thinks that's going to make me any happier about the magazine in her hand, she has another think coming.

"If you want me to finish this order, then I would put that away and pretend it never happened," I say, pointing my floral shears at the pages and snipping the air a few times.

"Don't lie. You know it's for a *very* important client," she says. "You'll finish either way. When have you ever blown off an order, little miss Anderson . . . *in Bloom.*"

She practically squeals that last part and I sigh, pulling the magazine out of her hand and shoving it facedown on the shelf beneath the counter. Of course, that lasts for all of two seconds before Regan's pulling it out to slide her finger across the high gloss cover.

"'ANDERSON IN BLOOM,'" she reads.

She trails her finger down to the subheading. "'Sometimes happily ever afters do exist.'" She lets out a dreamy little sigh at that and then hops up on the stool beside me. "Awww, that's so sweet."

"Don't remind me," I groan.

"Oh, I'm reminding you of this forever. It's going on the wall of the shop. Framed and everything. Maybe I'll blow it up onto a giant billboard and—"

"I will stab you," I say, punctuating my sentence with the snip of a stem.

"No, you wouldn't, because that wouldn't be very maid of honor of you," she laughs.

Yes, it's true, the very important bridal client that I'm making these floral arrangements for is indeed sitting right next to me at this very moment.

Johnny and Regan are finally making it happen.

They're having a stunning summer beach wedding tomorrow. One of the local hotels rented out their private beach and ballroom to them for a fantastic discount, on account of how Regan has been supplying them with event flowers for years at such reasonable prices.

It's a happy coincidence that their wedding date lines up with exactly when I wanted to be out of LA anyway—yes, I do split my time, coming back here whenever Nikki is filming. I don't think anyone can blame me for wanting to get out of LA when the cover hit. I can barely keep up with orders as it is, and half the people who come into In Bloom Too—our LA-based satellite shop—are just there hoping to catch me working or trying to catch Nikki stopping in with coffee, a morning routine she has taken it upon herself to keep up with on both coasts.

"Plus," Regan says, holding the magazine back up to my face, "you look *hot*."

I stop working long enough to examine the cover in more detail. I've been so worried about the things that I perceived as going wrong—a flower on my gown that slipped out of place in the cover image, my obviously photoshopped breasts that look a little *too* perky for someone braless and covered in rose petals, not to mention the fact that they used the photo of me growling and biting a carnation as a joke on the third page of the spread.

Somehow, despite all those little oddities, Regan is legitimately vibrating with excitement as she looks at it. It's maybe a little bit infectious. After all, it's not every day a florist sees their designs on a magazine cover, much less gets to be the one wearing them.

Regan flips through to the actual article. "'From red carpets and runways to the top of bestseller lists, Anderson Ducharme is having a year,'" she reads, pausing to look up at me. "I'll freaking say!"

I shake my head, struggling to focus on the arrangement in front of me in the face of her excitement. The wedding is tomorrow, and I want it to be perfect. I can't get distracted by—

"'Anderson walks into the hotel bar carrying a delphinium bouquet, which means pure happiness—something I learned while studying for this interview, knowing how important the meaning of flowers is to all of her designs.'" Regan pauses. "You did not bring flowers to your *Vogue* interview, you absolute dork."

"How could I not?" I ask, genuinely baffled. "If I didn't the first line would be 'Anderson showed up empty-handed like a monster.'"

"Oh my god, no wonder LA ate you up the first time," she laughs, because yeah, with the benefit of hindsight—and getting back in with regular sessions with Janet both virtually and in person—my past has been defanged enough that we can joke about it now.

It's not all funny, but . . . some of it is.

To say these last two years have been a period of growth for me would be the understatement of the century. Nikki's agent was able to finagle her publisher into scrapping the original idea and letting us cowrite the book together. They were over the moon to find out that they were getting both of us now, especially once they clarified it meant that we were splitting the same advance. Apparently, they already had such high projections for the book, they were maxed out on what they were offering.

I heard Britney's memoir got more, but, fine. I guess that's fair. She is the queen of pop. Or wait, was that Madonna? Either way.

Plus, Nikki didn't care that it meant she would get half as much—thankfully her finances are in a much better place than they were before. God knows that half of her advance is still way more than I've ever made in a year, even when I was on one of the top kid shows.

Our book, *The Nikki and Andy Story*, finally came out a couple of months ago. It turns out publishing time is *way* slower than regular time. Who knew? After it finally hit shelves, we did a little bit of press and touring together, which was fun ... but my new team knows that kind of stuff isn't really my thing.

Surprisingly, the hardest chapter, and the one we get asked about the most, is about Nikki's Oscar speech.

The first time we watched it together was about a month into the "reboot of our reboot," as Nikki calls it. I asked if we could and was not prepared for Nikki to immediately burst into tears at my request. It was hard for her to go back to the best and worst night of her life. It was also hard to watch, knowing she was at her lowest and loneliest that night. I wrapped her in my arms, her back pressed to my chest and my legs tight around her torso, as she held my iPad with shaking hands and pushed play on the old YouTube clip we dug up together.

Someone had turned it into a fan edit with an upbeat pop song playing quietly in the background. The juxtaposition of the song and Nikki's sad eyes as she thanked the Academy and Eliza and her director and castmates was jarring. She squeezed my arm tight as we got to the end of the speech, and the version of her on the screen said, "And to the person who couldn't be here tonight, I miss and love you. Thank you for all the flowers."

Nikki turned to me with wet eyes, setting the iPad aside to pull me into a hug. "They thought I had a secret girlfriend," she said, burying her face between my collar and jaw, and I nodded, remembering the headlines. "I was talking to you, Andy. I was always talking to you. You are the flowers. Your time, your energy, your love . . . all of you. My world wilted when you went away."

"I'm sorry I never watched," I said, pulling her back gently to kiss away her tears.

"I don't care about that. I don't care about any of that," she answered, laying me back on the bed. "We don't need the emails or the speeches or anything like that anymore. We just need each other."

We left what happened next out of the book, but . . . that doesn't stop people from asking questions and trying to guess.

Which is why, once we fulfilled what we were contractually obligated to, we took a break, sneaking off to another coastal town in a country where nobody knew our names just for a little while. Just to catch our breaths.

And now we're back to the real world. Nikki is scheduled for a bunch of solo stuff next month when she has time off from filming, and she has my enthusiastic consent. I'm all peopled out for the foreseeable future. Besides, I'm still the only one Gouda lets pet her.

I have to be honest, though, it felt weird having the book out in the world at first—especially once it hit all the lists and I realized just how many people were reading our story. I think in the past it would have freaked me out as bad as that brussels sprouts picture (which thankfully has been shoved way down in the search results).

Now, I'm embracing it.

I *chose* to put it out there. Me. On my terms. There's something powerful about that.

When the news first broke that we were doing the book together, people started digging into where I'd been a little more. Was it invasive? Yes. Was it also great for business? Hell yeah. In Bloom now has five employees to keep up with orders, plus our satellite shop has another four. I'm still the "master florist" here, even though I think it should be Regan. I don't really get a lot of time to do small, personal arrangements anymore . . . which is also why it feels so special to be able to make these for Regan's wedding.

Nikki's to blame for the red-carpet flower thing. Sending all of my work to her friends back in LA certainly helped get the ball rolling with things, but when she wore a flower gown I made to the premiere of her last film—a hilarious and biting movie where she was cast as Emma Stone's sarcastic sister—it really catapulted my work into the stratosphere.

Fashion houses started bringing me into their fold—first to accent their runway looks, and then to work with their designers to create living dresses, like the one I did for Nikki.

It's been overwhelming at times.

In the beginning, paparazzi were camped out in front of In Bloom hoping to get a glimpse of Nikki coming to visit. I had to give up the apartment over the shop as a result, but it's fine. We really needed the storage space, and the kitchen makes a great employee break room too. Most of that has died down now, though. Nikki's team feeds out so many official pictures—ones we both get to approve beforehand—that we've rendered pap pics pretty much worthless.

Still, I don't want them to know where I live.

I pull the magazine toward me, laughing when Regan tries to yank it back to keep reading herself. I skim the article quickly, curious if they kept in the part about future plans. They did—giving a nod to the documentary that Nikki and I coproduced about growing up in Hollywood. It got picked up by a streamer and will premiere in a month or two. It's the closest I'll ever come to being back on camera.

My days as an actress are *not* missed, but it's sure been fun to be beloved again.

I don't know how long any of this will last. I learned on the first go-round that fame is fleeting—an audience that loves you will turn on you just as fast—and also that generally it's probably better if I don't melt down in public ever again. We keep our public appearances happy and sober these days, thank you very much.

Needless to say, I spend a lot of time sneaking off here to work on projects in my old bedroom upstairs, which Regan has kept as an impromptu office for me. Now that she and Johnny have moved into her house together, I've been staying at his old place behind the garage whenever I'm in town. It's a little less cozy than my apartment here, but I love it just the same. Plus, it's behind all the tow gates for the impound lot he also runs, which means nobody can get in to bother me.

The bells over the door ring and I look up, grinning when I

see it's Nikki walking in. She's got on her standard shades and a hoodie that lets her move around here somewhat effortlessly—although less so lately with the publicity we've been getting.

I run over and wrap her in a hug, kissing her like I haven't seen her in weeks because . . . well, I *haven't* seen her in weeks. She's been away filming a guest role on a hot new TV show, and I've been here doting on Regan and doing all my best maid of honor duties. *It's only fair*, I think, looking down at the engagement ring on my finger. *She'll be doing it for us next year.*

"Hi, baby," Nikki says, pulling my hand up for a kiss. I'm not the only one who can't stop staring at our rings. Regan says it's just new, and we'll get used to having them, but I don't see how.

Nikki proposed a week before she left for filming—a simple, private affair after making me a quiet dinner at home—beating my plan to propose to her via skywriting by twenty-four hours. I still went ahead and made her stand outside and did the whole get-down-on-one-knee thing back to her, explaining after that it had been in the works for months . . . and also the skywriting was nonrefundable.

It's only fitting, I think—if we can fall in love twice, we can propose twice too.

Nikki reaches into her bag and pulls out another, more wrinkled copy of *Vogue*. "How's my little superstar feeling on her big day?"

"Too late," Regan says, holding up her own copy.

Nikki pouts. "You started teasing her without me? Tell me you at least didn't call her 'Anderson in Bloom' yet."

Regan shrugs. "You snooze you lose, Nik."

"It's not my fault that your future husband asked me to grab him a coffee on my way here!"

"Ugh, you spoil him." Regan rolls her eyes. "I told him to get his own damn coffee when he asked me."

"He told me you would say that, and he said I should ask you if you want him to finish restoring that 1967 Jaguar for your honeymoon, or if you want to drive across the country in your 'boring Civic'?"

"Point taken," Regan grumbles. "Thank you for caffeinating him, I guess."

Who would have thought? Nikki and Johnny are as thick as thieves these days. She probably talks to him more than I even talk to Regan, outside of wedding stuff. I think they relate to one another on the "hopelessly in love with someone who needed time" front. Nikki even used some of her connections through set designers and stunt people to help locate the perfect car for him to restore for their trip. It's pretty cute, honestly.

"You're welcome," Nikki says. "And I have coffee for both of you too in the rental car. I just wanted my hands free to greet my *fiancée* first."

"Oh, puke," Regan says, grabbing the magazine. "I'll give you guys some privacy. Give me your car keys—I want my latte. I'm going to go finish reading this in the park."

Nikki laughs and tosses Regan the keys before setting her bag down and wrapping me up in a proper hug. I jump into her arms and giggle as she slowly walks me back to sit me on the counter. Her fingers dig into my hips when I lean down and give her another kiss.

"I'm gonna call you Anderson in Bloom forever now. You know that, right?" Nikki murmurs against my skin.

"I'd rather you call me Anderson Colletti."

Nikki leans back, her mouth falling open in surprise. "Really?" she asks, as if she can't believe it. "You want my last name?"

"I want all of you, but yeah, the last name's a good start."

"Holy shit," she whispers, her face breaking into the most beautiful smile I've ever seen.

"I take it you like that idea?"

"I love it." She beams.

"Good," I say, pulling her in even closer. "So do I."

Acknowledgments

Thank you to: My agent, Sara Crowe, who is the best advocate an author could ever wish for, and my editor, Madelyn Blaney, for pushing me as a writer while somehow also making the revision process an absolute blast.

To my copyeditor, Martha Cipolla. To Jessica Cozzi and everyone else behind the scenes at Avon who helped bring this book to life. I'm so grateful for all your hard work.

To Jenifer Prince for creating such a stunning cover illustration, and to Amy Halperin for pulling it all together so flawlessly.

To all the florists in the Capital District who let me pick their brains about flowers and flower shop life. And definitely to the reader who wrote her name on a Post-it note and said I could use it in a future book.

To all my friends who have supported me over the years, especially Rory for constantly inspiring me (and trading pet pics); Kelsey, my constant movie date companion for better or for worse; Erik, my videogame compatriot who loves to tell me how many hours behind the average completion rate of our games I am (Is it a crime to be THOROUGH??? To enjoy the sound of

BREAKING GLASS???); Dahlia, for her friendship and advice; and to the Coven, who have been riding this roller coaster with me from the start.

To my family, for your unwavering support and love. I couldn't do this without you. Well, actually, maybe Brody should only get half credit since he moved eight hours away, and Liv should probably only get a quarter credit since it's technically her fault I draft half my books while sitting on ice-cold bleachers (but still, love you two to the moon and back).

And last but never, ever least, to readers, booksellers, librarians, bloggers, bookstagrammers, booktokers, and everyone else who enthusiastically shouts about books both online and in real life. I am beyond grateful for the work that you do.

Jennifer Dugan is an awkward romantic and a professional overthinker who loves writing stories about messy, complicated women and girls. Her debut novel, *Hot Dog Girl*, was called a "great fizzy rom-com" by *Entertainment Weekly* and "one of the best reads of the year, hands down" by *Paste Magazine*, although she is best known for *Some Girls Do*, her third young adult novel that took TikTok by storm. Her adult romances, *Love at First Set* and *The Ride of Her Life*, boast "the most hilarious disaster bisexuals you'll ever meet" according to the queen of *LGBTQ Reads*, Dahlia Adler, for *Buzzfeed*. Jennifer has also collaborated with artist Kit Seaton on several graphic novels, including the GLAAD Outstanding Original Graphic Novel Nominee, *Coven*.

Read more from
JENNIFER DUGAN

An irresistible enemies-to-lovers, grumpy/sunshine queer romcom for fans of *Delilah Green Doesn't Care*, about a wedding-obsessed city girl who inherits a horse farm from her estranged late aunt and clashes with the cocky, unfairly hot farrier who thinks she's going to run the barn into the ground.

A queer romcom for fans of *Written in the Stars*, in which a woman gives a drunken bathroom pep talk to a hot stranger, only to find out it's the bride-to-be she has convinced to leave her fiancé the night before the wedding.

DISCOVER GREAT AUTHORS, EXCLUSIVE OFFERS, AND MORE AT HC.COM.